Mac pulled to a st
a pair of giraffes an
a treetop picnic in t

The female seemed to give Tessa a knowing nod and then lowered her neck and nudged the baby. A family of three. At peace. Something stirred deep inside Tessa.

"Look at them, Nick," she whispered to their nephew.

"I saw. Now can we go fast again?"

Leave it to a restless teen to spoil the moment. Tessa wanted to stay there and watch. Never before had she been so hyperaware...so in tune with her senses. The way the air softly brushed her skin, the light snap of a twig, the smell of dewy grass and freshly rutted dirt, the striking blue and red of a bird taking flight from the acacia tree ahead of them. Everything around her was awe-inspiring. It didn't feel risky. It felt right.

She closed her eyes, took a deep breath and was enveloped by a warm, fresh scent that was uniquely Mac's. She quickly opened her eyes again. The stress, drama and romantic atmosphere of the Serengeti were getting to her. Mac belonged here. There was no separating him from the land and life that surrounded them. Mac and the Serengeti had an understanding. A symbiotic relationship.

A balance.

And he'd made it clear he didn't have room in his life for anyone else.

Dear Reader,

One of my favorite poems is Robert Frost's "The Road Not Taken." We all know journeys through life tend to be circuitous with many difficult choices along the way. More often than not, our choice of path is complex and the driving force runs deep. I look back on my own life (hindsight is a great teacher) and can plainly see which of my choices were based on fear, insecurities or even expectations...and which were made because I followed my conscience, listened to my heart and had the courage to be true to myself.

When faced with divergent paths, are you a risk taker? Someone who takes the less-traveled road? The beautiful thing about life is that it allows for change. A journey through life, after all, is about self-discovery. It's about learning from mistakes and righting the wrong. It's about connecting with those who share or respect our passions, ethics and values. It's about opening your heart to love in its many forms.

In this book, the hero and heroine are two very different people brought together by co-guardianship of their nephew. Mac is a risk taker...an adventurer who has convinced himself he's better off alone. Tessa, on the other hand, craves security...a need that led her to a marriage and husband she's determined to be loyal to. Yet both Mac and Tessa are facing internal and external battles between right and wrong. Both have made choices based on childhood experiences and both have now reached a crossroads where their choices will either drive them apart...or make them stronger.

I hope you enjoy this third story in my From Kenya, with Love series. My door is open at rulasinara.com, where you can sign up for my newsletter, get information on all my books and find links to my social media hangouts.

Wishing you love, peace and courage in life,

Rula Sinara

HEARTWARMING

Through the Storm

USA TODAY Bestselling Author

Rula Sinara

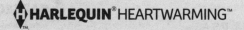

HARLEQUIN® HEARTWARMING™

If you purchased this book without a cover you should be aware that this book is stolen property. It was reported as "unsold and destroyed" to the publisher, and neither the author nor the publisher has received any payment for this "stripped book."

Recycling programs
for this product may
not exist in your area.

ISBN-13: 978-0-373-36787-0

Through the Storm

Copyright © 2016 by Rula Sinara

All rights reserved. Except for use in any review, the reproduction or utilization of this work in whole or in part in any form by any electronic, mechanical or other means, now known or hereinafter invented, including xerography, photocopying and recording, or in any information storage or retrieval system, is forbidden without the written permission of the publisher, Harlequin Enterprises Limited, 225 Duncan Mill Road, Don Mills, Ontario M3B 3K9, Canada.

This is a work of fiction. Names, characters, places and incidents are either the product of the author's imagination or are used fictitiously, and any resemblance to actual persons, living or dead, business establishments, events or locales is entirely coincidental.

This edition published by arrangement with Harlequin Books S.A.

For questions and comments about the quality of this book, please contact us at CustomerService@Harlequin.com.

® and TM are trademarks of Harlequin Enterprises Limited or its corporate affiliates. Trademarks indicated with ® are registered in the United States Patent and Trademark Office, the Canadian Intellectual Property Office and in other countries.

Printed in U.S.A.

Award-winning and *USA TODAY* bestselling author **Rula Sinara** lives in rural Virginia with her family and crazy but endearing pets. She loves organic gardening, attracting wildlife to her yard, planting trees, raising backyard chickens and drinking more coffee than she'll ever admit to. Rula's writing has earned her a National Readers' Choice Award and a Holt Medallion Award of Merit, among other honors. Her door is always open at rulasinara.com, where you can sign up for her newsletter, learn about her latest books and find links to her social media hangouts.

Books by Rula Sinara

Harlequin Heartwarming

The Promise of Rain
After the Silence

To the elephants and all living things that have endured unspeakable suffering. And to those whose hearts are filled with compassion and respect for all life...regardless of race or species. May your love heal wounds and make the world a better place.

Acknowledgments

To Claire Caldwell—a brilliant poet, writer and editor—for helping to bring each book in this series to life and whose patience and invaluable guidance gave me the courage to dig deeper... and reach *Through the Storm*.

CHAPTER ONE

HE WOULD COME after her.

Without him, Tessa Henning wasn't worth the dust left by a mercilessly harvested and exquisitely carved elephant's tusk, but once he discovered she knew too much, Brice would hunt her down just the same. He'd come after her because she was a traitor. He'd find her because she was his wife and he believed in gratitude and loyalty. He expected it. Brice had put her on a pedestal… made her feel beautiful and wanted at a time when everyone else saw her as awkward. He'd given her a life of luxury and security. He'd been generous.

He loved her.

She closed her eyes. She hoped it had been love all this time. Maybe it still was. Maybe she was wrong about everything. Brice had always been a decent man. A decent husband. Marriage involved trust. But didn't love and trust take two in a marriage? *Love* and *trust* were funny words. Tessa swallowed hard, but the lingering, bitter taste of uncertainty dried her throat even more. She needed to stop rationalizing.

Listen to your gut. Don't ignore your instincts this time. This isn't just about you anymore. There's a kid involved.

She took a deep breath, the kind she did in yoga class, then opened her eyes and took one last look around. The designer "organic eggshell"-colored paint she'd once thought made their bedroom appear clean and classy now seemed cold and painfully neutral. She ran her hand across the brown silk sheets that lay rumpled next to her duffel bag, making sure nothing she needed had been lost in them. Their silky touch was anything but soothing. It reminded her of how easily comfort and security could slip away. The pit of her stomach quivered.

"Just get Nick out of here first, then figure out what to do next," she muttered, trying to keep her nerve up. The sound of Nick's name grounded her and she rammed the last few bare essentials she'd piled on her bed into her bag, including her journal and the iPad she'd saved some work, research and personal files on. Nothing was *only* about her anymore. Not since her sister and brother-in-law were killed in an accident six months ago and her thirteen-year-old nephew became her responsibility. Well, hers and his uncle Mac's, but she'd pretty much assumed primary guardianship. It had been Mac's choice at first—a choice that preserved his rugged, bachelor bush-pilot lifestyle up in Kenya's Serengeti. Not that he was entirely delinquent as a guardian, but Mac had managed to convince her early on that there was no way he could raise Nick. He sent money instead.

But she wasn't complaining, exactly. She loved Nick and was glad he was a part of her life. Six months ago, she'd thought that having him around would be like having a part of her sister to hang on to. Things didn't turn out that way. For someone with no child-rearing experience, suddenly having a grieving teenage boy dropped into your life was like expecting a deer to raise a baby wolf. Still, a part of her hated that she was going to lose Nick if her suspicions about Brice proved to be true.

She slung her mini backpack purse onto her shoulder, grabbed the duffel then hurried down the curved marble staircase to the main level of their modern South African villa. The floor-to-ceiling window that framed a spectacular view of the Southern Ocean's crested waters never failed to take her breath away, but today the clawing waves seemed like they were desperate to capture her…to keep her from escaping. That same view made anyone who attended one of Brice's upscale cocktail parties jealous of what they had. Those guests didn't have a clue that his fortune had come at a price. Even Tessa didn't have solid proof, and hadn't even suspected Brice's illegal activity until recently, but she was *not* going to stand by and be a victim. Or watch others suffer at his hands.

The journalist in her had been screaming that something was off for a while now, but given all she was going through after her sister's death, her mind kept telling her to stay out of it, play it safe and take care of Nick. The problem was, there was no *safe* anymore. Home would never feel safe again. Tides changed and the undertow was deadly for the unprepared. She needed to be prepared.

At first, she'd thought Brice's increasing emotional distance, preoccupation with work and irritability were due to the change their daily lives had undergone when Nick came to live with them. She had thought her husband was avoiding the stages of mourning she and Nick had been suffering through, and she had decided not to confront him about it. She figured it would all pass and they'd find a new equilibrium; plus, it wasn't fair to make Nick suffer through their marital stresses. Not after what he'd already been through and not when his uncle Mac couldn't get over his bachelor-ness and take his nephew in. But since her initial suspicions, things had been getting worse. Maybe Tessa's imagination was working overtime and she was reading into the bits and pieces of a phone conversation she'd overheard when Brice didn't know she'd returned home early from taking Nick to one of his posttraumatic therapy sessions, but she needed to know for sure. If Brice was involved in criminal activity, no way was she going to let Nick live around him.

A door on the far side of the living room led to Brice's office. He kept it locked whenever he took trips, but Tessa had been planning today for over a month now. *Trust. Traitor.* She reached into her pocket for the key she'd made, then entered. His office had always made her nervous. Like a mother walking into a crystal display shop with a hyperactive child. Just about everything was made of glass or covered in it. The shelves. His desktop, resting on a sleek, sawhorse-style base with wooden drawers and files under either side. The decorative items between books. It had never hit her before, but now it looked as if he were being daring… seeing just how much load his life could take before everything shattered.

She went to his desk and wondered how he kept the glass fingerprint-free. She avoided touching the surface and opened the drawers. A credenza along the wall behind the desk carried his main computer. No doubt he'd taken his laptop with him.

She wished like crazy that she knew his computer passwords. One backup of his hard drive would be all she needed, but she had no time to guess and no clue how to hack.

She'd take anything, though—the last bank statement, receipts…anything that would put her suspicions to rest and prove Brice wasn't involved in dark business dealings. Prove that the man who'd swept her off her feet was still the same Brice she'd married. A charismatic and shrewd but moral and ethical businessman. Her *husband*. Yet the last words she'd overheard from that phone call still echoed in her ears: *No one can find out. I'll deny involvement with my last breath.*

The nape of her neck prickled as she rifled through his drawers, careful to leave everything looking untouched. She hated this: the sneaking behind his back, the spying… the adrenaline. Boy, did she hate adrenaline. The longer it took for Brice to notice something was wrong when he returned from his business trip in two days, the more of a head start she'd have. She cursed e-bills and cloud storage, then tried one last drawer. A small clear plastic container lay in the back, covered by a stack of manila envelopes. She lifted it out and stacked the envelopes in place. The container had at least six flash drives piled inside. *Maybe some things are too sensitive to store in cyberspace. Huh, Brice?*

Her cell phone ring tone sent her pulse scattering. She fumbled for it in her back pocket and checked the screen. *Katia.* Her editor must have already seen the article she'd sent her just an hour ago. Tessa took a second to steady her voice, then answered.

"Hey, Kat."

"Tessa, are you crazy? I can't publish this in tomorrow's paper. Have you forgotten who your husband is?"

Tessa pressed a hand over her eyes. Why had she bothered? Had she really thought the friendship that had grown between her and Kat would make a difference this time? How often had she been told "no" and to stick to her assigned fashion column?

"No, of course not. It has nothing to do with him," Tessa said, as she quietly closed the desk drawer.

The article had everything to do with him, but she wasn't stupid enough to mention his name directly. They wanted her to stick to her fashion column and she had. Only, instead of recapping the season's trends and giving her generalized opinion on them, she'd written about how outdated and deplorable the use of ivory in jewelry and home decor was, especially in an era of animal-rights awareness.

"How can it not?" Katia huffed into the phone. "Tessa, why do you think I offered you this column to begin with?"

Nice. Rub it in. Nepotism. She didn't write for the paper because of any talent. She wrote for it because Brice got her in.

"Not only is he on the executive board of this newspaper," Katia insisted, "he's the lead investor in half the companies you mentioned here. You have no proof. We'd get sued for defamation. I'm not losing my job over this."

"You won't *lose* your job. You'll be *doing* it. Isn't uncovering truths and raising awareness what journalism is supposed to be about?"

"Maybe for some journalists, but that's not the purpose of your column. That's not what your readers are looking for. If they want to read about crime, they'll turn to the front page. Your column is in the Arts and Home section. Remember that. Tessa, what's going on? This isn't how you write. Have you been sleeping? Watching too many crime shows?"

Only for ideas on how to rob her husband.

"Kat. Listen to me a minute. As my friend, not my editor. I know something is going on that involves some well-known business-men and politicians around here, and I have a really strong feeling it involves the illegal ivory trade. We can wave a red flag over the issue." She looked down at the thumb drives. If there was anyone she could trust, it was Katia. "I'm working on getting more solid proof. If you have to leave company names off for now, fine, but at least print the rest. Get the ball rolling. Attract atten-tion to the cause."

"Tessa..."

"Look, I have to catch a flight. I'm taking my nephew to his uncle's so that I can focus on this. Just post it. Making waves could be good for both our careers."

"Forget your career. Stop and listen to me." Katia lowered her voice. "Nothing is private here. I'm betting every email is mon-itored. You're playing with fire, and that's not like you. Be careful. It hasn't been that long since your sister and brother-in-law were killed. I think the stress is getting to you. Take a break. I can get someone to cover the column for a while."

"I don't need a break."

There was a pause and she could hear someone talking in the background and papers shuffling.

"Tessa, I have to go."

She started to object, but the line disconnected. Tessa cursed and jammed the phone back into her pocket. *You have no proof.* Why couldn't her instincts count for something? Apparently personal agendas trumped both friendship and truth. She took a deep breath. Katia was afraid to ruffle a few feathers. Well, Tessa was about to do a lot more than that. She grasped the USBs and stuffed them into her backpack, knowing full well they could end up being empty or useless, but she was running out of time. She wiped her damp palms against her beige khakis and tucked Brice's chair under the desk, but then pulled it back out and used the hem of her blue V-neck T-shirt to polish the drawer handle and the glass edge, just in case.

She locked the office behind her, then

climbed the stairs two at a time, slowing down only as she approached Nick's bedroom down the hall. She paused, slowing her erratic pulse with deep breaths before tapping on his door and cracking it open.

"Nick, you have thirty seconds or we'll miss our flight."

"I'm ready," he said, slinging his bag over one shoulder, swinging the door wide open and shoving past her. He was definitely taking after his dad in above-average height and already matched Tessa inch for inch. His jeans and dragon T-shirt were getting too short again. If only he'd let her take him to cut his hair a few inches to match. His blond side-swept bangs made it impossible to look him in the eye. His room looked like the latest hurricane had made landfall. Good thing Brice never bothered going past Nick's bedroom. If he had any idea there was a room in the house in a state like this, he'd die.

"Uh, are you sure you didn't forget anything you need? Toothbrush, perhaps?" And here she was afraid something had fallen between *her* bedsheets.

"No," he snapped, reaching around her and pulling the door shut.

"Okay." *Keep out. That won't be a problem.*

She followed him downstairs, letting him out first so she could set the house alarm. The taxi she'd arranged for earlier was idling in their circular driveway. Nick waited for her before getting in.

"You should be happy about taking a holiday."

The private school he attended—one of South Africa's popular and prestigious ones and the same one he'd attended before his parents were killed—gave its students ten days off in August. He'd complained plenty of times that one of his American classmates had told him kids back home got something like two and a half months off in the summer. How did parents over there survive that? How did parents survive, period?

Nick shrugged and gazed out the window at the passing shoreline as they headed for the airport.

"Whatever."

Tessa caught the driver glancing at her. Sympathy for Nick's attitude? Or recognition of whose wife she was and curiosity as to where she was going? She wouldn't doubt that half the drivers in their area answered to Brice. He tipped well, but he also had a great rapport with everyone. Which was why getting him to approve this trip had been so important. His approval meant less suspicion on his part and that alone would buy her time.

Brice had seemed relieved when she mentioned taking Nick out of town for a week. If Tessa had noticed anything since Nick came to live with them, it was that Brice had less patience for kids than she did. He hadn't been kidding when they'd had the infamous discussion about no kids right before they got married. But she loved Nick. He was her nephew...her blood. And Brice wasn't solely to blame on the no-patience front. Nick was a handful. A slurry of teen moodiness thickened with posttraumatic stress. Yet Brice *had* welcomed him into their home. That's why she was feeling morbidly guilty right now.

She smiled at the driver and tried to act as relaxed as possible, fighting back tears as they passed the neighborhood of midsize homes where her sister had lived. She noticed Nick looking over and her heart broke for not being able to tell him that his "visit" to his uncle might end up being a lot more than a visit…and that he'd likely not see his old neighborhood again for a long time. She placed her hand on his shoulder and he shoved it off. His constant rejections hurt. So she wasn't ideal substitute-mom material, but she was trying to do her best.

It's all going to be okay.

All that mattered was getting Nick to Kenya and then getting as far from the boy as she could. Because sooner or later Brice would realize this wasn't a vacation, and when he did, he'd be after her for answers…and there was no way she'd let Nick get caught in the cross fire.

MAC WALKER HATED being played almost as much as he hated owing anyone anything. But everyone—including Mac—had a price, and saving Air Walker Safaris from the red was a big one. He'd always gotten by okay. Up until now, the balance between booking enough paid charters to keep the cash flowing and still having plenty of spare time to volunteer free flights for herd observation or tracking for wildlife reservations or research and rescue camps in the area had been perfect. His safari charters hopefully raised awareness of endangered species while letting tourists take in or photograph the phenomenal world below. But his volunteer work? That's what he lived for. That's what he didn't want to sacrifice if AWS suffered. He liked the way his life was—he was on his own and in control. And no matter how many psychological games bigger, better companies tried to play with him, he wasn't going to give in.

He hated the fact that once anyone got wind of the good life or a diamond in the rough, they wanted a piece of it. Now every other flying junkie was trying to set up shop and cash in on the draw of Kenya's Serengeti and his books were beginning to show it. It made him sick that they didn't really care for the land, so much as the opportunity. He sat back, propping his dirt-crusted hiking boots onto the undersized wooden table that served as his desk, and studied his email reply to the latest franchise trying to buy him out. He deleted the colorful insult he'd added to the draft.

It wouldn't be selling out, really—except from his perspective. The companies trying to buy AWS positioned their offers as more of a partnership and a chance to increase business. No doubt the move would fund the kind of tender loving care his one true love—his chopper—needed, and he'd finally be able to add a second helicopter and pilot to his payroll. But the mere idea of giving up an ounce of control made him cringe. Sure, he was just a small charter business, but he'd never needed much to keep himself afloat before. He'd had a few extra expenses this past year. That was all. He just needed a small business boost and time to recover. He still had adequate savings to keep sending his share of support for his nephew, Nick. That was one of his priorities and the least he could do, but boy, did he need to start adding to the bank account. The numbers in the partnership offers were tempting.

Just not tempting enough. AWS wasn't on its deathbed yet.

But his gut told him it would happen sooner or later. The question was when. How many bridges could he burn before he lost all his chances at a deal that would keep AWS from going completely under?

For now, though, it was a risk worth taking to maintain his independence.

He took his feet off the battered wood desk and hit Send. Done.

He needed a drink.

And more customers.

He scrubbed his face with his palms and took one swig from a bottle of Scotch he kept in the short filing cabinet that helped support the end of his desk. Then he turned off his lamp and computer. His long-term lease at Hodari Lodge, one of the upscale tourist lodges near Amboseli National Park, afforded him a windowed office where tourists could browse brochures and sign up for tours. He also had adjoining private living quarters that were barely big enough for a man half his size. He'd divided his humble "single bed and bath" space with a curtain consisting of long orange and red cloths gifted to him by Masai friends after he'd located a young child who'd wandered too far from their village. The handiwork, woven with care, was a reminder of what was important in life.

He made short use of the basin and urinal that occupied the left side of the room, turned off the lights, sat on the edge of the single bed he dwarfed and pulled off his boots.

The chitter-chatter of insects and mellow cries of nocturnal beasts carried through the mosquito netting on the window he'd opened earlier. Potent sounds that fueled his blood and kept him company.

He leaned back against his pillow and started to tuck his hands behind his head but froze at the barely perceptible click of the door to his quarters. Shuffling steps were followed by the metal grind of his rusty file cabinet opening and the rustle of papers. Not a very quiet thief, but then again, few people knew he lived at the back of his office, and Sue, his assistant, never went past the front desk. She'd left much earlier and had promised to lock the door that opened to the lodge's foyer so he could deal with emails uninterrupted. He should have double-checked.

He slipped his switchblade out of his back pocket and rose. This had happened to him once before. The guy had been after his alcohol. Handing over his Scotch would be the least of Mac's worries. Losing his computer or the day's cash that he hadn't had the chance to bank would bite a lot harder.

He peered past a break in the Masai drapes and quickly noted that the dark figure was no match for his six feet. It looked more like the size of an older kid. Moonlight reflected off his bottle of Scotch at the back of the file drawer. Untouched. Not after the booze, huh?

One long stride and he had his hand over the intruder's mouth and their body braced hard against his. A faint trace of perfume or scented shampoo and the thief's curved shape gave her gender away and, admittedly, shocked the heck out of him. She gasped and dug her nails frantically into his forearm while trying, unsuccessfully, to kick her heels up at his knees. The little witch even tried sinking her teeth in him, but he twisted his hold and saved his skin. He held his blade just far enough from her neck so she could see it.

"Stop struggling and this won't get any worse."

Her chest heaved, but she obeyed. He flicked his blade shut with one hand, shoved it in his pocket and reached to turn on the light, then he flipped her around and pinned her against the closest wall.

"You have *got* to be kidding me," Mac said.

Tessa stared up at him with the same doe-like eyes he remembered, only now faint lines creased her forehead and a couple of early grays streaked through her long brown hair. She was still as beautiful as she'd ever been, but the past six months had clearly left their mark. She looked older than her thirty years...even more so than when he'd seen her at the funeral. Too many lazy beach days with fancy drinks did that to a person, didn't it? Okay, he was being a jerk, stereotyping her. He wasn't *that* judgmental. Not any more than she'd always been of his lifestyle. Maybe it really was the stress of her loss showing. That was something he did understand.

His brother, Allan, had been a pilot, too. He'd married his high school sweetheart, Tessa's sister, Maria, and when their Cessna had crashed just miles from their home in Cape Town six months ago, custody of their then twelve-and-a-half-year-old son, Nick, had been given to both Mac and Tessa. An arrangement that made no sense at all, given that she lived in South Africa with the millionaire husband she'd landed and he lived in Kenya's outback with no time or place to add a kid. The only explanation Tessa or Mac had been able to come up with had been that Maria and Allan wanted their child to retain ties to both sides of his family. Having the comforts of a mansion, great schools and both a father and mother figure on hand made more sense than uprooting him. Besides, as far as Mac knew, Tessa had plenty of time to spare, what with playing the butterfly wife and not doing much more than writing a fashion column once a week. Mac didn't have anything close to that kind of luxury.

"Can you please ease up on the man hold?" she panted.

Her face was pale and clammy. He'd scared her to death, all right, but she deserved it. Tessa Henning. In Kenya. In his cave. Unbelievable. He glanced down to where something glimmered against her skin with the rise and fall of her chest. A simple silver *M*...for Maria. He recognized the necklace as the one he'd helped his brother pick out for Maria's birthday senior year. Back when he couldn't afford a whole lot.

Mac released his hold and motioned her to sit on his desk chair while he stood akimbo between her and her only escape.

"What were you looking for, Tessa?"

TESSA SUCKED IN the corner of her lip the way she always did when she needed to think. This was Mac. She had to be on her toes. She waved away the entire situation with her hand.

"Looking for? Come on, Mac. Suspicious much? I was trying to find a plain sheet of paper to leave you a note to let you know that Nick and I arrived a few hours ago. He's in a room sleeping right now. We were hoping you could meet us early for breakfast and then take us up for a tour."

Mac folded his arms and raised a brow. Why had his confidence always irritated her? Standing there like that in his jeans and white T-shirt...like he was a model posing for a rugged photo shoot for one of her fashion posts. It just... She didn't like it. That was all.

"You broke in here and planned to write me a note," he said.

"Yes." Tessa nodded for emphasis.

"In the dark."

She kept nodding. She used to be so good at smart comebacks, but her nerves had clearly wiped out her memory banks. *You're such a dork, Tessa. Pull it together.* She cleared her throat.

"There's plenty of moonlight out and I thought lights out here were on some sort of generator timer. Aren't they? I was telling Nick on the flight that we might have to get some LED torches or brush our teeth in the dark."

"Cute. Really cute."

She smiled.

"Tessa." Mac ran his fingers through his short blond hair. Nick looked a lot like his uncle. "Seeing Nick will be great. But why in the world would you pay for a charter from Nairobi instead of calling ahead so I could pick you up? Couldn't you at least have left a message?"

"And ruin the surprise?"

He raised a brow at her. Okay, so even she knew Mac wasn't keen on surprises. She hadn't initially planned on sneaking into his office, but it was the one place she figured she could access a computer privately. She needed to do some research, but she also wanted to check if Katia had sent her an email. Maybe she'd changed her mind about the article. Tessa had forgotten her tablet charger. She should have searched her sheets better. As for getting here from the main airport in Nairobi...yes, counting on Mac would have been easier. And stupid.

"Look. I'm still not used to scheduling around school holidays, so this one crept up on us."

"I realize you've grown accustomed to the silver spoon and spa type of life and people falling at your feet, but I don't bow to anyone. Don't you think it's a bit presumptuous to assume I'm not already booked tomorrow morning?"

She hated—really hated—when people made her sound petty and self-centered just because she'd married a wealthy man. They had no clue about her marriage or what her life was like below the surface. As for Mac...he'd judged her and made fun of her since their school days. He used to call her

a hermit, chicken and nerd. She hated him
for that and had always resented the fact
that Mac, Allan and Maria were part of the
cool crowd she'd never fit into. They'd been
the kids who got invited to parties, always
looked trendy and weren't afraid to break
rules or play hooky when she didn't dare.

But right now, Mac's ego wasn't her problem. His cooperation was. She noticed the
top of a brochure sticking out from underneath a few envelopes by his computer.
AWS: Air Walker Safaris. He had his logo
embroidered on half his shirts and had given
a shirt and matching cap to Nick when he'd
come down to South Africa to settle things
after the funeral. Narcissistic company
name, if you asked her. Bet he'd had an easy
time coming up with that one.

Nick was a Walker, though, and she
needed to press the fact that he was the last
"Air Walker." No way could she bring up
having him stay with Mac permanently until
she could negate all of Mac's logistical ar-
guments against it. She needed Mac to suc-
cumb to his emotions regarding his nephew.
It wouldn't be easy. She needed to slip under
his radar and rob him of his bachelorhood.

When they'd gained custody, Mac had made it quite clear that raising a boy while being both a bush pilot and tour guide wouldn't work in any way, shape or form. His refusal to take Nick was just one more reason why she resented him. Mac—who lived for spontaneity, change and challenge—had backed off when it came to raising a kid. And he'd assumed that just because Tessa was married, had money and a house and was female, she was mother material. He'd implied that she had more time on her hands—between manicures—than he did.

There were no words for how much she loved and cared about Nick…and no regrets for the time she'd gotten to spend with him. She truly wanted to do right by Maria, but taking on a traumatized child had terrified her, and months of dealing with his depressed moods had left her drained. Mac did care about his nephew. She knew that, just like she knew that if something happened to her, he'd figure out a way to blend Nick into his life, whether he wanted to or not. She just wished he'd taken on some of the load from the beginning. And in his eyes, he had no more reason to take on raising Nick now than he had six months ago when he'd left him in Tessa's hands.

"Are you booked tomorrow?" she asked.

His lips hardened and he clenched his jaw. "No."

"I guess it's all good, then. I promised Nick a holiday and I'd hate for him to be disappointed or, God forbid, bored. He's been a bit depressed, and I figured a last-minute surprise trip would be fun and good for him," she said, getting up from the chair and brushing past Mac. He wrapped his fingers around her arm. They were calloused and worn...and warm against her skin.

"Just how long do you plan to stay?" he asked.

Did he mean her and Nick? Or just her? Bringing up the Nick situation right now with the mood she'd already put Mac in wouldn't be smart. No, Nick and Mac needed some bonding time...if that was possible with their personalities. And with Mac's history of volunteering with wildlife organizations, he was the only person who might be able to help her figure out what was going on with her husband. She knew without a doubt that Mac was on the right side of the law when it came to poaching, but then again, Katia had refused to help her. Mac might have his own agenda, too. Ultimately, she could only count on herself. So much for skipping out on computer science classes in college and not learning something useful…like navigating computers beyond the basics. Where *did* one learn how to hack?

She looked at his hand—he let go—then she let out a breath and tucked hers into her pockets to calm herself. She glanced around his cramped quarters. He wasn't kidding when he said he didn't have room for Nick. But he'd have to make room or find a new place because the way Tessa's life was unfolding, Nick living with her was no longer an option. Not with her life crumbling around her. She angled her head at Mac.

"A week tops. Then I promise I'll be out of your hair."

For good.

CHAPTER TWO

MAC HAD AVOIDED touching his Scotch again last night. With Tessa around, he needed to keep his head on straight. But finding her in his office, bracing her—not *em*bracing, he reminded himself—against his chest… The memories the evening had stirred up were worthy of a full-bottle hangover. The way she'd fallen into his arms at Maria and Allan's funeral. How she'd sobbed against his chest and he'd buried his own tears in the crook of her neck. She'd never liked him much back in their school days, and he'd never cared for her lifestyle after marriage, but at that moment, no one else in the room—other than perhaps Nick…and Tessa's parents—had understood what she and Mac were going through. In that moment, he'd imagined a connection…an understanding between them that had never been there before.

Then she'd begun pounding his chest and screaming about how much she hated him for encouraging Allan to propose to her sister. That her sister would still be alive if they weren't related. She'd buckled to her knees after that.

Half of him had wanted to take off and the other half had wanted to wrap his arms around her and pick her up. But Brice had beaten him to it. He was the one she needed to lean on, anyway. He was her husband. Her safety net. Mac... Mac apparently wasn't even a friend. He was nothing but a co-guardian. A brother-in-law she didn't like. He still remembered the crushing pressure in his chest when he'd watched Brice rush over and take her in his arms. Mac had lost his brother. Opening up and sharing his pain with Tessa hadn't been easy. He'd let himself be vulnerable. Then she'd turned on him. He'd never forget that.

Mac's trip back home to South Africa had been rife with raw emotions. There'd been a lot to take care of and the need to focus on Nick had helped him ignore the punch to his gut every time Tessa's eyes met his as the lawyers sorted their siblings' wills out. He wasn't sure why she'd always hated him so much. At the time, he wasn't sure he'd ever get over losing Allan, but thinking of Nick put his pain in perspective. The poor boy was orphaned. Allan and Maria's funeral had been hell for all of them on so many levels.

This visit was different, though. They were on Mac's turf this time.

Nonetheless, this week was going to be hell, too.

Mac washed down a couple of aspirin to dull the throbbing in his temples and turned his computer on for a quick email check. Prior to the arrival of his surprise visitors, he'd planned to lie low and work on some marketing niche ideas or a new design for the brochures he'd last updated six years ago. He needed an edge before the lodge owners let some big shot come in and take his customers. He didn't normally care what others thought of him, but Tessa was the last person he wanted knowing that he was just getting by. She'd always acted standoffish and better than him in school. After marrying Brice, she really *was* better off—socially and financially.

But what was bothering him more was that he'd bought into her holiday excuses for being here. It wasn't until she'd gone back to her room, leaving her scent behind to taunt him, that he realized she must have ulterior motives. She was up to something...or that husband of hers had put her up to something. Like trying to convince him to take over raising Nick. Or perhaps Big Business Brice had sent his trophy wife to convince him to sell out to his latest investment idea. He'd never liked Brice Henning. The guy was too polished. Too perfect and careful. As far as Mac was concerned, shiny surfaces hid things...like polished diamonds hid defects and rough pasts, or like a calm sea glistening in the moonlight hid sharks. He simply wasn't the kind of guy Mac cared to share a beer with, not that Brice would stoop to drinking beer and socializing with a small-beans pilot.

Still, Mac sincerely felt Brice and Tessa had the better setup for raising a kid: being close to Nick's school, material comforts and all. Plus, Nick had needed access to good counseling after his parents' deaths. He'd needed to stay close to the friends he had for peer support. No one wanted the tragedy to send Nick veering along a downhill path. Mac had been doing his share, sending as much money as possible to support his nephew because Walkers took care of Walkers. Regardless of wills.

The money Nick had inherited had been put in a trust for him, but after paying off the debts his parents had, he and Tessa had agreed that the majority of the amount left needed to be saved for his college education. It had been the only thing he and Tessa had *ever* agreed on.

He hovered his finger over his mouse, then gave into his lack of focus and logged out.

Mac locked his window, grabbed his AWS cap and headed out the door, this time making sure to lock his quarters behind him.

"Morning," Mac said, taking the mug of hot coffee Sue Bekker held out. He leaned an elbow against the low counter that divided the front desk from the rest of the office. "Sweetheart, you're spoiling me."

Sue blushed and patted his arm.

She was the mother of his old friend, Dr. Anna Bekker, who ran the Busara research and rescue camp for orphaned baby elephants. Sue was a skilled, albeit sometimes forgetful, woman who'd battled depression. But ever since she'd reconnected with her daughter and moved from America to live in the Serengeti and work for him, she seemed to embrace life. Something about the region did that to a person. Life here was simple, raw and beautiful. He loved it.

"Well, I figured you'd need it this morning," she said. "They came in asking for you. The brunette said they were family," she said, nodding through their glass office doors toward the pretty woman and lanky kid who stood facing one of the lodge's attractions: a floor-to-ceiling wooden wall carved with images of wildlife, including a herd of elephants the park was so famous for.

Man. Nick had shot up in six months. He had definitely inherited the Walker gene for height. Couldn't tell much about his face from where he stood. Not with all that hair hanging over it. The boy made a final crease on a flyer-turned-paper-airplane and shot it at the wall. His aunt mouthed something, but he ignored her, walked over to a stand

of safari brochures and reversed the stacks
in their holders. Mac couldn't claim fame
as having been the world's easiest teenager.
He'd been hell with wings. His gut told him
karma had just caught up with him.

Tessa looked ready for action with her
hair pulled back into a tight ponytail and
a mini backpack slung stylishly over one
shoulder. She was fidgeting impatiently with
the pocket of her carpenter-style—and no
doubt designer—khakis and what looked
to him like the same stormy-blue shirt she'd
had on last night. She picked up the plane
herself, then scanned the lodge, as if worried
they'd get kicked out. The kid was pushing
her buttons like a pro. She glanced impatiently at her watch.

*Well, a man has a right to coffee first,
Princess Tess.*

He took a long swig. Tessa turned and
spotted him. *And the day begins.*

"That's my nephew out there," he said,
breaking eye contact with Tessa. He didn't
share a lot of family information with anyone, but Sue did know he'd lost his brother
in a crash.

"Oh! Well, go spend time with him. I have

things covered here. Go. Go." Sue waved him off.

Mac gulped the rest of the coffee down, then set his cap on his head and his hand on the glass door, but Tessa beat him to it. She slipped inside with Nick. An unwelcome fresh scent and all-encompassing energy filled the room. The same energy he'd felt when he'd set eyes on her at Maria and Allan's wedding. The same energy that had filled his quarters last night.

He'd been stunned by her transformation when he saw her arrive at their siblings' wedding. If that wasn't enough, Maria and Allan had called out for them to join them on the floor after their first dance. The way she'd felt in his arms then was the way she'd felt in his arms at the funeral…and again last night. He didn't like reacting to her. Didn't want it. Didn't understand it. They'd never gotten along. It was probably nothing but "hard to get" vibes challenging him. Well, she wasn't single anymore. Vibes or not, she was off-limits.

"Hello again!" Sue greeted Nick and Tessa a bit too enthusiastically.

Mac held out his hand to shake Nick's

and pulled him into a one-arm hug, slapping his back.

"Hey, man, good to see you."

"Yeah."

Guess the feeling wasn't mutual.

"Sue, this is Nick, my nephew, and Tessa, my, um…his aunt. My sister-in-law." He scratched the back of his neck as brisk handshakes were exchanged. He needed air. He held the door wide open.

"It's nice to meet you. Would you like some coffee? It's freshly brewed," Sue said, returning behind the front desk. He was *not* having them linger for coffee.

"We already had breakfast. Thanks, though."

"If anyone comes asking for me specifically, catch me on the radio," Mac said. He hesitated, then added, "And don't forget to reschedule that group tour package for later this afternoon."

"Group tour?" Sue looked understandably perplexed. Mac set his hands on the counter and leaned close, winking for good measure. The guilt for putting the glow in her cheeks was justified by desperately needing to signal her to play along without Tessa or Nick cluing in.

"Yes, you remember…the *magazine photographers*…and confirm tomorrow's customers while you're at it. Please."

It took a second for her to catch on.

"Oh, yes, I remember," she lied.

"Great. What would I do without you? Oh, and Sue, if you need to leave the office for whatever reason, don't forget to lock up," he added, ushering Tessa and Nick out the door.

"Of course. I always do," she said, appearing even more perplexed.

Right.

Mac didn't have the heart to tell her about last night, considering he had things under control. He had much bigger issues to deal with right now. He let the office door swing shut behind him.

"How've you been?" he asked, ruffling Nick's hair in the hopes of reading his face. Nick ducked away from his touch.

Don't touch the hair. Got it.

"I'm fine. Not here by choice, but whatever," Nick said, hanging his head as he spoke and stuffing his hands in his pockets.

Tessa watched intently with her lips

pressed together. She closed her eyes briefly, in an apparent apology for Nick's rudeness, then wrinkled her face at Mac in a "would you like to deal with this every day?" expression.

"*Whatever* works for me," Mac said. "Seeing as you two beat me out here, how about you help me run a check on my chopper and then we can head up? I'll give you a taste of piloting if you want."

Guy stuff. Right? Didn't every kid like planes, trains and the whole array? Tessa gave him an almost imperceptible shake of her head. Mac caught on right away. He pinched the bridge of his nose. This was why he wasn't good parent material. Guy stuff...except, maybe, when the kid's parents had been killed in a plane crash. Hadn't the flight over bothered him? Or maybe it *had* and that's why Tessa was cautioning Mac. Then why'd she mention a tour last night? Unless Nick hadn't said anything about not wanting to do an air tour until this morning.

Mac rubbed the cramp in his jaw. It didn't matter. Accidents happened. The kid couldn't stay grounded for life. Flying was in his blood. But Nick needed to feel in control again and Mac, more than anyone, understood that.

"What about a quick tour of the lodge and the gardens? Maybe a short hike," Tessa suggested.

"Sure. We don't have to go up if flying bothers you, Nick," Mac said. "I assure you, my girl is safer than driving a car, but I can understand fear and..."

"I'm *not* afraid," Nick said, raising his voice. "You think I'm some stupid wimp or something? I hate it when everyone treats me like a baby. I didn't say I was afraid, Aunt Tessa. I said I just didn't feel like it. I made it here on a plane, didn't I?"

"Yes, you did," Mac said. Touchy one. "I'm just giving you options. I can get a jeep, take you on foot or take you up...anything you want, depending on what you'd like to see."

"Then just do whatever Aunt Tessa wants and get us back home," he said, storming away. Mac and Tessa watched as he cleared the building and made his way onto a lush terrace of grass and trees, then stopped cold when two vervet monkeys approached him, begging for food. He took several steps back.

And then a few more, flattening his palms against the wall he'd backed into. Yeah, the kid was *clearly* not a wimp.

GET US BACK HOME. Tessa's stomach twisted at Nick's words. The poor kid was about to hurdle another life change—because of her. If she'd simply turned a blind eye and kept her suspicions to herself, they'd both be back at home in South Africa, safe and sound. Well, *maybe* safe. That was questionable. Now she had no idea when or if she'd ever have a home again. And Nick… his home was going to be here and he didn't even know it.

"Do we rescue him?" Mac asked. The corner of his mouth twisted into a wry smile as the monkeys tried cornering the poor kid. Mac was enjoying this?

"Of course we do," Tessa said, swatting his arm. Preying on Nick's pride was mean, although she had to admit that perhaps he understood teen boys better than she did. She certainly wasn't a model guardian. No doubt Mac would do better. "Just don't tell him we are," she said, heading for the terrace.

Mac followed her out, tossed the pair of

squealing beggars a couple of peanuts from his pocket and told Tessa and Nick to head around the corner of the building. The scent of honeyed flowers from a nearby vine wafted on the breeze as they cleared the courtyard area. The rustling shade from a cluster of fig trees welcomed them down a path that gave way to a large clearing and a chopper that had to be his. They still had to walk out to it, since it was parked a safe distance from the lodge itself. She caught Nick actually giving his head a jerk to flick his hair out of the way for a better view. The helicopter was mostly white with a dark green strip down the side and big green lettering that said AWS.

It looked way too small for comfort. Tessa's pulse quickened and her stomach clenched. The situation, desperation and the need to set an encouraging example for Nick were all that had gotten her through the trip here. Still, she'd left imprints on the arms of her seat during the flight over from Nairobi. But a helicopter wasn't a commercial plane. A person didn't feel air turbulence in a big plane the way they did in a little one. She knew that firsthand. She'd never forget the one time her sister and Allan had convinced her to go for a ride in their Cessna. It had been the first and last time. And now, knowing how their lives had ended, the idea of touring in Mac's helicopter was hitting home. What had she been thinking?

You can do this. Don't think about Maria. Trust Mac. He won't let anything bad happen. He's been flying forever. Allan had been, too.

"Not your kind of chariot?" Mac whispered over her shoulder. Tessa jumped and slapped her hand to her chest. Then she took a deep breath and studied the chopper.

"It's perfect actually," she said, forcing a smile. "Show us why Mac Walker decided to call this place home."

This was it. She was in all the way. Now all she had to do was get him to agree to keep Nick. Doing so would mean swallowing her pride and sharing her worries about Brice. That also meant confessing that her life wasn't turning out to be as stable and perfect as she'd hoped or let on. And to reckless Mac of all people. That was akin to begging for "I told you so." As if Mac Walker weren't cocky enough. She might as well hand him an extra serving of ego on a silver platter.

CONSIDERING THAT THIS trip had been her idea to begin with, Mac never thought Tessa would be the one scared to go up. Five minutes in the air and Tessa was still gripping the sides of her seat and she hadn't opened her eyes once. Nick, on the other hand— sitting up front with Mac—had raked his hair out of his face repeatedly to take everything in. Mac resisted suggesting that Tessa loan his nephew her hair elastic.

Maybe being up here was good for the kid. Exposure therapy. A way to remember taking flights with his parents. Kids were more resilient than grown-ups gave them credit for. Tessa, however, had turned into a more cautious person, rather than a stronger one.

Mac spoke into his headset, giving them his usual tour spiel and pointing out the lay of the land and the view of Mount Kilimanjaro in the distance. He identified the wildlife herds they spotted, but was pretty sure

Tessa didn't hear a word. Too bad. Her loss. She was missing out on some spectacular scenery. She leaned to one side and rested her forehead in her hand.

Please don't barf in my bird.

"You need an air sickness bag back there?" he asked, hoping she wouldn't make a mess. She scrunched her face but shook her head. He told her where they were kept in the back, anyway.

"Can we land for a few minutes?" Her mouth clamped shut as fast as the squeaky words left her lips. Boy. She really wasn't doing so well. Mac altered course.

"Camp Jamba isn't far. Hang in there."

Camp Jamba was not a luxury tourist attraction—especially not for a Tessa caliber of tourist—but it was his favorite place to get away. A small camp, nice and remote with minimal offerings. The owners, Mugi and Kesi Lagat, were an older couple who'd become good friends to Mac over the years. More like family. And if this whole trip of Tessa's was about trying to snap a teen boy out of his funk, then a taste of the rustic life might just do the trick. Come to think of it, taking him to Busara for a day to help out with baby elephant rescues wouldn't be a bad idea, either. Nothing like helping others to make a person appreciate their own life. The good and the bad.

"What are those?" Nick asked, pointing at a grazing herd, several members of which sported formidable black horns that rose high off their heads in a graceful curve.

"Grant's gazelle."

"Cool. Can you see them, Aunt Tessa?" Nick asked, louder than necessary, into his mic. He turned to his aunt, who sat huddled in the back with her eyes still shut. "Oh. Never mind. You okay?"

"I'm fine, Nick. You have fun. I'm fine."

"We're almost there, Tess," Mac added, noting the beads of sweat forming on her forehead. The camp came into view as they cleared a mass of trees. He really wanted her on the ground and out of his baby before she got sick.

He landed in his usual spot and gave them the clear when it was safe to hop out. Tessa ran straight for the bushes.

Getting her *back* to the Hodari Lodge was going to be very interesting.

TESSA'S LEGS WOULDN'T stop shaking and

they'd been on solid ground for a good fifteen minutes now. She sat on an overturned log that served as a bench near the entrance to Camp Jamba—the kind of camp that catered to granola-loving tree-huggers, from what she could see. She sure hoped they had a jeep and driver here. The thought of going back up in the air made her hands hot and head cold. *We landed in one piece. We landed in one piece.*

Nick had followed Mac inside, clearly more comfortable with watching wildlife from the air than from the ground. She glanced back at the small, earthy-looking, thatched-roof cottage that Mac told her was both the main office for the camp and the owners' home. Guests, she assumed, rented one of the framed tents, fashioned from sticks and tarps, that dotted an area about ten yards from the main house. A stone-lined dirt path led to each one and a grove of elephant pepper trees kept the area cool. The entire camp was situated on a low rise overlooking a branch of what Mac had said was the Mara River and a formidable expanse of the Masai Mara grasslands beyond.

She closed her eyes and the fluttering

shadows that danced against her lids soothed her nerves. The sounds that surrounded her kind of reminded her of the music they played in her yoga meditation class at home. A person didn't need earbuds or music here. The air was filled with song so complex, so mesmerizing, it could never be man-made. It was magical. It soothed her motion sickness. She'd never been more out of place, yet she'd never felt so unexpectedly at peace. She was surprised that anything related to Mac's life could make her feel that way.

She was simply overcome with relief from having successfully fled her house in the Cape with the flash drives. She was projecting that emotion onto Mac's wilderness. That was all.

Wow. She'd actually taken a risk and made it this far. She had to admit the feeling was a little thrilling. A bit empowering. Mac was the last person on earth she'd ever confess that to. But it wasn't over and risks came at a price. She knew that better than anyone.

"Drink this," Mac said, walking up and handing her a soda. "They're getting more bottled water later today and I didn't want to risk the well tap on you, even with a filter in place. The bubble in this will make you feel better in any case." She reluctantly opened her eyes.

"Thanks," Tessa said, taking the cold bottle from him. Her fingers touched his. She ignored the ripple in her chest and rubbed her fingertips up and down the icy dew that had formed on her bottle. She drank and immediately felt her stomach settle. "Is Nick okay?"

"Yes. He's browsing some wood carvings and a few things they have for sale, souvenir-wise. They don't really have a gift shop. When real guests are here, they put out things like T-shirt samples on the porch, but keep the inventory inside their home."

"I didn't give him any of the rand I converted to shillings yet."

"Not a problem. He's just looking."

They both sat quietly, taking in the exquisite view of acacia trees and a herd of elephants passing them in the distance. The leaves of the pepper trees rustled overhead and the chatter of a million animal languages vibrated through the air in a lulling rhythm.

"So this is why you live here," she said. A hint of admission was easier to take than awkward silence.

He nodded.

"It does make for nice meditating," she allowed.

"And it's free. Always amazes me that people will dish money out for things to help them relax, yet they never bother to try going for a walk or sitting somewhere like this."

"Not everyone has access to a place like this. Or even a backyard. You really like prejudging and making assumptions, don't you? For your information, group meditation classes do have their benefits. They're motivating and supportive and they really help with anxiety. I even took Nick to one."

"Bet he loved that."

She pressed her lips together and turned away. No, Nick had hated it, but Mac didn't need to know.

"I'm sorry about cutting our flight short. Obviously I've flown before—not in a helicopter and I avoid small planes, but big ones I can handle—and I didn't expect to react the way I did. I was never good at going out on boats with my parents, either. Not even when I was little. At first, it was the motion sickness. Later on it was the nightmares I'd have about them out there on their own. I should have never, ever watched movies like *Jaws* or *The Perfect Storm*." She took another sip. "This mental image of Maria and Allan crashing flashed before me after we took off and I couldn't get rid of it."

Mac etched the dry ground with the end of a stick.

"Don't worry about it. It happened to me a couple of times after the funeral. I had to work a little harder at putting it out of my head and getting in my pilot's seat. When someone calls you and needs help, it makes putting your fears aside easier. The nerves and memories do hit you in random spurts, don't they?"

Tessa dug the heel of her sneaker into the ground and ran it back and forth forming a coffin-like trench. Any bigger and she'd be saving Mac the trouble of figuring out where to hide her body once she spilled the truth. She pulled her ponytail loose and scratched her scalp.

"I'm leaving him with you, Mac," she

said, keeping her eyes on a herd wandering so far off in the distance that she couldn't identify them. "I'm so sorry, but I need to leave him with you. He doesn't know yet."

She finally braved a glance at Mac. His jaw was popping like there was no tomorrow as he stared at the dirt just beyond his boots.

"And I had just started to think you were actually coming out of your glass cocoon to enjoy the world around you. That your maternal instincts had kicked in full throttle. Yet you've planned all this—this trip—and failed to discuss your decision with either of us. Nice one, Tess."

"Trust me on this," she said.

Mac stood abruptly and turned on her.

"I do *trust* on a case-by-case basis."

"Brice isn't father material. He doesn't have the patience and he's so busy he's never around. Nick deserves better than that. He needs a male role model. He's miserable with me, Mac. And I... I have work I need some time to focus on."

Mac narrowed his eyes.

"Are you trying to tell me Brice is mistreating him or something? And that you have more important things to do than care for Nick?"

"No! Brice is simply not present and I can't do this alone." It was true that Brice hadn't exactly been an attentive husband or guardian lately, but that was a separate issue. "Nick simply doesn't mix in well with our life. Our lifestyle is too…"

"Sterile?" Mac offered. She glared.

"If you care at all about Nick, you'll take him in. At least for a while," she said, trying to soften the blow but knowing full well that "a while" would turn into "until he's a legal adult."

Mac sat back down and scrubbed at his face.

"I'm about to take on a lot more work, Tessa. Largely, so I can continue to provide for his expenses. There's no way I can keep an eye on him and make sure he's not freaking out at every turn when an animal shows up. They kind of tend to around here. Plus, you saw where I live. And school. He may be on holiday right now, but you can't rip him out of his school at this age. We agreed he needed to have his peers around him."

"Yes, we agreed, but things have changed, okay? I tried…"

"No!" Nick appeared at the door to the cottage looking like an irate bull. Tessa and Mac both leaped off the log. "You liars! You selfish, little…" The trail of cussing that ensued had Tessa covering her face while Mac tried to get a calming word in edgewise. With the kid's anger-fueled lungs, half the Serengeti had probably just gotten a ripe lesson in original insults.

"Nick, calm down. Let's talk. Nothing has happened yet," Mac said with his palms held up. "And you owe your aunt exactly nineteen apologies by this evening or I might rent you a permanent tent right here at this camp."

"Nick, I was going to talk to you, but…" Tessa tried adding.

"Both of you need to just shut up," Nick persisted, pacing and gripping his head as he yelled. "You make me sick! I hate you!"

"That's it. Tessa, come with me," Mac said, leading the way to the cottage. "You, Nick, park it on that log until you get in control. No control, no inside. No flight back. Got it?"

Tessa hurried after Mac, shocked at how

he'd handled their nephew. For one thing, Brice had never ordered Nick to apologize to her. He didn't feel comfortable reprimanding him. Nick had had plenty of outbursts before and not once had Brice intervened as Mac had. Not for her sake or Nick's. He dealt with Nick's outbursts by telling her to take him to see a different therapist.

She briefly greeted the owners—Mugi and Kesi, if she'd caught their names correctly. Her mind was on Nick so she wasn't paying attention. She apologized for anything they might have overheard, then glanced out the window. Nick had actually listened to Mac and was sitting on the log, rubbing his hands along his jeans.

"Will he be okay out there alone? What if he runs off?" she asked.

"He's surrounded by wildlife. Trust *me*, Tessa. He won't move more than two feet from that log unless it's to run toward this door."

CHAPTER THREE

NICK LASTED NO more than ten minutes and the look on his face made Mac feel like scum, but the kid had gone over the top. No wonder Tessa was begging Mac to take over. Had Brice not been supporting her in raising him? Mac understood what Nick had to be going through. Around the same age, Mac's mother had abandoned the family, and his father, left to raise his sons on his own, had always favored Allan as the son with potential. His parents may have been alive when he was a teenager, but his world had been turned upside down just the same. Mac had left the Cape long before his father, a South African air force veteran, passed away, and their last encounter had not been on the best of terms. He and Allan had become close brothers because they really could only count on each other. But as much as Mac had hated his father's overly strict and emotionally removed parenting style at the time, he knew firsthand that what Nick needed were boundaries. Without them, the kid was going to be as lost as Mac had been.

Mac exchanged looks with Tessa as they listened to Nick's fifty-percent-sincere apology—a percentage Mac figured was pretty good for a teenager.

"Apology accepted," Tessa said...maybe a little too quickly. "Nick, you know I loved your mom. She was my sister and she trusted me to do what's best for you. I had to make this call."

Nick simply chewed the inside of his cheek and turned away, his nostrils still flaring.

"Well, clearly these aren't the makings of a *real* holiday, so why don't we abort the rest of today and head back to discuss this," Mac suggested. A *family discussion*. The phrase hit him from out of the blue, and he almost laughed out loud at the notion. The three of them were like three stray puzzle pieces from different boxes that would never fit together, let alone form a picture of a family.

"Yeah. I want to go back," Nick said.

"First, tell me where a guy is supposed to pee around here without a lion biting his…"

"Hey!" Mac held up a warning finger and Nick chose not to finish his sentence. Something about Nick's attitude made Mac want to keep the fact that the cottage actually had a flushable toilet to himself, but he resisted blurting the few ideas he had on where else to go pee. There were always bushes with lurking predators.

"If you ask politely, Mr. or Mrs. Lagat will show you a bathroom you can use," Mac said.

Nick left a dust cloud in his wake. Tessa rubbed her arms.

"Can I get a ride back on wheels? I'll pay for the service," she said.

"I'm usually the service people use to get out here. The camp does have a jeep, but it's typically used to take guests out on safari."

"Well, I'll tell you what. You go on. We'll stay the night. But I really need to see if someone here has a charger I can borrow or a computer I can use. I have to check my emails and take care of a few things, and there's no way I'm getting back in your helicopter. Someone can fetch me tomorrow in a jeep."

"Hate to break it to you, darling, but there's no internet out here, and do you have any idea how much longer it would take to get back by jeep?" Mac asked.

The Tessa he'd known hadn't been quite so clueless. If anything, writing for their school paper had given her a smart—albeit nerdy—image. Living with money had spoiled her. She'd had a soft heart for animals in shelters back then and always posted articles about school fund-raisers and food drives to help support them. She'd even taken home one too many herself. She told him they kept her company. Maria had been more of a social, outgoing type than Tessa and spent much of her time at school events, and their parents were often away at sea. Maria had been a lot like them. Much like Mac's brother had followed in his father's footsteps. Tessa, not so much. He'd kind of felt sorry for her.

Mac had tried reaching out to Tessa since his brother hung around her sister all the time. He'd even attempted to draw Tessa into their crowd, but she hadn't wanted anything to do with him. He made her nervous for some reason, so he'd backed off. He still was around a lot, though, because of Maria and Allan dating. He'd once overheard Tessa having an argument with her sister in her bedroom; she'd cried about wanting to be more than the latch-key daughter of adrenaline-driven parents. She was fed up with them prioritizing work over spending time at home with their daughters, and risking their lives at sea. She'd been royally ticked off at him when she opened her room door and found him lingering in the hall. Allan's plans for hanging out in their backyard were cut short when Mac told him they'd better leave before Tessa killed him.

And then there was the time during Allan's senior year when Mac had tagged along to visit Maria and fire up the grill. He'd gone inside to grab a drink and ran into Tessa freaking out. Her computer crashed before she had the chance to save her English paper that was due the next morning. He insisted she use his essay, which would have no doubt been worse than hers but was better than nothing. He ended up writing a second one and turning it in after the deadline.

His father gave him a lot of flak for the late penalty, but Mac figured he'd have picked on something about his grade regardless. Seeing the relief and gratitude on Tessa's face had been so worth it. And he'd obviously mistaken it for a truce. A friendship. Right now, Tessa was looking at him with the same wrenching expression as she had that night.

"No internet. For real? Not even for an hour a day or dial-up or something?"

She was obviously desperate, but Nick, who'd just returned from using the facilities and overheard her...he seemed absolutely horrified.

"We could knock you out for the flight," Mac said, scooping up a fist-size rock and bouncing it in his hand.

Tessa glared at him.

"You're not even funny," she said. "Why is it you think you're so funny?"

He grinned and winked at her.

"Because I am." He tossed the rock into a nearby bush and cranked his neck. "Come on, the Tessa I knew was a survivor. I'm betting you can suck it up and manage the trip. With puke bags in hand."

"It's not happening," she said. "My head is still spinning."

Mac whipped his cap off and put his hands on his hips. He needed to get back to work. This was ridiculous.

"Be reasonable."

"I am being reasonable."

"I'm not staying here all night, Aunt Tessa," Nick warned. "I could get bitten by a venomous snake or something. Or get eaten alive. What happened to doing what was best for me?"

Mac had to hand it to the kid. He knew how to manipulate and guilt-trip like a pro.

"Yep, what he said," Mac added.

"You two are ganging up on me?" Tessa asked. "I'm telling you, I'm not going back. I mean, not in that flying tin can. Nick is free to return to the lodge with you."

"On second thought, nothing like a night out under the stars to make a man out of a boy. Camping here would be good for you, Nick. A new experience." Mac smiled at his nephew.

Nick stormed back to the cottage. Mac was grateful that Mugi and Kesi were staying inside to give them some privacy. He'd given them a signal earlier when Nick had lost his composure. Not that Mac cared what anyone thought of him—sort of—but his friends meeting his nephew and Tessa for the first time *was* turning out to be a little embarrassing. Mac lifted his cap, scratched his head, then set it back in place.

"I tell you what," he said, sitting back down next to Tessa. "Why don't you go inside, chat with the Lagats and check on Nick. You have some explaining to do. At least out here he won't run away. Maybe after a longer rest, you'll be ready for the flight."

She dropped her head into her hands.

"You don't understand, Mac."

"I could see if Kesi can brew up one of her concoctions to help with your stomach. She's very skilled with herbs."

"I need to get back," she said, her hands muffling her voice.

Oh man. Was she crying? He hoped not. This was why he lived alone. He silently swore, then rubbed her back. It was instinct. An act of comfort. Brother-in-law to sister-in-law. But she shivered when he made contact and he quickly pulled back.

"That would be the point," he agreed.

"Get back and clear up the Nick situation. Clearly you can see this whole idea spells disaster." If she wanted to go back, then why was she arguing about it? Why couldn't women make sense?

"I'm messing up your scheduled flights. I'm so sorry," she said, raising her head.

"My…oh, yes…my customers. The photographers. Right. Um, no worries. I'll radio Sue and tell her to take care of things. They won't mind rescheduling."

"Mac, can I trust you?"

"I got you here in one piece, didn't I?"

She turned and, this time, she wrapped one of her hands around his. The sight of her slender fingers braided with his wiped out his train of thought.

"What's going on here, Tess? This isn't just about Nick, is it?"

She shook her head and licked her lips. Too close for comfort. Was Tessa Henning coming on to him?

"I may be in trouble. Possibly even in danger. Not one word to anyone, Mac, until I have a chance to figure this out. Promise me."

He nodded because how could he not. She wasn't flirting. She was desperate again. It must be some pretty deep trouble for her to have brought Nick here. Tessa looked over her shoulder, then back at him.

"Mac, I think Brice may be involved in an ivory smuggling ring."

Crap.

Mac pulled his hand out of hers. Ivory smuggling? He got up and she leaped after him.

"Not a word to anyone, Mac. Not yet at least."

He turned on her, bringing his face within an inch of hers and lowering his voice. He hadn't noticed any campers, but one never knew and voices carried around here.

"Do you have any idea what you're saying, Tess? The implication? This better not be about some marital spat or a ploy to justify uprooting Nick."

"Is that how little you think of me? Why would you assume the worst? I came to you because I want Nick in a safe place if this turns into a legal fiasco and the media comes down on us. Or worse. And because I thought I could trust you with this. Allan used to brag about the work you've done with the Kenyan Wildlife Service, helping to catch poachers, and about how you've volunteered for animal rescues in the area. I thought maybe you'd know something. Or know who I can trust among the authorities, because don't believe for a second that Brice can't pay for silence."

Mac pulled back a few inches. His pulse pounded in his temples. His brother had bragged about him? They were close, but Allan had always been so much like their father, critical to a fault. He played the role of big brother, but bragging about Mac was pushing it. The fact that he'd told anyone he was proud of Mac was an unexpected punch in the gut.

"You can trust me, Tessa. That's not the point. You're talking about murder here. Brutal poaching. Tessa, ivory smuggling is an illegal and deadly trade—and deaths aren't always limited to elephants. I won't lie. Brice isn't my favorite person. He's just not my type, but he's a smart businessman. Too smart to get involved in shady dealings."

Tessa closed her eyes and shook her head.

"I know. It all sounds surreal, and I assure you I didn't come up with this overnight. I *know* it's dangerous. Why do you think I'm here with Nick and not still back at our home?" She pulled her hair back into a ponytail like she meant business. "I stole some drives from his desk before leaving. I have no idea what's on them, but I couldn't take a chance. If he's involved in something like this, I need to know."

Yep, she meant business.

"You took his files?"

Damn it. Tessa's suspicions could turn into a full-blown disaster. If she was right.

"He thinks I'm here visiting with Nick."

"Until he discovers what else you brought with you."

"He's out of town for a few days. Which is why I need to find out if there's anything important on the drives as soon as possible. I can always put them back if they're clear and he's not home yet. Maybe it's nothing. Maybe I misunderstood what I overheard. It's a lot of maybes, I know. I need to find out the truth. He's my husband, Mac. I could ruin his life. If I'm wrong, I don't want him knowing that I doubted him."

"If you find proof that backs up what you're saying, then what'll your next move be? Have you thought that far? What are you planning? To disappear? Turn him in and ask for official protection?"

She didn't answer.

"Okay, then. We're staying here tonight," Mac said.

"What?"

"We're staying. I need to hear details, whatever you can tell me, and we're a lot less likely to be overheard by the wrong ears—and I don't mean Nick—out here than back at my office. I'll call Sue and tell her we're… somewhere else…camping out." He didn't want Sue blurting anything to the wrong people. She was too trusting.

Mac pinched the bridge of his nose. Come to think of it, if things went south, he couldn't leave Sue at the mercy of anyone searching for them. She'd be safer visiting Anna and Jack at Busara for a while. Spending time with her grandkids. He was going to need to call Anna and Jack and make arrangements for getting her there, since he was not ready to leave Tessa and Nick alone. Not until he had a better grasp of the situation. Unfortunately, staying here also meant

Air Walker Safaris would be losing business. Business he couldn't afford to lose.

"I'll ask Mugi and Kesi to keep quiet, too. If you need anything, you can trust them."

"Mac. Thank you."

"Don't thank me yet. Just hope Brice doesn't come home early."

TESSA HAD TO admit Mac was right. Lying low at Camp Jamba was a smart idea. Brice knew they were traveling to see Nick's uncle, but she had told him they were meeting Mac in Nairobi. The rest of the trip to Hodari Lodge she'd paid for in cash. Mac's office would be the first place he'd come looking for her if there was incriminating information on those drives. Still, it bought her a little time. Camp Jamba was another step removed, which meant even more of a buffer between them and Brice. But she wouldn't get any closer to confirming her suspicions out here.

Maybe she should have told Mac what was going on last night in his office...where a computer was available. She drank the last sip of her soda. No. Her instincts had kept her from doing so. She needed to trust her gut. He wouldn't have listened then. She wouldn't have been able to dish the note-writing excuse to him. Just as he'd pointed out that more modern conveniences would have made running away easier for Nick, the same could have applied to Mac. He could have acted in defense before listening to anything she had to say about Nick or Brice. Maybe she needed to trust her gut more often.

The aroma of spices and the warm char of open-flamed cooking drifted past her, a solid reminder that she'd been too nervous to eat breakfast this morning—a saving grace considering how she reacted to not being on solid ground. She went inside to thank the Lagats for letting them stay, but soon realized she needed more fresh air.

The flaming Serengeti sun burned directly overhead and a chicken, of all things, ran past her, squawking like it was being chased by an invisible predator until it found the safety of its flock under a fig tree. Maybe her mind was also making up things to fear about Brice. Did she subconsciously want out of her marriage? Was she looking for reasons to leave?

There was no point in procrastinating any longer. She couldn't let Nick hate her. She couldn't let him think she didn't want him around or that she had priorities greater than him. True, she had to make a decision to leave him with Mac, but not for the same reasons her parents had left her alone so often. They were so busy with their aquatic research that they couldn't focus on their children, too. She finally understood how important their work was, but back then she'd been like Nick. Just needing someone to be around…a safety net to catch her as she muddled through her teens…a home and family like all the other kids had. As a child, she'd wanted to feel secure and not have to worry every night—especially during storms—that one or both of her parents might not come home.

She wanted to be that safety net for Nick, but right now, the only way to keep him safe was to pull that net out from under him. And hope Mac was there to catch his fall.

The air vibrated with the trumpeting of elephants in the distance, as if they'd heard her thoughts and were trying to share their wisdom about motherhood and the delicate cycle of life.

If only she spoke elephant.

As a child, she spoke to her adopted cats and sometimes believed they understood her. They'd give her a sign: a lazy blink or a sedating purr that rumbled deep against her chest.

She needed a sign now.

The roar of a lion had her turning quickly toward the path to the cottage. Mac stood on the front porch, leaning against the wooden log that supported the thatched overhang, watching her, the piercing blue of his eyes intense and knowing. Maybe it was the way the Kenyan sun had left its warmth on his skin or how stubble shadowed the hard lines of his jaw, but the way he looked at her sparked a smoldering ache in her chest. She swallowed hard to extinguish it. If only Mac hadn't wanted to get away from home so badly. Maybe they would have eventually become friends. But he'd wanted to escape and explore and she'd wanted—needed—stability.

And now she didn't even have that.

Was this her sign? That the one thing—

the one person—who would make her and Nick's life whole and balanced was the one man she'd turned away from years ago? The one man who knew how small, insecure and insignificant she used to be? She stared down at her feet as she walked up the path toward him.

Life could be so cruel.

CHAPTER FOUR

"HEY. DON'T TOUCH that yet."

Mac gave Nick a warning look and didn't break eye contact until his nephew pulled his hand away from the basket of fresh, warm chapati.

"What? It's there to eat, isn't it?" Nick said, eyeing the traditional flatbread like a hyena with its tongue lolling out. The boy was acting spoiled, like these were free-for-all breadsticks at an Italian restaurant, but this wasn't a restaurant. They weren't campers paying for a safari stay. Those meals were served outdoors. Come to think of it, Mac didn't think he'd ever been just a guest here. They were dining in the Lagats' home. Very dear friends who deserved respect.

"It's there to eat after Mugi and Kesi join us and you thank them for the meal. It's called manners," Mac said, glancing at Tessa to read her reaction.

"We don't always have sit-down meals," she explained. "Brice isn't usually home for dinner because of work, and Nick is so hungry after school that he stuffs himself then. And then again about every hour after that," she added, smiling at Nick. Her attempt to soften him up with good-natured teasing went right over his head.

Mac looked pointedly at both of them. He remembered well the consuming hunger that would hit him as a teenager during bouts of raging hormones or growth spurts. It had to be the closest a guy could get to understanding pregnancy cravings. It hadn't been unusual for him to eat an entire roast down to the bone—by himself—and then get hungry again soon after. So he got it, but that didn't excuse bad manners or lack of respect.

Nor, as far as he was concerned, did living on riches. He'd seen one too many kids come through Hodari Lodge with families who could afford the place and then some, acting careless and entitled. No nephew of his was going to act that way. Losing one's parents wasn't an excuse, either. Life wasn't always fair, but a kid had to grow up understanding how to handle punches like a man—with morals, honor and dignity.

Wow. He was sounding like his own father.

There had to be some give and take, though. Mac leaned back in his chair and rested his palms on his khakis. Who was he to judge Nick's behavior and attitude when he'd willingly left him with Tessa and Brice? In a convoluted way, he was just as guilty as Brice when it came to putting a lot of value on money. As a millionaire investor, Brice wasn't around to be the quintessential family man because making money was his priority. And Mac wasn't around because he needed to make money to live and help support his nephew. And given Air Walker Safaris' financial state, Mac knew full well that money was important. However, some people didn't have their priorities straight. Need and want were very different things.

But Mac's ideals and values were essentially meaningless if he wasn't around to instill them...to set an example. Even if staying in South Africa was best for Nick on so many levels, in the end, all Mac was doing was sending his nephew money. He wasn't really in a position to judge Brice, or his own father, for that matter. Or Tessa.

He rubbed his jaw against his shoulder and stretched his neck.

"Yes, well, consider this a lesson in manners. The Lagats are like family to me. It doesn't matter that they just met you. You've been invited into their home because anyone I care about they care about, too. That's the kind of people they are."

Nick slumped back and looked away from both of them, arms folded and face flushed. The rims of his eyes turned pink. Poor guy was fighting for control. He'd never asked for any of this. Not losing his parents. Not being here in the middle of nowhere. And certainly not being juggled between the only two people in the world he had left.

The last time Mac had been in the same room with him, Nick had not quite hit thirteen yet and he'd retreated into himself. He'd changed a lot since the days after the funeral. It was like he was ready to discover himself…but he didn't know how. And his safety net was full of holes. Apparently, so was Tessa's. Good thing Mac didn't need safety nets. Not having to rely on anyone had been his most liberating discovery as a young man. Maybe that's what Nick had to learn.

Tessa was nibbling on the corner of her lip. She shook her head ever so slightly as she studied the back of Nick's head. Everyone was feeling disappointed and frustrated. No one felt in control.

"Hey, man," Mac offered. "Wait until you try Kesi's cooking. Trust me. It'll be worth the wait."

"No more waiting," Mugi said, coming in the back door with a large bowl of what appeared to be a vegetable curry. Mouthwatering aromas permeated the room and lingered, despite the soft breezes floating through the screened windows and doors. He set the plate on the old wooden table and smoothed the simple black-and-brown patterned *dashiki* shirt that Mac recognized as the one Kesi had recently made. She'd made him one, too, only she'd chosen a brighter yellow-and-orange pattern for Mac, saying it was because he liked to be in the sky with the sun. Kesi was right behind Mugi with several more dishes.

"Kesi makes the best chapati. She cooks it in an iron pan over an open flame out back. Please, help yourself," Mugi said. "And this is vegetable and potato curry and this other dish is *sukuma wiki*. Fried onion, tomato and spinach."

"My gosh, this looks like it was so much work. I wasn't expecting a vegetarian meal. I'll admit, I was prepared to just eat bread and claim to not be hungry, out of politeness, but boy, am I relieved. I'm starving. We didn't mean to bother you," Tessa said.

"It's no bother when it comes from the heart." Kesi smiled and laid her worn hand on Mac's shoulder. "Any family of Mac's is family of ours."

"Thank you," Tessa said, dipping her chin. The corner of her mouth tipped into a grateful but slightly sad smile.

Mac felt her kick his boot lightly and raised his brows. Her eyes opened wide and pink spread to her cheeks. She glanced sideways at Nick, and from his abrupt thanks to Kesi and Mugi, Mac figured she'd kicked the wrong foot the first time. He couldn't resist messing with her. He tapped hers back, anyway.

Tessa did her best to ignore the way the corner of Mac's mouth lifted lazily after he kicked her foot under the table. If he added that flirty wink he was famous for in school, she'd scream. *Don't...don't...* He did it. She took a deep breath and turned her attention to the Lagats. She knew Mac wasn't really flirting. She was a married woman. He'd never even gone out with ex-girlfriends of his buddies back in school. But he had always enjoyed giving her a hard time. If it was at all possible for a sexy wink to be aggravating, he'd just pulled it off. Why did that not surprise her?

"You look a lot like Mac did when I first met him, Nick," Mugi said with a deep chuckle. His accent was highlighted with a different quality than Kesi's musical voice. Tessa couldn't place it. He sat down at the end of the table and eyed Mac to his left and Nick to his right, then scratched his graying sideburns. Tessa had no idea why, but the scene struck her oddly as one of grandfather, father and son.

"I look like my dad," Nick said, raising his chin as if to uncover his face and prove his point. He totally had his mother's chin.

"I'm not surprised, given your uncle carries the same blood," Mugi pointed out. "I never met your father, but I can already see pride runs deep in your family. It makes a man strong, if not stubborn."

"Stop giving our Mac a hard time." Kesi laughed at the opposite end of the table, closer to Tessa. She wore pants and a white cotton top embroidered around the neck. A printed scarf was wrapped around her head and beaded earrings added beautiful traditional touches to her outfit. Her style would have made a great subject for one of Tessa's fashion columns. Kesi couldn't have been much younger than Mugi, yet her warm skin had such a youthful glow.

"Are you two calling me stubborn? *Me?*" Mac asked. "I don't know what you're talking about." He took a piece of chapati, tore it and offered half to Nick. Nick took one bite and immediately reached for another piece.

"Oh, should I tell embarrassing stories of the first time you landed here?" Kesi smiled as she waved her hand across the table. "Please, everyone, fill your plates and don't be shy. There's enough for seconds and thirds."

"I think I need to hear this story," Tessa said.

"Yeah. Embarrass Uncle Mac. *Please*." The way Nick's lopsided smile mirrored Mac's was uncanny. She wished she had a camera.

"Did he run out of gas and get stranded?" Tessa ventured.

"Worse. He ran out of gas on the wrong side of the river," Kesi said. "You tell them, Mugi. I love hearing this story."

"They don't want to hear it," Mac insisted.

"Yes, we do," Tessa and Nick said simultaneously.

Mugi laughed and put his elbows up on the table. He leaned a few conspiratorial inches toward Nick and jerked his head at Mac.

"Your uncle here was out on his first flight in the area. No passengers. Just him…a fledgling." Mugi chuckled. "So he had lost his bearings and realized he was too low on gas to make it back safely. According to him, he had been told over the radio that there was a camp nearby, but the trees had just greened up, lush enough to make spotting this place from the air difficult. So he went for a clearing…but not the one where you landed today. No, this one was across the river. Kesi and I were sitting at the edge of the camp watching the various herds make their way upstream for water when we saw him land. Now, mind you, where there's prey, predator is not far behind."

"So you called out to him?" Nick asked, chewing more slowly.

"Of course not. We just watched to see what he'd do. After all, even lions have babies to feed. He was just part of the food chain we were observing in action. There's no television out here. A guy needs entertainment."

At that, Nick stopped eating and stared at the older man. Kesi covered her mouth with one hand to keep from laughing out loud and squeezed Tessa's arm with the other. Tessa struggled to keep a straight face.

"Remind me never to put my life in your hands," Mac said, spooning curry onto the rice in his dish. He looked like he'd heard this story more times than he cared to.

"Let him finish," Kesi said.

"Okay, so we did call out—not that it helped," Mugi confessed. "I called and asked if he needed assistance. Surrounded by hungry, thirsty wild animals and blocked by a river that most certainly hid jaws of death, Mac answered that he had everything under control, but thanks, anyway. So we watched him strut back and forth assessing the situation and too stubborn to admit he needed help. That's when the lion roared less than ten yards away."

This wasn't funny anymore. Tessa parted her lips, but Nick jumped in.

"For real? What happened?"

"He wet himself," Mugi said.

"As in he fell in the river?" Tessa asked.

"No. As in, he *wet* himself," Mugi repeated.

Everyone burst out laughing. Even Tessa couldn't hold it in, but the best part was seeing Nick relax.

"Did *not*," Mac said. "I got splashed when the herds panicked."

"You say that if it makes you feel better." Mugi sniggered.

"Did you kill it?" Nick asked. "The lion?"

Mac's face sobered.

"I don't kill anything unless I'm forced to put it out of pain and misery," Mac said.

"Not even for food?" Nick asked.

"Not even for food anymore. I have nothing against anyone who eats livestock raised humanely and taken with gratitude, but I personally have seen so much merciless killing that I've lost my taste for meat. Now, if I were forced into a situation of self-defense, that would be another matter."

"But you *were* in danger," Tessa said.

"I was unprepared. No gun. No tranquilizers."

"No way," Nick said. "How could you be so stupid?"

"Hey. Watch what you call me, huh?" Mac said, then he grinned. "I was *very* stupid."

Nick smiled right back and pushed his hair out of his face.

"So what *did* happen? After he wet himself," Tessa asked, raising one brow at Mac. He'd never live that down. Indiana Jones and the Moment of Doom.

"He was rescued by a woman," Mugi said.

"Ooooh, shame!" Nick hooted and clapped.

Tessa looked at Kesi in surprise.

"You swam across the river and rescued him, Kesi?"

"No way." Kesi laughed. "Mugi wasn't really just watching. He had a radio on him and had called a researcher we knew was studying elephants in the area and who we'd heard, over the air, was nearby that day. She drove up in her jeep just in time, but Mugi did have his rifle ready and aimed just in case."

"Wow," Nick said. Tessa shuddered at the scary, albeit funny in retrospect, situation Mac had been in. But she'd always known that he'd wanted adventure. Even in high school he'd loved adrenaline rushes. He used to skip school just to go for a swim that involved diving off cliffs; there was the time he'd taken off in his father's car before he had a license to drive. All of it used to fry her nerves. Especially when her sister went along for the fun of it. But Tessa knew he also took risks just to rebel against his dad and to prove he didn't care what anyone thought of him. He'd wanted a life where he'd be putting his life at risk. The exact opposite of what Tessa had always wanted. They still were opposites, which was why raising Nick *together* was so impossible.

"Rescued by a woman." Tessa folded her arms and shook her head.

"Dr. Anna Bekker isn't just any woman, though," Mac said defensively.

A twinge of jealously she had no right to feel pinched Tessa's chest. More of an insecurity, really. Mac had no respect for her or her lifestyle, but this rugged, elephant-rescuing Dr. Bekker *wasn't just any woman.*

"He's right," Kesi added, turning to Tessa. "There's nothing ordinary about Anna. Around here, her orphaned elephant rescue camp is becoming legendary. Mac should take you two to visit Busara. I'm sure she and her wonderful husband and adorable children would love to meet one of Mac's relatives."

Tessa had no rights over Mac—neither did she want any—but she couldn't help but feel a little relieved that Anna was married. Nonetheless, a part of her wished Mac could see her as "not just any woman," too. Then another part of her wondered if any of those baby elephants had been orphaned because of Brice. If they had been, then she was living off his blood money. Markets were all about supply and demand. That made her part of the pain and injustice Mac devoted his time to fighting. She rearranged the food on her plate, suddenly losing her appetite and unable to meet his eyes.

She needed to find evidence and stop what was happening…or she was as good as an accomplice to murder. Murder of the very lives Mac was so intent on helping to save.

TESSA SCRUBBED A dish in the soapy water, rinsed it and passed it to Kesi to dry and put away. She'd insisted on helping clean up while the guys went outside to do some maintenance on one of the guest tents. Kesi explained that they did whatever they could to conserve water. Although they had a well, they also used a cistern to catch rainwater. The couple also had some solar panels in place to take advantage of the plentiful sunlight. Tessa admired the gorgeous mosaic backsplash behind the sink and the unique strands of wooden beads that hung to the sides of the kitchen window instead of curtains.

"Your kitchen is beautiful and so…" She fumbled for the right word, realizing belatedly that anything she said might be taken the wrong way.

"Unexpected?" Kesi offered.

"Well, yes, but I don't mean it in a bad way. You have incredible taste in design and decorating. It's just that I expected anything out this far to be more basic, only because I'd imagine getting some building items and finishing touches out here would be difficult." She hoped Kesi understood. She never intended to sound rude or snotty. After all, she'd grown up in a house no bigger than this cottage. Maybe that's why she liked the atmosphere here. "Your home has so much character. There's a welcoming comfort about it."

Tessa meant it. There was a spirit to the place that, despite all the luxuries that had become hers when she'd married Brice, she'd never felt in her own home. Mac was right. Their place was a little on the sterile side. Like her and Brice's modern, minimalist style, there was no clutter here, yet the wood and stone, with splashes of color from woven pillows and practical accents like the herbs Kesi had hung to dry along one of the kitchen walls, gave the cottage an earthy warmth. She pointed to a stunning painting on the far wall. She'd seen a couple of others in the living room that looked like they'd been done by the same artist. The lighting in the kitchen made it easier to see Kesi's name at the bottom. "You painted that?"

"Yes. I like to dabble in water colors. It's relaxing," she said.

"You have a gift. It's beautiful. I should have known you had an artist's eye from how nicely you designed the entire place."

"Thank you," Kesi said. "Some of the touches were indeed special ordered, and some we brought out here ourselves. Most of the wooden furniture was handmade and carved locally, but a few pieces were from before we lived here. I'm a retired architect. In fact, when Mac's friends, Anna and Jack, decided to upgrade from the tent Anna had raised their first child in on her own at Busara, I helped them out."

A dish slipped from Tessa's grip but she saved it from breaking.

"You're an architect?" She needed to work harder at keeping the surprise out of her tone. Kesi didn't seem fazed.

"Yes, and Mugi is retired from law. I met

him in England, where he went to school. I wanted to see the castles, and he happened to be on the same tour. The rest is history. No pun intended."

That explained the hint of something different in his accent.

"Why would you decide to retire here?"

Tessa handed her the last dish and dried her hands.

"Why not?" Kesi said, ushering Tessa out to the front porch where they could enjoy some tea. "I take in this scenery and it reminds me of what home is all about. All the rush, demands and pressures of careers and city life fade away out here. We lived that life. Had our fill of it, and yet, left it feeling empty. I never had children—though we did try—a fact that took my parents forever to get over. Our lives had been about our careers, but neither of us felt settled. We never felt like we were making a difference or that we'd achieved our purpose, despite some of the pro bono cases Mugi used to take on. This place seemed like it had been waiting for us. It started as nothing but a couple of tents, but we wanted to build an environmentally conscious experience. A family-friendly camp where, if children came along, they could learn about water conservation, wildlife habitats, endangered species, solar energy...you understand the idea."

"Ecotourism," Tessa said, recalling an article she'd read not long ago in the very paper she worked for. The one Brice practically owned. Ironic.

"Exactly. Kenya is our home. Our ancestors walked this land. We figured if our purpose wasn't to raise our own children, then maybe it was to help educate others. To save the land left to us by past generations. Then, out of the blue, Mac landed in our lives and it was as if all the pieces had fallen into place. He's like a son to us."

The pieces of a puzzle.

Tessa nodded and looked over at the men patching a hole on one of the tents. Kesi had wanted children but couldn't have them, and now she saw Mac as a son. And Tessa never wanted kids for fear of the risks involved—the worry, the potential failure to give them what they needed—and now she had Nick. Kesi followed her gaze.

"Those look like mere tents, but they're quite nice inside. Each is raised on a platform because of the rainy season, so there are carpets and beds with linens and even water. It makes it easier with children. I suppose we're kind of like a Serengeti bed-and-breakfast. Our next guests aren't booked for a few weeks, so Mugi has been wanting to take care of repairs before they arrive."

No guests for that long? So much for Mac telling her they couldn't use the camp's jeep to get back. *Liar.* She had to admit, she was kind of glad about it. She'd needed to slow down. Catch her breath. Plan. The past few hours had indeed given her a breather. But she was also anxious to find out what was on those computer drives.

"So this place isn't as rustic as it seems at first. It's like the best of everything." Tessa chuckled. "Does that mean you have electricity?"

"A generator we only use as needed."

"A television?" Tessa asked, wondering if Mac and Mugi had been telling Nick the truth or if they had been messing with him, too.

"No. No television. It just wasn't a priority for us and we want guests taking in their surroundings. Getting lost in the experience."

"Ah, then no computer."

"Of course we have a computer and basic internet, for safety reasons if anything, and so we can keep up with news as well as letting the world know we're here. Mugi, being a lawyer, insisted."

So Mac knew all along that they could lie low and still check out the flash drives she'd taken. When was he planning to let her in on it? She was starting to wonder if she could trust him at all.

"Is it safe here? I mean, with all the wild animals...and I've heard that poachers aren't really as under control as some think," Tessa ventured, not wanting to give her real concerns away.

"Wild animals? We have to use common sense. We take precautions similar to most safari groups. Poachers? We haven't had a problem near us, though it's true—unfortunately, they're out there. Busara and some other reserves deal with the orphans left by poachers all the time. All the more reason to provide places where the public can get educated and in touch with nature. The more memories they make here, the more likely they'll be to care, even after they return home. One person can make a difference."

One person. Was Tessa one person making a difference?

"Life's funny, isn't it?" she said in a near-whisper.

"What do you mean?" Kesi asked.

"Just that you've been so generous and kind. We crashed your day and took it over unexpectedly. If you need us out of the way, just say the word."

"Nonsense. Stay as long as you like." She motioned to Mac, who was involving Nick in the repair. "It'll be good for them. See? Male bonding. You were hoping they'd get along. Weren't you?"

"How did you know?"

"I'm good at reading people."

A moment of silent understanding passed between them.

"Everything happens for a reason. Even airsickness," Kesi said.

She was right. Everything did happen for a reason.

It was the reasons that always eluded Tessa.

CHAPTER FIVE

MAC STOKED THE logs in the fire pit until the flames danced like Masai tribesmen dressed in their bright red and orange colors. The pit, encircled with local lava rocks, was set up in a clearing not far from the guest tents. A mix of wooden stumps and folding chairs surrounded it. He'd helped arrange those rocks and seats so that guests would have a nice place to congregate for after-dinner drinks and stories. Mugi always did love telling stories with dramatic flare.

Nick was already sleeping in the tent he was sharing with Mac, and Mugi and Kesi had gone to bed. Tessa stared at the flames with her knees tucked against her chest and her chin resting on them. Her hair glistened in the firelight like the river's surface on a full moon. He looked back into the fire. He had no business noticing those sorts of things. At least not in a way that stirred unwelcome feelings of nostalgia and longing. As a teen there'd been something about her that drew him in, but she'd always kept her guard up good and strong.

It didn't matter. Mac was a loner. He lived for the present and future. Not the past. Tessa wasn't his type, anyway. The only thing they had in common was custody of their nephew. She was another man's wife—a fact that, ever since she'd shown up in his office the night before, he had to keep reminding himself of…and that bothered him to no end. The sense of loss…the fact that she'd never really cared for him and his attraction had never been reciprocated…he could handle all of it when she was in her own country, but he'd made Kenya his and she'd crossed his boundaries. Tessa crossing any boundary and pulling a stunt like this had thrown him off-kilter. The Tessa he knew would never have done that. The woman sharing the campfire with him was a whole lot more appealing, way more interesting…and very taken. The smoke and flames had to be playing hypnotic tricks on him. He rubbed his eyes, remembering that he hadn't really slept the night before.

"What are we going to do about all this?" she asked.

Obviously she was talking about her situation with her husband, but for a split second, he thought maybe she'd heard his thoughts.

Perhaps mind-reading came with raising a kid together.

A log popped with a long hiss and crackle and he pushed it toward the center of the pit. He'd never forget the time she'd taken Maria and Allan's side about his first trip to the Serengeti. She'd told him he should listen to his dad and brother and stay put. It was only a week before he was scheduled to leave to do volunteer work for the experience and flight hours...and because he'd needed a break from his father and brother breathing down his neck about what he was going to do with his life. Real men made a lot of money, they said. Enough to support their families. According to them, working for free made as much sense as a hare curling up with a cheetah at night for warmth.

History had a way of repeating itself, didn't it? Tessa had sided against him before. She'd never agreed with his choices. Why should she care about his opinion now?

He eyed her carefully across the flickering tips of the fire. Burned once, twice shy. For all he knew, Brice had sent her. How convenient would it be if they couldn't see the files on those drives and there was no proof but her word? Or if the drives were fake? Maybe this was all a ploy because her husband didn't want an ornery teenager in his house. Did Nick clash with their uppity lifestyle? Or were her intentions even darker? What if Brice *was* involved in ivory smuggling and Tessa was embroiled in her husband's business right alongside him, like a good, loyal wife...but was having second thoughts? Maybe she was getting scared and trying to save face by making herself seem innocent. Was she playing the victim? She'd never been the type to stand up to anyone or risk losing the people in her life. If Brice had asked her to do something that went against her values, would she have been strong enough to say no?

She used to express strong opinions on animal welfare in their school paper, but after she got married, she'd settled on a fashion column. Maybe she'd given up her integrity and dreams for money. She could be here to use their shared custody of Nick to draw him into their sick game. Or she could be here as a spy, trying to get him to reveal inside information about the wildlife reservations, rescue and conservation groups in the area and the Kenyan Wildlife Service's plans against poacher activities. Or maybe her marriage had simply gone south and she was looking for excuses to come running to him for help and support because she didn't want to be alone. Tessa had always hated being alone.

He took the last swig of his beer and set the bottle in the dirt next to him.

"Let's see. What *are* we going to do about all this?" he said. "I'd say the safest thing would be to give me the drives you have. I'll check them out while you and Nick stay here. If there is indeed incriminating information on them, in what's bound to be a phenomenally dramatic and dangerous operation, I'll turn it in and help catch Brice red-handed…then kill him. In self-defense, of course, because something tells me he's used to getting what he wants and won't give himself up peacefully."

Tessa had dropped her feet to the ground and sat there gaping at him.

"Are you crazy?"

Mac shrugged and leaned forward.

"Guilty of being stupid once or twice in my life and a bit stubborn, but no, not crazy."

"Then don't make fun of the situation and don't go painting Brice out to be some superruthless alpha villain just because he's rich and powerful. He was always kind and good to me. I'm not sure why he's involved in all this or to what extent, but I know when I married him he was a smart, stable and talented man."

Touché.

The air tasted bitter and even the insects, whose rhythmic humming had been loud enough to mask their whispers, hushed. Mac wanted to walk away, but doing so would add power to her words. What Brice was, Mac wasn't. His father would have liked Brice. She knew it, too.

She covered her face and shook her head. "I'm so sorry. I realize how that sounded. It was uncalled for. I've just been so stressed and confused."

He forced the corners of his mouth into a

smile that fought against the weight in his chest.

"No worries, Tessa. I'm quite confident with my God-given gifts. I don't need riches to prove anything or to compensate for anything else." Now he was really smiling. "As for you marrying rich—kudos to you, baby. But running away from home tells me that you've questioned marrying him. So how about a game of 'Get Tess to Confess'? Are you really here because you suspect Brice? Or because you're having marital issues and deep down, all these years, you've found me irresistible?"

OF ALL THE egotistical—Tessa scowled as Mac got up and came around the fire, then reached into his pocket and tossed a coin on the ground between them before sitting on a log next to her. She was so not playing *that* game. The one he'd made up senior year.

When his brother and her sister, who'd gone off to the same college, had announced that they were getting married, she didn't take it well. She'd known they'd get hitched sooner or later, but Allan was a daredevil like all of the Walker men, and she didn't want to have to worry about Maria. She also knew marriage would mean her sister would visit home even less, and with their parents gone most of the time, Tessa would be alone more. They had asked her and Mac to help plan wedding stuff back home. She was so unenthusiastic about it that Mac had taken to teasing her, as if he needed an excuse. He'd started this habit of tossing a coin and telling her if it landed on heads and she answered a question from him honestly, he'd take care of whatever wedding arrangement she didn't want to deal with. If it was tails, she'd have to go for a swim with him—in the ocean. He knew full well she only swam in pools. The beach was where waves pushed you under and the currents pulled you out. She feared dying in the same manner she feared her parents would. Mac would take his shirt off anyway and egg her on. A shirtless Mac always left her flustered. He probably knew it, too.

It was a lose-lose scenario as far as she was concerned. At one point, when the coin had landed on heads, he'd asked her if she was glum because she had a secret crush on his brother. Gross. Or if she was jealous because no guy had even asked her to date. And every time it landed on tails, he'd rip his shirt off and make her skin heat up in a way she'd have never admitted to. He'd actually called her a wimp a time or two, when she refused to go swimming.

He tossed the coin.

"Let's see. No wedding planning responsibilities to take off your shoulders, so what do we bet on?"

"I'm not playing, Mac. Nor am I lying to you, so there's no point."

"Come on. Afraid of the truth or that I'll take my shirt off and drag you down to the river?"

"Don't flatter yourself."

"Ouch."

"You know the rugged, risk-your-life adventurer was never my type." No doubt he still sported rock hard abs. The mental image made her cheeks burn.

"Right. I'm just the guy everyone runs to when they need help that involves risk. The one who's expendable."

"I never, ever wanted you putting your life at risk. That was the point." Man, he ticked her off. She got up but his fingers wrapped gently around her wrist.

"Shrug it off, Tess. I was just trying to get you to let your guard down. Come on. I've always given you a hard time, haven't I? It's how we are."

She turned around and studied his face. The creases the sun had left around his eyes made him look wiser and those around his lips, more jaded. He rubbed her upper arms, and there was nothing but a calming reassurance in the gesture. Nothing inappropriate. So why was she feeling his touch all the way down to her toes? This was *Mac*, for crying out loud. Maybe she just missed having someone around who knew her sister the way she did.

"Sit. Tell me what happened," he said, nudging her back down. She sat and took a deep breath, the smell of smoke and grassy plains reminding her that Brice couldn't hear her. She was safe here. She'd succeeded in getting here in the first place, and that had to mean she was stronger than anyone had ever given her credit for. Didn't it? Stronger than she gave her*self* credit for. She scratched the bridge of her nose.

"Everything was okay at first. He's always treated me well, Mac. He has always been there and taken care of everything. He's smart and has never been anything but kind to me. I mean, yes, he liked throwing private cocktail parties and obligatory business dinners, none of which I enjoyed. I played along because it was the least I could do. He provided. If he wanted me to throw a dinner, how could I say no? Especially when some were for the staff at the paper. The one he encouraged me to write the fashion column for."

Truth be told, she had asked if she could do an environment and animal welfare-related column. Had even told him about the work she'd done in high school for the paper and for shelters and the fact that she was currently involved in fund-raising efforts for them, but he'd said the paper's readership was more fashion-oriented.

"Don't you hire caterers and maids, anyway?"

"No, actually. Cooking is something I've always been good at. I had to do a lot of it growing up. And Brice hates the idea of anyone poking around his possessions to clean. It's his one pet peeve."

"So you keep the house."

He made it sound like she was Brice's maid. There was nothing wrong with cleaning your own house. Brice had never wanted children—not even cats—and with only the two of them in that massive house, she needed to tend to something other than him or herself. No amount of coffee dates with other wives or shoe shopping, nor her once-a-week column, could fill her time. Deep down, she wanted to do something meaningful, something she really cared about. But instead, she cleaned.

"I do my own thing, too," she said defensively. "My work at the paper and organizing fund-raisers for various charities. Brice thinks that's good publicity for his companies, but I do it because I enjoy it. Plus, I've been handling Nick's needs."

"Are you still rescuing cats? Taking in strays?"

"No. Brice doesn't want pets destroying the house or putting off guests with allergies. My role as Mrs. Henning is to wine and dine potential clients of his. When no one's around, I sit at this table we have overlooking the ocean and—never mind."

She couldn't believe she was about to embarrass herself and tell him that she'd stand at that massive window and pray for her parents to be okay out there at sea and to return home safely. Same wish she'd always had growing up. Mac was so like her parents. Their rush... their raison d'être...was the sea. Mac's was the wild expanse of earth and sky out here. And hers...she'd never been able to pin down her purpose, passion or place in life. Even her love of journalism had stalled at her fashion column. Katia had always rejected any other pitches she'd made. And her contract with the paper prevented her from submitting articles anywhere else. Her parents and Mac had callings that made a difference. All because of some contractual covenant not to compete, hers never would. Unless she went up against Brice, which she'd never dared to do before. She ran her finger against her dry lips. Mac stretched his long legs in front of him and crossed his ankles.

"I saw your column once. Online," Mac said.

Tessa closed her eyes and felt heat creep

up the back of her neck. She held her breath and waited for the criticism she knew would follow.

"What of it?" she asked.

"Nothing." He shrugged. "It's just that you used to write opinionated stuff in the school paper. You created quite a storm with the one report on how the cafeteria's vegetarian menu wasn't so vegetarian, after all. Shocked the heck out of me. Didn't think you had guts. I was pretty sure it would get you suspended."

"I can't believe you remember that."

"How could I not? It was one of the few times you showed a little courage. Writing about fashion? I don't know. Just surprises me, is all."

"It's not like I never dressed well." Maybe she knew how, she just never did. Jeans and a sweatshirt had been more her speed than miniskirts and heels. "So fashion's not your thing," she continued. "It is for a lot of people."

"Four-inch heels and leopard-print leggings? Yeah, not sure I could pull off the look."

"Very funny."

He was right, though. Writing made her feel courageous. It was the one way she felt comfortable speaking up or taking action. Brice's influence had gotten her the opportunity to put her words out there—it just came with limits and no control.

"Anyway," she said. "Shortly after Allan and Maria's funeral, things began to change. Brice grew more distant, but I didn't care at first because I needed to be alone. Losing my sister crushed me. I was emotionally and physically drained, but Nick came first. So the fact that Brice was around less and less, taking more trips and coming home later at night, was a bit of a blessing in disguise. He was supportive of Nick living with us. He understood, yet there was palpable tension when both of them were in the house. Brice was less equipped to deal with Nick's emotional state, on top of the usual teen challenges, than I was. At least whenever Brice wasn't around, I didn't have to spend time placating him." She hoped Mac picked up on the fact that *he* hadn't been there to help with Nick, either.

"I hate to bring it up and don't jump on me for asking, but how do you know he wasn't having an affair? That it isn't still going on right now? Watch all of this have nothing to do with poaching and everything to do with another woman."

Tessa forced her lips shut before she could spit out the response he deserved. Her throat tightened. She should have expected as much from Mac. It only proved she'd never be more than an awkward, wimpy nerd in his eyes. What cut even deeper was that the very same suspicions had crossed her mind. What did that say about her self-worth?

"Why? Because I was never the girl a guy wanted to ask out, let alone one to land a husband? You think I can't hold on to a man?"

"I didn't mean it like that. Usually, when a guy is scarce without reason, an affair is a possibility. The fault being on him, not you, Tess."

She shuffled her sneaker in the dirt. Why did being around Mac make her feel like a teenager again? Unsure of herself, needing approval and struggling to think clearly in his presence. She scratched her upper lip. She was an adult now. She had a career…a voice. *You're in control here, Tessa. You're not a kid anymore.*

"I can't be one-hundred percent sure," she said, "but I don't think he is. He trusts me to take care of things like paying the bills. I've never seen anything out of the ordinary on our bank statements. Of course, he could be smarter than that, but I've never smelled perfume on him or seen lipstick, and if something was going on there would be rumors going around by now. Okay, I'll admit, the same thought crossed my mind at first. Who wouldn't wonder when their spouse's behavior changed so drastically? But then about a month ago, we had a cocktail party. The usual, except there were a couple of men I hadn't met before. New business associates, presumably. Nick was in his room, where he always hides during these parties. He hates them, too.

"I went up to check on him and came down the back stairs to the kitchen, not knowing that Brice was having a private talk with someone in the walk-in pantry by the steps. At first, I thought he was with one of the guests, but then I saw from behind that he was on his cell phone. I didn't think anything of it until he began saying things like, 'No one can find out,' and 'You're on your own if there's a leak.' My gut told me to keep quiet and back up the stairs. I did, but my heel caught on my long dress. I stumbled, he heard me and he turned. I pretended I was just coming down."

Tessa took a deep breath. The memory of that moment, the instant panic and churning in her stomach, came back. Adrenaline had helped her keep her wits about her, but she knew in that second that something was very wrong. Her skin had prickled like fire ants were crawling up her arms and her chest had gone ice cold.

"Did he threaten you, Tessa?"

She looked at Mac and pressed her fingertips to his jaw to stop him from popping it up and down. He stopped.

"No. He gave me a gift. He hesitated when he saw me and ended the call, then pulled a box out from his tuxedo pocket. It was a fountain pen."

"A pen? I would've expected diamonds from Brice," Mac said.

"Oh, it had diamonds on it, all right. Mac, this fountain pen had a solid gold nib and the barrel looked like hand-carved ivory. It was studded with diamonds. It was a work of art, but I was in shock. I remember the word *ivory* leaving my lips and he immediately explained that it was 'humanely harvested'—his words—from elephants who had died of natural causes."

Mac let out a string of expletives and began pacing with his hands on his hips.

"I know," Tessa added. "It doesn't make it okay. I didn't believe him for one second, but I had to fake gratitude because a part of me wasn't sure what was going on. I felt sick just looking at it, but tried to seem appreciative. I had no idea if he'd bought into my act or if whatever he was dealing with would put Nick in danger. I felt overwhelmed and all I could think was that I had to be smart. He told me he'd gotten me the pen because he knew how much I loved to write in my journal."

"He was buying you," Mac hissed.

"Don't you think I didn't wonder if that's what was happening? I didn't want to be bought. I've never wanted to be bought." Tessa fought the tears burning her eyes. She swiped at them and swallowed back their saltiness. "Whatever you might think, I didn't marry him for his money. I wasn't after his materialistic life. All I wanted was the sense of security he offered. I didn't want to hurt inside anymore, Mac. That pen was the ultimate sign that he didn't know me. My own husband and he doesn't know or care about who I really am."

Until that instant, she wasn't sure if *she* had really respected or known who she was. She'd gone to bed that night unable to stop thinking about the fact that the only person who'd ever understood and accepted her for who she was deep down was her sister, and she was gone. That night, she'd also decided that she had her limits and cruelty was too high a price to pay for staying safe. Turning a blind eye would make her just as guilty.

"This trip he's on is to China."

"All sorts of business takes place in China," Mac said. "Still not proof."

"I know. I know, but do you really think these are all a bunch of coincidences? Come on, Mac. You can't deny a possible link between China and ivory dealings. And why an ivory pen of all things?"

Mac didn't answer because there really

wasn't an answer. She knew these weren't coincidences. Not with Brice's dealings at the art gallery. His choice of gift had been calculated and deliberate, but the Henning connection to the art gallery was more information than Mac needed to hear. She had to be careful about what she shared and what details she kept to herself.

"Did you ever love him?" Mac asked.

"I thought I did. I've been doubting myself, wondering if he's really involved. Maybe the pen had nothing to do with the call and his only crime was ignorance. But even if that's the case, then I don't know him any more than he knows me."

"Then I guess there are two big questions here," Mac said. "Is he innocent, and if he is, after all this, will you stick to your promise of 'till death do us part'?"

CHAPTER SIX

MAC PEERED OUTSIDE the cottage window. Nick was wiping the Camp Jamba jeep's dipstick on a rag. Mugi was standing next to him, demonstrating how to do an oil change and general checkup on the vehicle. Nick seemed to be having a good time. He'd even stopped looking over his shoulder nervously at the monkey who'd been chattering persistently in a nearby tree.

"He's starting to fit in. It didn't take long," Tessa said from the stool next to him as they waited for the Lagats' personal computer to boot up.

They'd both confided in Mugi after breakfast and his first piece of legal advice was to make copies of everything on the drives before handing them over to any authorities... and not to hand them to just anyone. It was a sad fact, but too many "officials" out there were easily paid off.

"There's a good kid under the wall he's put up. He'll come out sooner or later," Mac agreed. "If anyone can reach him, it's Mugi. They seem to be getting along."

"My guess is he would take just as much interest in you showing him what all those buttons on your chopper are for."

The computer screen flashed and its start-up page began loading.

"Don't push it, Tessa. You know I can't be his main guardian right now. You saw where I live." Tessa had done her share of confessions last night. It was his turn. If she ended up thinking any less of him than she already did, so be it. "The fact is, I can't afford much more right now and business hasn't been what it needs to be for me to barely break even. Helicopters aren't cheap. There's gas and maintenance involved. A place to ground her. My office space isn't free, either. I love what I do, but business has slowed down because of competition, and if I can't focus on turning things around, I'll lose Air Walker Safaris by the end of the year."

Tessa frowned and stopped rocking side-ways on her stool.

"I'm sorry. I didn't know."

"It's not your problem."

It wasn't anyone's problem but his. Air Walker Safaris going under would prove to the world that he wasn't good enough. That his father had been right about him. But the worst part was that if he couldn't fly, his friends in the area who were dedicating their lives to wildlife, and who were counting on his volunteer efforts, would pay the price, too. Friends like Anna Bekker. He wouldn't be able to take them on herd-spotting flights or to make population estimates or to spot the bloody trail of poachers and help to rescue the babies who were left defenseless—worthless without tusks or skins large or luxurious enough for harvesting. He couldn't let that happen.

"Maybe not, but we need to figure something out. It's not just about me not being enough for him. If things don't go down well in the near future, I may not be safe for Nick to be around."

"I won't let it come to that," Mac said. He meant it, too. He'd help her get to the bottom of this, so that she could carry on liv-

ing safe and secure with Nick. Somewhere.
Everything would go back to normal.

Tessa looked back out the window, and
Mac followed her gaze. Kesi was offering
Nick and Mugi a plate of *mandazi*. Nick
took a careful bite of one of the triangu-
lar doughnuts and then grabbed three more
in one hand. Kesi threw her head back and
laughed at him.

"Have you ever wondered why Maria and
Allan chose the two of us as coguardians?"
Tessa asked. "I mean, obviously we're his
only close relatives… My parents couldn't
take him in—not on a boat—but why didn't
they pick one of us? Why both? They had
to have known we'd be torn on what was
best for him and that we wouldn't agree on
anything. They *knew* we lived in different
countries."

"Maybe they did it on purpose. Maybe
they thought Nick would keep their two
families together. His paternal and maternal sides. Maybe they thought we'd learn
to get along for his sake. Kind of like what
some married couples do. They think having
a child will fix everything and keep them
together." Mac's mother had tried that route,

but ended up leaving both of her sons with their father.

She never came back.

He and Tessa weren't married, though.

Tessa cocked her head at him but didn't say a word. She knew all about his mother. It had been school gossip for a while. She tucked her hair behind her ears and rubbed her palms against her jeans.

"Maria was so angry with me when I got married," she finally said. She had a faraway look in her eyes and a sad smile. "She didn't even want to attend the wedding at first. She insisted that I was making a huge mistake. That I wasn't following my heart."

Mac let her words sink in. What had her heart been telling her to do? Mac knew first-hand that sometimes following one's heart simply wasn't a good idea. Sometimes the heart's fantasies needed to be balanced by the mind. That balance was an elusive thing, though. In high school, his heart used to tell him that Tessa needed someone around. That she needed protecting and needed to be kept from feeling utterly lonely. It told him he was attracted to her, not that he would have admitted it. Not then. Not now, either.

But his mind had set him straight. It had registered her reactions to him and warned him to pull back. True. He'd been a jerk to her at times, but that defensive, cocky attitude had saved his heart.

"What did my brother think?"

"He agreed with her. They teamed up against me in a mini intervention. For some reason, neither one of them felt that Brice and I fit well together." She met Mac's eyes but he didn't agree or disagree. He wasn't about to. None of his business.

She pulled her shoulders back and sat a little straighter.

"I guess we can just agree to put Nick first and hope Maria and Allan aren't regretting their faith in us from their graves," she said.

He almost missed her chin quivering as she ducked her head and pulled a small, plastic box full of flash drives from the backpack purse she kept close. She handed them over. He took the box. Kesi used to always tell him that everything in life happened for a reason. Well, there were plenty of good reasons why he was neither married nor a father. His life was better this way. No one was going to turn him into the hardened man his father had become after his mother left them.

"Here it goes," he said, sticking the first one into the computer's USB port and waiting for the external drive to show up on the screen. This old machine was painfully slow.

"I'm guessing he hasn't shared his passwords over pillow talk," Mac said.

Tessa rolled her eyes but didn't look at him. "No, he hasn't."

He tapped several keys and then a few more. Nothing got him in.

"Sheesh. He's not fooling around. This flash drive is encrypted."

Mac tried the others. All encrypted. He sat back.

"I hate to break this to you, Tessa, but I'm no hacker. I wouldn't even know where to begin. We're never getting into these files. We should just turn them in and let the authorities try. They have professionals and computer programs designed to do this sort of thing. I have connections."

"We can't do that. We don't even know if these drives have anything to do with ivory smuggling. I can't go turning my husband into the government without finding out more first. That was my plan. Otherwise, I could have marched right over to the authorities back home."

He raked his hair back and glanced at her sideways.

"I thought you were trusting your gut on this. I thought you'd overheard him."

"Ask Mugi. None of that would be enough evidence in a court of law. I'm not ignoring my gut entirely. That's why I'm here. But I can't go destroying his life, then turn out to be wrong. False accusations are serious, especially with something like this. You said so yourself. He could turn around and sue us both for destroying his business reputation. We'd lose everything, and where would that leave Nick? What about Air Walker Safaris? Brice could ruin you. Or what if he is guilty, but without solid evidence against him and whoever he's working with, he gets off? We'd become targets. We need to be careful."

Mac put the drives back inside their box and wrapped it in his fist. He held his other hand out.

"If you want my help, Tessa, then we need

to do this my way. All the way. You need to trust me."

She licked her lips and glanced at his palm.

"Come on, Tess. Take a risk. Trust me… for Nick's sake."

She nodded and placed her hand in his.

"Okay. Your way. For Nick."

A YELP ESCAPED Tessa's throat as a rut in the road sent them bouncing hard against the jeep's worn seats. She braced against the olive green frame and held on for dear life. So much for foregoing air travel. Mac had given her the choice: a quick chopper ride or the camp's jeep. She'd given him a rough time about not being totally honest about ground transportation when they'd first landed at Camp Jamba, but going back to Hodari was a moot point now. Something told her the helicopter might have been a smoother ride. Kesi had made her a cup of herbal tea before they left. A delicious blend of ginger, mint and honey. She'd even packed her a thermos of the brew. Luckily, despite how fast Mac was going, her stomach didn't bother her the way it had up in the air. Or maybe the herbs were really doing their job.

"Please slow down, Mac. We don't want to be vulture food," she said.

"Go faster! This is amazing!" Nick screamed. He held both hands up in the air the way kids let their inner daredevils out on roller coasters. "Whoo hoo!"

A beautiful, tan-colored herd raised their heads in unison at the sound of his voice, their black-spiraled horns held high above the tall grasses. Two seconds later, they took off running in the same direction the jeep was headed. Mac slowed to a more reasonable speed.

"Those are impala. They're great jumpers," he called out over the engine noise.

As if on cue, one of the impalas leaped gracefully into the air, avoiding a mass of bushes in its path, and cleared a phenomenal distance before landing just behind the rest of the herd. They were like a group of Serengeti dancers: stunning and dramatic against a backdrop brought to life by an artist's brush.

"They're so lovely. Are they endangered?" Tessa asked.

"No, but too many species here are. Some that most people have never heard of and some more recognizable. Black rhinos and elephants to name a few. And Rothschild's giraffe. World's tallest land animal." He pulled to a stop and pointed toward a pair of giraffes and their baby enjoying a treetop picnic in the distance. The female turned her elegant neck and Tessa could have sworn she was staring right at her from beneath those luxurious lashes. She seemed to give Tessa a knowing nod and then lowered her neck and nudged the baby lovingly. A family of three. At peace. Something stirred deep inside Tessa.

"Look at them, Nick," she whispered.

"I saw. Now can we go fast again?"

Leave it to a restless teen to spoil the moment. He definitely had Walker blood in him. Or perhaps it was a testosterone thing. Tessa wanted to stay there and watch. Never before had she been so hyperaware…so in tune with her senses. The way the air softly brushed her skin, the light snap of a twig, the smell of dewy grass and freshly rutted dirt, the striking blue and red of a bird taking flight from the acacia tree ahead of them.

Everything around her was awe-inspiring. It didn't feel scary or risky. It felt right.

She closed her eyes, took a deep breath and was enveloped by a warm, fresh scent that was uniquely Mac's. She quickly opened them. What was that about? The stress, drama and romantic atmosphere of the Serengeti were getting to her. Nick's therapist had said something about kids often retreating into fantasy worlds to escape the pain of reality. He'd told her to keep an eye on him in that regard. Clearly, she needed to keep an eye on herself. There was still a chance, though tiny, that her husband was innocent. Even if she were single, Mac wasn't her type. Was he? He belonged here. There was no separating him from the land and life that surrounded them. Mac and the Serengeti had an understanding. A symbiotic relationship.

A balance.

And he'd made it clear he didn't have room in his life for anyone else. And honestly? She didn't want a rebound relationship. After all this, she was starting to appreciate the simplicity of being alone in a way she never had before.

"We should move on," she said, shaking away her thoughts. "It would be great for Nick to see more endangered species. You can impress your biology teacher," she said over her shoulder.

"Who cares? Have you *seen* Mrs. Beechum? She looks and acts like she's half croc, half baboon. I hate that class."

"Oh my gosh, you are so right." Tessa laughed. "But don't tell anyone I agreed with you. I shouldn't agree, but who can hear us out here? A croc and baboon. Wow. I think you may have a knack for genetics."

Nick stood up in the back of the jeep and cupped his hands around his mouth. "Mrs. Beechum is a crocoon!" he screamed, then bounced back into his seat with a wide smile on his face and a sparkle in his eyes. "Can't get me in trouble, Uncle Mac. It's a made-up word. It only sounds like a cuss word because I'm brilliant."

Mac chuckled and shook his head at both of them.

"You two are something else," he said. He restarted the engine and stepped on the gas. "Just don't repeat it at school."

"Of course I will. In front of the entire class—on the last day."

"No, you won't," Tessa said, coming off her laughter high. "Get it out of your system here. Don't get yourself in trouble and don't ever be rude or hurt someone's feelings." She was pretty sure that he was kidding, but not entirely. With Nick, she never knew. What was it the therapist had told her? That kids' brains weren't fully developed until their mid-twenties? So they were prone to making bad choices and taking unnecessary risks. Did that explain some of her past...and Mac's? That would mean her brain wasn't fully developed when she married Brice. Oh, come on. She was fishing. Her parents married right out of high school and were still happily together.

"Mrs Beechum doesn't have feelings," Nick said. "You should have seen her last test."

"Nick," Tessa warned.

"You're so gullible, Aunt Tessa."

She made a face at Nick and then at Mac for laughing in agreement. This was the most fun she'd had and the most relaxed she'd been in years. Mac and Nick playfully ganging up on her was a good thing. Guys bonding. The two of them would be all right.

"We have our share of wildlife reserves and safaris down in South Africa—haven't you two been?" Mac asked as he maneuvered the jeep around a granite outcropping.

"A school trip to a zoo once. My parents flew me over one area, but all I remember seeing were lions. I was just a kid at the time," Nick said.

Mac and Tessa shared a smile subtle enough for Nick not to notice. *Just a kid.*

"You know, I don't think I've ever visited one," Tessa said. "I probably haven't visited half the places tourists flock to. It's that way everywhere, isn't it? You get caught up in your everyday life and completely disconnect from the world around you. It's easy to take the things you're surrounded by for granted. I had an American classmate once who'd never seen the Grand Canyon or Statue of Liberty, yet she'd already seen all of our attractions and I hadn't." Tessa turned in her seat as she caught sight of a rhino grazing in the thicket off the road.

"True," Mac said.

"Where are we headed, anyway?" Nick asked.

"To visit a neighbor. Speaking of which, it looks like we have a visitor." Mac eyed the rearview mirror. "Now that's a good-sized cock. You want me to slow down so you can get a close look?"

An ostrich raced after them with black-and-white wings flared and a determined expression on its face.

"Speed up," Tessa said.

"I thought they were supposed to be shy. What happened to sticking its head in the ground?" Nick called out over the revving engine. He held onto his seat, Tessa-style.

"They'll get down on the ground if threatened, and when they do, their necks aren't as visible against the sand. They don't actually bury their heads. It's an optical illusion."

"Feel free to speed up a little more, Mac," Tessa insisted. The massive bird was gaining on them and she didn't like the fact that Nick was in the back.

"Don't worry," Mac said.

She felt the jeep pick up speed, but the ostrich reached the end of the jeep and tried poking at it with its beak. It was like a scene out of *Jurassic Park*. Tessa reached back and grabbed Nick's hand, jerking him toward the center of the seat, away from the side the bird was on, but suddenly, it broke off its chase.

Tessa pressed her hand against her chest.

"Are you okay, Nick?" she asked. His mouth hung open as he watched the bird shrink in their wake.

"That. Was. Incredible. Now, that's something everyone at school is going to hear about," Nick said.

She hadn't seen him so full of life since his parents died. And for all the therapy bills, what he'd really needed was a high-speed chase by a male ostrich. Go figure. Mac kept one hand on the steering wheel and rested the other on her shoulder. His touch soothed her racing pulse.

"I knew we'd lose him. The ostrich, not Nick," he said with a wink. "The males are very territorial and we may have passed a nest, but they're sprinters. Kind of like cheetahs in that they run out of steam."

"I wasn't worried."

"You sure about that? Should I 'get Tess to confess'?"

"I was petrified," she immediately said, removing his hand from her shoulder and setting it back on the steering wheel. Not only was she not about to take a dip in a croc-infested river, but she also didn't trust herself to keep her eyes off Mac if he took off his shirt.

He merged onto a dirt road that looked like it had seen a little more traffic than the one they'd been on. The jeep cleared a hill, and a large, bustling camp surrounded by sprawling acacia and fig trees and overlooking the river valley beyond came into view. The jazzy sound of a band of elephants carried through the air as if to announce their arrival.

As they approached, the figure of a petite woman with light hair emerged onto the porch of a single-story home that blended into the landscape in a Frank Lloyd Wright way. She had a baby strapped to her back in a colorful sling and held the hand of a child with a mass of vibrant, curly hair that bounced as she hopped up and down, pointing toward them.

"That," Mac said, "is the Busara Elephant Research and Rescue camp."

CHAPTER SEVEN

MAC PULLED UP in his usual spot and got out of the Camp Jamba jeep in a single move that avoided opening the finicky driver's side door. He opened his arms to hug Pippa as she came barreling toward him.

"Hi, Uncle Mac!"

"Hey, squirt." He ruffled her hair, then sized her up. "Have you really grown two feet in the past two weeks? Or is Ambosi hiding in there?" He reached for her hair again and parted her curls as if conducting a search. She giggled and ducked away. He'd known her since she was a baby, back when Busara was nothing but a couple of framed tents and a few pens where Anna kept and treated baby elephants found injured or orphaned by poachers. At the time, Pippa's father, Jack, was living in the US and had no idea he had a daughter being raised in the wilds of Africa.

Teasing spunky little Pippa had become a routine, even now at her precocious seven years of age. Ambosi was a three-legged vervet monkey who'd fancied Anna from the moment she first gave him food when he'd hobbled into her barely set-up camp.

"No, silly. Ambosi is too busy with his new girlfriend." She rubbed her hands together mischievously and crinkled her pert nose. "Mommy said they might have babies."

"Is that so?"

"Yep." She peered over his shoulder. "Are those your friends you said you were bringing?"

Mac shifted as Tessa walked up. Nick lingered closer to the jeep, his bangs once again hiding most of his face.

"Pippa, this is Mrs. Henning, an old friend, and that is Nick, my nephew. Anna, this is Tessa."

"I've heard so much about this place. It's an honor to meet you," Tessa said, shaking Anna's hand.

"Oh, thank you. It's really not much. We just do what needs to be done," Anna said.

"She's too humble," Mac said.

"Says the man we can't get by without," Anna added, patting his arm.

"How's Noah been?"

"Sleeping very well, thank goodness. I can feel the wet drool on my shoulder, so my guess is he's dozed off again."

"He's adorable," Tessa said.

"Hey, Nick, come say hello."

Nick shuffled over and shook hands, back in his moody shell. So the kid was a bit shy around people. The opposite of Pippa, who studied Nick shamelessly with her arms crossed. She tipped her head to the side.

"Nice hair," she said.

Nick shifted his feet and his face flushed, but he shrugged.

"You, too."

She grabbed his hand without asking his permission and tugged him away from the jeep.

"Come on. I'll introduce you to each of the elephants. They all have names. And Ambosi. He's a monkey and watch out because he likes to throw things at strangers. And my friend Haki. He's human."

Mac shook his head and chuckled as Pippa dragged Nick away.

"This should be interesting," he said. "I say we forgo rescuing him and let Pippa have a little fun."

"You're something else," Tessa said.

"She's quite the big sister, let me tell you," Anna said. "Fearless and not the least bit shy. Sometimes I wish she had just a little of both. A happy medium."

The way Tessa smiled in disbelief almost made him feel like they were real partners. Like parents watching their child.

"I don't think I've ever in my life met a more adorable little girl," Tessa said.

"Thanks. You two come inside. I'm betting you need a break after the trip over." Anna glanced between him and Tessa. "Jack will be back from Nairobi soon...and then we can talk."

TESSA FOLLOWED ANNA into her house. It was much bigger than the cottage at Camp Jamba. The living room had a large window overlooking the valley and she couldn't resist walking up to it for a better view of a family of elephants mud-bathing by the riverbed. A large kitchen opened onto the living room, and a painting that Tessa immediately recognized as Kesi's artwork hung on a wall over a casual lounging area. Mac had told her about how impossibly rustic and minimal Busara had been when it all began. This home, new as it was, kept the rustic, minimal feel despite its comforts.

"This is really nice," she told Anna. "Kesi told me she helped design it."

"She did, and she was amazing to work with. I'm still getting used to all the space." Anna smiled. "I was so accustomed to tent life, this felt like a strange luxury, but I have to admit it has been nice. And being able to share it with our best friends who live and work here, too—Niara and Kamau and their son, Haki—has been perfect."

Ah, so that's why it was so large. The sections on either side of the main area, she guessed, were two separate family wings. Until she'd seen the Lagats' cottage and now, the Busara house, Tessa had never imagined that living out here, in the middle of nowhere, could seem so normal. If anything, both places, for all their isolation, carried more of an atmosphere of community and family than her home in South Africa. More than her entire neighborhood, for that matter.

"Well, hello again." Sue appeared from one of the rooms down a short hallway, closing the door quietly behind her. "I left Niara some crackers and ice to help with the nausea. She said she just needed to lie down for a bit," she told Anna.

"Thanks, Mom. I'll check on her again soon. First trimester," Anna explained to Tessa. "Please, have a seat. Make yourself comfortable. Can I get you anything?"

"Oh, no, thanks. I'm fine." She honestly didn't think her stomach could handle anything. Anticipation over the discussion they were supposed to have with a friend of Mac's who he believed could help, had her on edge. She wanted this all over so she could have peace in her life again.

Anna sat down on a small sofa and skillfully slipped the cloth carrier and baby off her back. He complained, but she had him tucked against her and nursing within seconds. Tessa tried to appear nonchalant. Maybe a little too hard. She knew nursing was totally natural and a good thing, and her discomfort wasn't about the unexpected glimpse of Anna's breast. Tessa had seen plenty of them for crying out loud. It was the act that took her by surprise…and the sudden realization that no matter how many articles she'd read on breastfeeding or how much she'd learned about it in school, she'd never seen it done in person. Well, there was this mama cat at a shelter once. And that cute baby monkey she'd spotted clinging to its mother and nursing up in a tree at Camp Jamba. But even Maria had bottle-fed Nick because of a post-partum infection that required medication. She'd insisted that formula was safer than drugs, even when the doctor had said breastfeeding wouldn't hurt the baby. So watching Anna's baby nursing was a first. Anna leaned down and kissed her little boy—Noah, that was his name—on the head.

Something stirred in Tessa. Something she'd never felt before. She'd never given babies and nursing much thought because she'd never planned to have kids. Nick was a different situation, but babies? Could she ever do what Anna was doing? Have children and care for them from infancy, as fragile and dependent as they were?

Her mom once told her that she'd nursed her for as long as she could…about six months…before she resumed her work trips out to sea with Tessa's father. They'd hired a nanny to help with the girls during those early years, and yes, her mom did return home more often when they were little than she did once Tessa and Maria had reached their teens, but she hadn't cared for them like this. Here, Anna had managed to blend her work and family seamlessly. And seeing Noah's tiny hand pinch her chest as he nursed was indescribably wholesome. Now she understood why Mac had said that Anna wasn't just any woman. He was right.

"Come on, have a seat," Anna said, motioning to the other half of the sofa. Oh, man. Had she been staring? Tessa gave a polite smile and sat down. Mac had excused himself early on and said he was going to rescue Nick. Tessa knew he was rescuing himself. Mac wasn't a girl-talk kind of guy.

"How old is he?" she asked, smiling at Noah.

"Just turned nine months," Anna said. Her mom brought a tray with cups of tea from the kitchen, set it on the wooden coffee table and sat with them.

"I'll burp him for you when he's finished," Sue said.

"Thanks, Mom." She handed her a burp cloth but let the baby have a few more minutes." She turned back to Tessa. "So, how are you liking it out here?"

"It's nice," Tessa said, forcing herself to take her eyes off baby Noah. He was so precious. Why couldn't she think straight? *It's nice?* Really? "I mean, obviously, you know, I could be here under better circumstances, but the country is beautiful and Camp Jamba is lovely. The Lagats have been extraordinary." She glanced at Sue. Did she know why Tessa was here? Maybe she'd said too much.

"They're special people," Anna said. "And yes, I'm sorry that you lost your sister and brother-in-law." Okay, so Sue wasn't necessarily in the loop. Luckily, Anna had smoothed over what the "circumstances" might be without a flinch.

"Thank you. It's nice that Nick is getting to see some other kids here, even if they are younger. It's not easy for a thirteen-year-old to be stuck with a bunch of grown-ups."

"Well, Jack's brother-in-law, Ben, now

lives in Nairobi and his oldest daughter isn't much younger than Nick. Maybe if you come back to visit, Ben can bring his family and the kids will have a chance to meet."

Tessa nodded and reached for a cup of tea. She took a sip and it was sweet, minty and soothing.

"Mmm. This is nice," she said.

"There's plenty," Sue said, taking Noah from Anna and resting him against her shoulder. Anna untangled the ends of her ponytail from his little fingers and straightened her blouse, then took a cup for herself.

"The Mac I've come to know," Anna mused, "would stop anything he's doing at the drop of a pin just to help friends and family. He's a good partner to have when it comes to raising a teen boy. From what he told me when he called, you've been amazing since Nick lost his parents. His words, to be exact." Anna looked at her from beneath her lashes as she took a sip.

Tessa was speechless. Mac had told Anna that she, Tessa, was amazing? Why hadn't he ever told Tessa that? And the idea that Mac was a good partner threw her, too. He'd contributed, financially, to raising Nick, but he hadn't really been there the past six months. He was really making up for it now. Is that what they were? Partners? Her and Mac... on the same team. That tilted her world as much as watching Noah nurse. She didn't want children. Nor did Brice, for different reasons. Even if she ever changed her mind, something she'd never considered until a few minutes ago, he wouldn't change his. He'd made that clear.

"That's generous of Mac to say. I'd be lying if I said it was easy, but I think getting him far away from home for a break might be the catalyst he needs to see that there's still life beyond the loss he's endured. You know?"

"I do."

"Hello. Have I missed all the fun?"

A beautiful woman dressed in a loose, geometrically patterned dress entered the living area and smiled as she held her hand out to shake Tessa's.

"I'm Niara. You must be Tessa. I'm sorry I didn't come out sooner to meet you." She sat down on a chair across from the couch.

"Nice to meet you. I hope you're feeling better," Tessa said.

"Much. It just comes and goes like magic. I wish I had a pregnancy like yours," she told Anna. "She didn't even throw up once."

Tessa grinned at Anna.

"It's all the animals I work with. I'm completely desensitized to odors. Jack, on the other hand, turned the oddest shade of green the first time Noah needed a diaper change. You should see him handle it now, though," Anna said.

Tessa almost choked on her tea, trying to picture Brice changing a diaper. For that matter, she wasn't sure she could picture *herself* doing one. They continued to joke and tease the men behind their backs.

"I overheard him telling Kamau about it over a game of chess. I burst out laughing. Kamau claims that diaper changes are nothing. Let's see what he says after he tries his first," Niara said.

Tessa had been told that Kamau—aka Dr. Kamau Odaba, a field veterinarian working with Anna—was Niara's husband, though not her son Haki's biological father. Haki was already a little boy by the time Kamau had fallen in love with Niara, so their second child was going to be a new experience for

Kamau. He was off tracking one of the elephant herds they were studying. The mention of his name reminded her she'd come here on business. She wasn't really a part of this group. She was merely a visitor. Why did that bring her down?

She was loving these women. The whole situation felt surreal...as if she'd always known them. Anna, Niara, Sue and Tessa bonding over breastfeeding, tea and funny stories about their husbands. Tessa would have never pictured sitting around like this and thoroughly enjoying herself.

"I'm afraid I'd make the men look professional," Tessa said.

"No younger siblings that you ever changed diapers for?" Sue asked. An enormous belch burst from Noah's baby mouth and everyone raised their eyebrows, then laughed.

"No. Just an older sister," Tessa said as she set her cup down. "I managed to avoid diaper duty as Nick's aunt after he was born."

"Would you like to hold him?" Anna asked. She was up and scooping Noah from her mom's arms before Tessa could answer.

"Oh. Sure. But I haven't held a baby since Nick was born."

"Here you go." Anna settled Noah in Tessa's arms and guided her hold on him, then sat back down beaming.

Tessa looked down. Heaven help her, he had an indefinable scent that made her want to nuzzle him and bottle it up for keeps. He was sleeping, yet his hand wrapped around her finger and he squeezed. She was done for.

She could hear the main door opening. She glanced up just as Mac walked in. He tipped his chin to greet everyone in a "let's get to business" way, but he stopped in his tracks and did a double take when his eyes met Tessa's. A man she assumed was Anna's husband bumped into him from behind. Mac shuffled out of the way, but had the strangest expression on his face as he looked at Noah and then back at her. Tessa felt her cheeks heat up, but couldn't pinpoint why.

Right behind Jack appeared a man with a military cut, well-worn fatigue pants and a black T-shirt that emphasized shoulders that filled the doorframe.

Tessa's stomach sank. Who was that? Mac

had told her they were only meeting with Anna and Jack and maybe Dr. Odaba, Niara's husband, since they were involved with rescuing elephants and tipping the KWS on any poaching patterns or activity they picked up. But bringing in a stranger? One who clearly looked "official"? She felt like cornered prey. Just how many people had he involved?

All comfort Tessa had enjoyed moments ago evaporated and suddenly the room felt cramped. She handed Noah to Sue, who'd stepped over to pick him up.

Tessa needed to get Mac outside. Alone.

MAC KNEW TESSA would freak out when she saw Ben. He hadn't mentioned bringing him because he was afraid she'd lose her nerve. But seeing her cradling Noah had freaked *him* out on a primal level. Tessa as a mother. Tessa and child needing protection. His Tessa. His child. His family. The images came at him like artillery fire. He whipped off his cap and raked his hair back. *Have you lost your mind?*

"Ben," Anna said, getting up and giving Jack a kiss on the lips and Ben a kiss on the cheek. Her voice broke through and Mac inhaled, ready for reality. "Jack didn't tell us you were coming. How are Hope and the kids?"

Ben cocked his head and the corners of his lips turned up.

"They're great. The kids are loving living in Kenya and Hope said to remind you that if you need anything—especially you, Niara—she'll come ASAP."

"She's the best. You'll all have to come out to visit soon."

"You bet."

Ben's new wife, Hope, was a doctor specializing in pediatrics and rural medicine. She'd met him in the States, shortly after the tragic loss of his wife had left him—an ex-marine and single dad of three—clueless about parenthood, struggling to cope with his grief and dealing with his oldest daughter's retreat into a shell of silence. Hope had been a blessing in their lives. Ben had never thought he'd fall in love again, but not only had Hope healed his heart, his children had opened hers. Now his daughter was speaking again and their world was complete. Mac knew Jack and Anna loved that Ben and his children had moved here from America and could visit more often. It was good to have family around.

"Tessa, this is Ben Corallis, Jack's brother-in-law. He works in Nairobi with the US embassy to help with Kenyan law enforcement training, including the Kenyan police and KWS—the Kenyan Wildlife Service. He also spent several months when he first moved here working with a private group of US military veterans who train and work alongside KWS teams to apprehend poachers. Not only can he help, he has personal connections and knows who we can trust," Mac said, hoping to keep things under control. Tessa's chest lifted visibly.

"Hi," she said. A single word. Tessa was nervous for sure, but Mac felt confident. Ben was as sharp as they came and with his special-ops marine background and his position at the embassy, not only could he be trusted, he'd never let anything bad happen to his family and friends. Plus, Ben had quickly earned the respect of the Kenyan officials and soldiers he'd trained and worked with. They trusted him and this wouldn't be the first KWS poaching investigation he'd been involved with.

"I'll take Noah with me for a nap, if you don't mind seeing if Pippa and Nick are hungry or at least staying out of trouble," Niara said to Sue, taking Noah from her arms. "We wouldn't want Ambosi—or Pippa, come to think of it—tying poor Nick to a tree." Her son, Haki, who was a few years older than Pippa, had gone with his new stepfather on his first field rounds.

"Leave it to Pippa," Sue said. She shook Ben's hand on her way out and Niara waved and disappeared down the hall.

"Kamau just radioed in and said he'll be late. Why don't we all get started? The dining table is probably the best place," Mac said, motioning everyone to sit down. They headed toward the table. Tessa scratched her palm as she took hesitant steps to follow the group. Mac put his hand on her back and nudged her to the free chair at the end. Ben had helped himself to the opposite end and Jack and Anna sat side by side. Mac sat near Tessa.

"So, is everyone ready to catch a criminal?" Mac asked, wanting to gauge Tessa's reaction to him labeling her husband as if it were a done deal. She frowned slightly, as if she wanted to argue with him, but not in front of the others. Mac pulled the thumb drives out of his pocket and slid the clear plastic case across the table to Ben. "I'm officially turning these over to you. Let us know what you find out, if you can get in."

Ben propped his elbows on the table, eyeing the drives but not picking them up. Instead, he looked squarely at Tessa.

"I understand that you have reason to believe your husband, Brice Henning, is involved in illegal ivory trafficking."

Tessa glanced at Mac, then at Anna…and then at her hands.

"I, um. I don't exactly know what…"

"You either suspect him or you don't," Ben deadpanned. The man meant business. Good. Mac was counting on that. "I'm a busy guy, and I'd much rather be at home with my wife tonight than sleeping here, so tell me now if you're planning to waste my time with cold feet."

Anna raised her forehead in surprise and even Jack narrowed his eyes at his brother-in-law. Maybe Ben did want to be with

Hope, but he didn't have to embarrass Tessa or pull bully strategy on her.

"Ben," Mac said. Ben held up a hand to warn him not to interfere. Fine.

"So," Ben continued, "is he involved in blood ivory trade or not?"

"I don't know for certain," Tessa said, folding her arms around her waist.

Ben leaned back in his chair and splayed his hands.

"I understand loyalty and feeling nervous about turning in your husband...or maybe about what will happen to you, but my guess is—since you're here—you want to do what's right. Look, whatever your involvement is with his activity, I'll make sure my contacts are aware of your cooperation. Chances are, it'll weigh strongly in your favor when it's all said and done."

"What exactly are you accusing me of, Ben?" Tessa blanched. "I'm not guilty of anything!"

Anna and Jack looked taken aback by Ben. Anna was about to speak, but Jack put his hand on hers and whispered something in her ear.

Mac closed his eyes briefly and flattened his lips.

"Then what's your husband guilty of?" Ben pressed on before anyone could jump in.

"I said I'm not one hundred percent sure," Tessa said. "That's why you're here."

"Why do you suspect him of being involved in the ivory trade?"

"Things I've overheard. Behavior. Gifts he's been giving me. I know something is going on."

"That's not evidence. You know what I think? I think your husband is a smart guy and he sent you out here as a spy. That's why Mac found you at his computer your first night in Kenya."

Tessa's eyes widened and she flashed them at Mac. He didn't say a word. Yes, he'd told Ben about that. Ben needed to know everything if he was going to help. Mac might not like his methods, but the guy was an ex-marine and security specialist. He knew what he was doing.

"I'm *not* a spy."

"Having Nick around was the perfect cover-up, wasn't it?" Ben grabbed the drive case and tapped its corner annoyingly against the table.

"No! Keep Nick out of this. What's going on, Mac?" She turned to Ben. "Why are you talking to me as if I'm guilty?"

"No need to be defensive if you're not." Ben raised one brow. "Just a few questions, that's all. Kind of suspicious that your husband happens to have investment control and/or influence in strategic companies and businesses, such as a lucrative jewelry store chain, an art gallery and a newspaper or magazine or whatever you call that kind of reporting. And you just happen to write for it. Did Brice send you because of your connection to Mac and the nature of Mac's work?"

"No!"

"Is there a chance he married you because of both your connection to Mac as well as to his brother and your sister, considering their work and assistance with wildlife tracking in South Africa?"

"Oh, my God." Tessa gripped the table and shook her head. "I refuse to believe that."

"I have to ask, Tessa," Ben said.

"Tess. Just tell him what you know." Mac wiped his hands over his face.

"Do your kids and wife even *like* you?" Tessa asked, the color rising in her cheeks.

Ben grinned.

"Mrs. Henning," Ben said, ignoring her jab, "how long have you known about Brice's activities?"

She let out a breath and sat back.

"A while. At least, I've suspected him for…"

"So you were aware, but didn't bother to tell anyone? Don't you think that makes you an accomplice?"

Tessa rose from her chair.

"Sit down, Tessa. You need to tell me the truth. Everything." Ben stopped tapping the drive and leaned forward. "Either you spill it here, or you can come back to Nairobi with me until we get to the bottom of this. I came here alone because Mac asked me to, but make no mistake—I have a KWS team itching to jump on a solid lead, if this turns out to be one. There's no turning back at this point. You're in deep. Now's not the time to hold back. If they're to take action, missing information will only put you and your nephew in more danger."

"Tell him everything, Tessa. Tell him about the pen. Anything you can remember. It might make a difference even if you don't think it matters," Mac said.

"You expect me to believe you haven't already told him all that? I'm assuming you have," she said.

"The gist, yes, but I left the details to you."

He watched her as she recounted what happened the night Brice gave her the ivory-and-diamond pen.

"Where's the pen now?"

"I locked it up away from the house. At a spa center I go to. I wasn't sure if it'd serve as any kind of evidence and didn't want him getting rid of it if that was the case."

"What else?" Ben asked.

Mac was starting to wonder what Ben was sensing from her. Was there something she hadn't told him? Had Mac let his guard down and given her the benefit of the doubt to the point he could no longer tell if she was hiding something?

Tessa rubbed her nose and studied the

ceiling for a long minute before matching Ben's gaze.

"The art gallery you mentioned. There is a small group of investors and their wives who go in to give our share of input to the head curator on what pieces to consider for display. Some pieces are by private showing only. There's a secure, keypad-protected room at the back where those showings are done. No one goes unescorted." Everyone was silent. Waiting. Tessa cleared her throat. "I'm part of that group."

Oh, no. No way. Mac scrubbed his jaw and stood, shaking his head. He went over to the window and stared out. He knew where this was going. It wasn't good.

"I'm listening," Ben said.

"The idea is for the investors to have some artistic, aesthetic input. At least, that's what Brice told me the first time he asked me to join him. I write about fashion. It made sense. I was flattered to be asked to help, to tell you the truth. He valued my opinion."

So she wasn't as shocked as she'd led Mac to believe when she first saw the pen Brice had gifted her.

"Why didn't you mention this before? To me?" Mac asked, turning to face her.

Tessa picked at her nail and kept her face averted. "I signed my name in approval of things."

A hush filled the room. Mac could hear Anna's lungs deflate.

"What things?" Ben asked.

"Statues. Carvings. Some of them looked like solid ivory. Some only had pieces incorporated into different semiprecious stones or other materials."

Mac covered his face with his hand. She'd signed her name. She had blood on her hands. She was part of a trail. No wonder she hadn't brought it up before. *Damn, Brice.* He'd taken out an insurance policy. Anyone who knew about any ivory dealings had their names linked to it in such a way that if they tried to bring anyone down, they'd be implicated, too.

"When did you start doing this?" Ben asked.

Tears pooled in her eyes but she sniffed them back and raised her chin.

"Three years ago. But the visits were only a couple of times a year, at least for me. I didn't know. What I mean is, the first time I went, I felt uncomfortable. I didn't want to disappoint Brice after he'd explained that he was including me in an important business deal. Still, I asked if it was real ivory. I tried to sound like I was impressed, not suspicious. The curator said, 'Isn't it amazing how deceiving looks can be?' and that was it. After we left, Brice assured me the pieces weren't real. He said they were resin. That it wasn't about the material. It was about the artist's vision. I believed him. I wanted to believe him. A part of me still wants to," she whispered.

"And why should I believe *you*? Why should I believe you didn't know exactly what you were doing? Or that you aren't trying to manipulate me right now. Playing it safe. Protecting yourself. Giving yourself a way out," Ben said.

Playing it safe and protecting herself would be classic Tessa, for sure. But Mac couldn't wrap his head around the idea that she'd be a party to illegal activity. Not knowingly.

"How many people still buy an exotic pet from a pet store and don't think twice about how it got there? Are they guilty or ignorant?" Tessa asked. "How many people pay top dollar for a dog or cat from a breeder, while thousands are in line waiting to be put to sleep if they're not adopted or fostered from shelters? Guilty or ignorant? I'm telling you, I'm here because I didn't know. Because now I *need* to know. I finally became suspicious enough that I acted on it." She looked at Anna and Jack and Ben. "You're all parents. Can't you understand that I wouldn't stand by and let Nick be in a dangerous situation?" Tears streamed down her face.

Anna got up and pulled a cotton napkin out of a console table against the wall. She gave it to Tessa to wipe her face, placing her hand briefly on her shoulder before returning to her seat.

"For what it's worth, Ben, I believe her," Anna said. "No, I don't have evidence. Call it a woman's intuition, but I do know I'm not perfect. I wasn't born knowing about elephants. Of course, I knew about the danger they face as a species before I first came to Kenya, but it wasn't until I'd seen, first-hand, a brutally killed and bloody mother and her orphaned calf nearby that the impact of poaching really hit home."

Ben reached into his shirt pocket and pulled out a stack of photographs and slid them across the table to her.

"Then let's make sure Tessa here understands how serious this is," Ben said.

Tessa wiped her nose, then picked them up. She immediately covered her mouth with the napkin. Mac glared at Ben and went around the table and stood behind Tessa. What he saw was sickening, but sadly, nothing new to him. Tessa slowly went through the nauseating, bloody, faceless images of poached elephants and piles of confiscated tusks on fire. One showed a watering hole dyed red by the bodies that lay along its banks.

Mac had seen the gory remains of poaching firsthand more times than he cared to. As gut-wrenching as the photographs were, they didn't convey the stomach-roiling stench of rotting flesh or the mourning cry of an orphaned baby elephant standing helplessly near the body of its mother. Pictures didn't fire your defense instincts the way standing over a freshly massacred bull did—

knowing ruthless, evil men weren't far away. Mac scrubbed his lips and went back to the window. The kids laughed outside as one of Anna's orphaned rescues picked peanuts off the tops of their heads with its trunk. Children. It didn't matter what species. They needed guardians...protectors. They needed guidance. Most of all, they needed a chance to *be* children. No kid deserved to suffer the loss of a parent. Ben's kids had. So had Nick and all the baby elephants at Busara.

"You see," Ben said, after silently watching Tessa process the images. "I don't believe in mindless, sick violence. Not when it comes to people *or* animals. There's no defense for what you're looking at. No amount of money justifies it. There's not an ivory sculpture, piece of jewelry or even so-called 'medicinal' powdered rhino horn out there on the black market that makes this okay. You're looking at greed and murder. Ask my friends here at Busara just how much pain and loss poaching causes."

"It's heartbreaking," Anna said. "We have the *Endangered Species Act* and other laws and international conventions—and it still happens. There are wildlife collectors and dealers out there who just won't see the light. About one hundred thousand African elephants were killed by poachers between 2010 and 2012. You and Mac are from South Africa. Surely you heard about the recent case where an investor pled guilty to selling illegal ivory. It's a huge problem. And the thing is, an elephant cow's gestation is almost two years. That makes recovering from population loss that much harder."

Tessa nodded.

"That South Africa case was part of a bigger operation," Ben added. "And there was another one a few months ago to intercept wildlife trafficking through customs. We're talking about a problem up there in scope with narcotics. And just like there are undercover narcotics agents out there, there are undercover agents posing as collectors and poachers. It doesn't matter how long it takes—if I can pass tips on, someone can eventually work their way in to places like your art gallery to make a behind-the-scenes purchase. And if it's real ivory or rhino horn or anything else, they'll get caught."

"And if I'm wrong?" Tessa asked.

"What if you're right?" Ben said.

Mac sat back down next to her. What were the chances that Brice had had contact with the investors in that South Africa case Anna mentioned? Tessa's chest rose and sank. She set the photos down and looked up. Her eyes were red and hollow and he wanted to wrap his arms around her like he had when her sister died.

"Okay." She rattled off the names of individuals in the group, the curator and the gallery address, while Ben made notes. "I never wanted to be a part of anything like this," she whispered. "I had no idea what Brice's businesses were about when I married him. I'm here because I can't stand by and do nothing."

She glanced at the pictures on the table and tears spilled down her cheeks. "Do you have any idea how hard it is to accept that the person you loved and thought loved you…the one you slept beside at night… is a complete stranger capable of being involved in something so cruel? That the person you admired and trusted might turn on you? Can you not understand why a small part of me might doubt my own suspicions?" Her voice cracked, but she went on. "I may not be as confident or accomplished as he is, but I do have moral boundaries. I'm trying to do what's right. That's why, before coming here, I tried submitting an article that raised some red flags about local companies turning a blind eye to their product sourcing. Things like blood diamonds included."

"You're saying you actually submitted an article to the paper you write for, but it was declined?" Ben asked.

"Yes."

"Can you give me the name of the person who turned it down?"

"She's innocent. I know it. She's a friend and…"

"Her name."

"Katia. Katia Pollier."

"I find it interesting that she refused it. Sounds to me like someone in power is dictating what you write and what gets published."

"No one tells me what to write."

Ben raised a brow at her.

"Okay, not as long as I stay restricted to this fashion column I'm assigned to." She looked at the ceiling again and scratched her neck. "Katia told me to be careful. Right before I left. That's what she said when she got back to me about the article. I forgot."

That was the first Mac had heard of that. He exchanged glances with Ben, Anna and Jack.

"We all agree there are too many connections to ignore, but even that isn't enough to pin anyone down. Yet," Mac said.

"There are a lot of powerful people involved at various stages of the ivory trade," Anna said. "If Brice doesn't want to create a trail that leads to him, he won't fund poachers or limit himself to suppliers in South Africa. Past seizures and arrests have shown that buyers don't necessarily use suppliers in their country. These people have an intricate web system in place, making it very hard to trace illegal activity beyond the poachers themselves—that is, if they're caught red-handed. Unfortunately, Busara isn't the only sanctuary that has seen a rise in poaching fatalities and orphans in the past six months and the increased activity hasn't only been in Kenya. It's everywhere. Tanzania, South Africa...the entire region."

"I agree," Ben said. "We're dealing with an ivory mafia. That's how these people work. There's a hierarchy. The untouchables and the expendables. Loyalty and betrayals. We may never have enough for a takedown. Even if one group is caught, others will still be out there. But if these drives have contact lists or anything like that, they would be invaluable. All it takes is a little insider information. A broken link in the chain."

"Wait a minute. You're implying that she go back to him and act as intelligence? No way," Mac said. "Don't do it, Tessa. I draw the line there. It's too dangerous."

"I'm referring to the drives, Mac. Not sending her into the lion's den."

Tessa sat wide-eyed with her hands on the table. Her lips parted, but the door swung open before she could say anything. Kamau stood there with bloodstains across his shirt.

"Sorry I missed the meeting. We've had another killing. Anna, I need you at the clinic. We have a little guy being unloaded now."

Anna shot up and ran out behind Kamau. A little guy. Another baby elephant orphan. Another child who'd be mourning.

Just like Ben's children. And Nick.

The room was silent.

The photographs on the table said it all.

THE RIDE BACK to Camp Jamba was quiet. Neither of them was prepared to discuss anything in front of Nick. Tessa didn't even want to talk to Mac. He'd just stood there and let Ben take her apart. Tessa wiped the corner of her eye and pretended her hair, windblown from the open-air ride, had irritated it. She reset her ponytail and took a drink from the thermos tucked between them.

Ben had shown a softer side after Anna, Kamau and Jack had left the room to check on the baby elephant. Mac had looked unsure, telling her he'd be back and then running off to help them. And she was left at the table with Ben. Talk about awkward. He'd given her a quick apology for being rough... and for her sister's death...and then Niara had walked into the room with baby Noah. Thank goodness. She'd been surprised by the way Ben took Noah from her and started playing with him like a big old teddy bear. Then he'd given Tessa a lopsided grin and pointed out that he was pretty sure his wife and kids liked him. Of all things incomprehensibly male...

But even after the tension had let up in

the room, it hadn't let up inside of her. Tessa hated how unsettled she still felt.

If Brice was involved with poachers, she'd walk away and never look back. She'd never set foot in her house again. The whole thing made her sick to her stomach. To have shared a life with a man who'd sanction and profit from such horrific acts…her throat tightened and her chest ached. But what if he turned out to be innocent? Would he forgive her? Or was all of this a red flag telling her something was fundamentally wrong in their marriage?

And the mention of Allan and Maria had her head spinning. That wasn't possible, was it? Had she been the family's weak link all this time? A family of brave individuals who were willing to live on the edge if it meant making a difference…and she was their Achilles' heel. The point of entry for anyone who wanted to use them.

Her head hurt and throat burned. She wanted to curl up on her cot, close her eyes and dream that none of this was happening.

Mac had said that they needed to make it back before nightfall, but he kept an even pace. No thrill rides this time, despite Nick's begging. According to Sue, around Pippa, Nick had acted like he'd worked with animals all his life and wasn't apprehensive at all. Tessa was sure it was all bravado. Still, it was good to see him more confident. A flash of red caught her eye and her mind pinged images of the bloody carcasses she'd been looking at.

"Wow, look! What's that?" Nick propped himself up on his knee in the backseat for a better view. Off to their left, hundreds of men decorated in white paint, red cloths and dyed hair and beaded necklaces streamed down a distant hill and around rocks and shrubs like the meandering flow of molten lava. Tessa could hear chanting even from their remote vantage point. Mac pulled to a stop and twisted in his seat.

"Those are Masai. They're taking part in one of the later stages of their coming-of-age rituals. The end goal or reward is to become a Masai warrior."

"Cool. Like prove you're a man by hunting or surviving in the wild on your own?" Nick asked.

"Oh, it's a lot more involved than that. They do need to prove themselves worthy warriors, but it's a long process that involves kids around your age undergoing an *emuratare* ritual—getting circumcised without anesthesia—living at an *emanyatta* or warriors' camp for ten years away from your family and eventually moving to a ceremonial house where they'll drink a mixture of ox blood, beer and milk before officially becoming warriors."

Nick winced.

"Glad you're not a Masai teenager?" Mac said with a laugh.

"Uh, yeah."

"It may sound bad to you, but it's their way, their culture, and it means something to them. We have to respect that. And by the way, you don't need to hunt to prove you're a man. Honor and compassion make a man. I'm betting your dad taught you that," Mac said.

"Yeah, he did."

Tessa remembered watching the news with Nick last month, dumbfounded over the greedy, recreational killing of Boni— a beloved cheetah mother who researchers were tracking—while she was out teaching her cubs how to hunt. She knew from Nick's outrage then that he sincerely understood what Mac was saying now.

But the mention of Nick's dad deepened Tessa's depressed state. What would Maria have done in her shoes? Would she have spoken up sooner? Marched straight to the authorities the second she got suspicious? Or would she have walked on eggshells like Tessa, wanting to act but worried about disrupting life as she knew it—especially if she was wrong. Was it about innocent until proven guilty or protect the innocent first and figure out the guilty later?

Mac restarted the engine and resumed their course for Camp Jamba.

The sun was low on the horizon, its final rays glistening against the peak of Mount Kilimanjaro on the horizon. A quiet thirty minutes later, a flicker of light reassured her that they were approaching camp. She turned to let Nick know, but he was lying on his side in the back of the jeep sound asleep, despite the bumps and ruts in the road.

What would Nick think of all this if he knew what was really going on? He was at such a fragile time in his life because of both the loss of his parents and the normal growing pains that came with surviving the teenage years. The mood swings. Self-discovery. One thing was for sure: he was a lot stronger than she'd been at his age. Maybe even than she was now.

MUGI AND KESI had dinner waiting, but Nick was so groggy he simply stumbled toward the tent he was sharing with Mac and collapsed on his bed. Mac made sure their mosquito netting was in place and returned to the house, only to be told that Tessa had excused herself without eating a bite, saying she was going to bed early.

Their drive to Busara had been nice. He'd felt like they were a family on an outing... or at least relatives on an outing. The ride back wasn't the same at all and now this? She had to eat *something*. He wasn't worried about Nick after the way he'd stuffed his face at Busara before they left, but Tessa had barely eaten. Even after Ben had put a hand on her shoulder and explained that he was only doing his job and he'd contact them when the contents of the drives were uncovered.

"What happened? She seemed upset,"

Kesi said as she filled a plate with food. "Trust me, when a woman loses her appetite and her eyes look dim, she's either sick or upset—and she wasn't sick."

"Did things not go well with the meeting?" Mugi asked as he sat down and filled his own plate.

Mac stared at his untouched food. As usual, it looked delicious. His flagging appetite took him by surprise.

"The meeting was rough," he said. He sighed and scratched the back of his neck. "My contacts with KWS will probably be pissed off at me for handing over the drives to someone else. We're on the same page, but you just never know. I trust them, but I trust my friends more, and with something like this, I trust Ben implicitly. He was tough on her, though. He said that once they secure evidence, they'll share it with the right people and work to bring the ring down. So at this point, it's out of our hands. Ben did ask us to give him a few more days of lying low. He'd prefer it if we—or at least Tessa and Nick—didn't return to Hodari Lodge until he did some basic checks on her husband. Just to make sure they're safe. I think the meeting was a bit much on her and the idea of drawing things out didn't help."

He picked up his fork, then set it back down.

"You do know you can stay here anytime, for as long as you like, don't you?" Mugi said.

"Mac, he's right. I realize you men don't like to pour your hearts out, so take it from me. You're our only family. That's what you mean to us. A friend, yes, but family, too. Stay as long as you want."

"We understand the logistics of being at Hodari. Having a safer place for your helicopter, saving gas and all that, but consider this your home. If you're ever able to swing living here while maintaining your office there, you don't have to ask. Nick is welcome to live here, too. He reminds me so much of you. It would bring back memories," Mugi said.

"Thanks," Mac said, clenching his jaw so the well of emotions would settle down. He wanted to say more, but the words wouldn't come out. Living here with Nick? Sure, it'd solve the space issue, but not the fact that the kid was thirteen and in school. He needed his teachers and a social life. And where would that leave Tessa? He was fairly certain the only reason Kesi and Mugi hadn't extended the offer to her was because, so far, she was still married. She could end up staying that way, too.

Not that Mac assumed they'd all live together if she left Brice. Why had he let his mind go there?

"I know you care about her. Have faith that things will turn out however they should," Kesi said. Mac frowned, picked up his fork and stuck it in a potato on his plate.

"You're wrong, Kesi. I only care because she's my sister-in-law and co-guardian."

"She cares, too. She's just confused and hurting."

"She's married. Off-limits. I have rules about things like that."

Kesi pressed her lips together, then set the plate she'd filled next to him.

"And you should. I respect that about both of you. So eat your dinner and then take this plate to her tent for me."

He glanced at the plate and hesitated, the unbitten potato still on his fork.

"Or," Kesi said, "take her the plate first, then come and eat. We can wait."

Mac set his fork down and scooted his chair back.

"I'll, uh, take it to her now…you know…so she gets it before falling asleep." He picked up the plate and utensils and started for the door. "Um, go ahead and eat. No need to wait for me," he said, motioning at the table. The napkin he carried dropped to the floor when he fumbled with the screen door handle. He hung it on a hook meant for rain ponchos. "I'll wait for her to finish and bring the plate back. Wouldn't want to attract animals or flies," he said.

"Mmm-hmm." Kesi waved him off.

Mugi chuckled and dug in.

Tessa lay on her bed staring at the black, burnt-orange and red patterns woven into the area rug that covered the tent floor. These really weren't ordinary tents. The bed, likely a cot underneath it all, was soft and cool with natural cotton linens. Mosquito netting was gathered overhead, hanging from the canvas ceiling so that it could be gathered aside or drawn around the bed like curtains. Her notebook sat on a small, carved wooden table, short enough to be used as a desk. She'd tried writing something, thinking it would either distract her or give her an outlet, but nothing came. She couldn't even bring herself to journal what had happened in the past few days. Her brain was fried. Crisp and dry like Amboseli during a drought. Even her soul felt drained. Completely parched.

She shifted onto her back, bunched her pillow under her neck and hugged one of the small decorative pillows embroidered with a traditional tribal pattern. If she waited long enough, surely the soft night sounds would soothe her to sleep. She was so ready for a new day. A new life.

Let go, Tessa. If you want a new life, have courage. The sound of Maria's voice in her head and the simultaneous crunch of footsteps approaching her tent had her jerking herself up onto her elbows. Had she in fact dozed off? *It's nothing wild. It's probably Nick, awake and hungry again.* He didn't need to be wandering alone in the dark. Maybe he thought she was over at the cottage. She sat up and slipped her feet into her sneakers.

"Tessa? Tess, are you awake?"

Not Nick. Her lungs deflated.

She knew sooner or later she'd have to sit and talk things out with Mac; she'd simply hoped it wouldn't be tonight. She was too tired and needed time to take in all that had happened. She got up and pushed open one of the tent flaps. Mac stood in the light of the full moon that sparkled in the treetops behind him. His expression was awkward and uncertain. He held out the plate.

"I brought you dinner."

"I told Kesi I wasn't..."

"You *said* you weren't hungry, but I know you are, Tessa." There was a silent pause. "Please," he whispered.

The look in his eyes was intense and overwhelming, and his voice pleading.

"You didn't believe me," she whispered back, not wanting their voices to carry. "You let Ben make it sound like I was an accomplice. You didn't even try to defend me. You just stood there. If you knew me at all, you know I'd never participate in animal cruelty. Being rich doesn't make me heartless or materialistic."

She was no longer whispering and didn't much care.

Mac set the plate down on a small end table flanked by two director's chairs just outside her tent. He moved one of the chairs closer and took her hand, pulling her gently toward the other chair until she sat. Then he let go. She folded her arms, safe from his touch.

"Listen to me, Tessa. He needed to ask those questions. He warned me he would and asked me to not interfere. He was also keeping an eye out for hints that you were being blackmailed or coerced. Look, the guy was a special-ops marine and works with top officials at the US embassy. He has traveled with them to meet with delegations from KWS in places like China. The embassy has been supporting projects to combat wildlife trafficking and poaching in Kenya and elsewhere. Tess, he's our 'in.' He can help us. I trust him."

"But you don't trust me."

"Did I want to hear your answers? Yes. I won't lie to you about that. Despite what you think, living out here doesn't make me a reckless risk taker. It makes me cautious and deliberate. A survivor. Yes, I know you from when we were younger, but how much of our adult life have we actually spent together? Can you blame me for wanting to see how you handled the questions? The thing is, you're a survivor, too. You just don't give yourself enough credit. And you've done your share of not trusting me."

"If I didn't trust you, I wouldn't have brought Nick to stay with you."

"If you trusted me, you would have contacted me and told me you couldn't keep him right from the start."

"You would have said no before we got here. You've been quite clear that he doesn't fit into your life."

"Be reasonable. Where is he supposed to go to school? Down at the river? The kid's afraid of shadows."

"If you wanted to raise him, you'd figure out how. Look at Anna and Jack. They live in the middle of nowhere, too, yet they're raising a family just fine. I'm sure they have homeschooling plans set up for their kids," Tessa said.

"That's the only kind of schooling they've known. I'm not about to isolate a thirteen-year-old right when his social life is supposed to take off."

She splayed her hands and took a moment to respond.

"Fine. So you're saying I should find a place to move on to with Nick and start from scratch as a single parent? Have you seen how he reacts to me?"

"That's not what I'm saying." Mac scrubbed his face, then looked at the moon. He closed his eyes. "I don't know. I don't *know* what we should do."

"So what happens now?" she asked, her voice tired and hushed again.

"We agree we can trust *each other*." He softened his tone and took her hand. "We agree we both love Nick and want what's best for him. That means that, whatever happens and wherever any of us are, we keep in touch. We share what's going on. We talk."

Her eyes shimmered in the moonlight and she nodded.

"Because you must know that I'd give my life to keep you and Nick safe," Mac said.

She closed her eyes and tears spilled from

the corners. She reached up to wipe her cheeks but he beat her to it.

"Me, too. I want you both happy and safe," she said.

"We figure out how to give Nick the best life we can give him."

"That goes without saying."

"You eat your dinner," he said with a quirk of his lips.

That made her let out a stunted laugh. She picked up the plate and took a bite of chapati.

"Agreed," she said, mid-chew.

His eyes tracked her lips, then he quickly looked up and cleared his throat.

"No matter what happens, we agree to be friends," he added.

"Okay," she said slowly. "Friends."

CHAPTER EIGHT

TESSA PINCHED A wooden clothespin and secured her shirt to a line strung between two trees. She reached into her pocket and pulled out another pin. She was wearing one of Kesi's embroidered blouses. She'd packed nothing but one spare set of undergarments and an extra shirt in her backpack when she'd left home. Luckily, she hadn't stashed her backpack at the Hodari Lodge. Nick, on the other hand, had left his. Kesi surprised him by sewing him a shirt just like Mugi wore, only considerably smaller, so that his could be washed.

"I don't like that they're not back yet," Tessa said.

"Don't worry. Mugi is very careful." Kesi dunked a bed sheet into a large rubber tub of soapy water and scrubbed it between her hands, shifting her hold every few rubs. "He won't take him far. It's good that Nick learns about the plants and dangers. Let him get exposed."

Tessa couldn't help but glance down the path they'd taken that morning. Mac had actually gone on a flight round after getting a call from one of the research camps north of them. He wasn't back yet, either. She and Kesi had been doing everyday chores around the camp. Tessa had felt ridiculous when she admitted she'd never done laundry in a tub, nor had she ever harvested food from a garden, but she'd assured Kesi she wanted to help out and learn. In return, Kesi had admitted that when they first moved out here, she had a lot to learn herself.

"I'm just worried about wildlife encounters," Tessa said.

Kesi slopped the sheet into an adjacent bucket of rinse water.

"Mugi is armed and trained as a guide. And he's fully aware of dangers, so I promise, they're relatively close by. He takes guests out all the time."

"What if they ran out of gas?"

"He has a tank in the back of the jeep. And a radio, my dear. Nick is probably having more fun than he ever has. He's a teen-ager. They get bored."

Nick had been in the worst mood that morning. He wasn't a morning person to begin with, but he was in a rare slump. Glum. Irritable. Hormonal…if Tessa had to guess. He'd been doing so well. Maybe Mugi had been right. A little excursion would do him good.

"I guess. Maybe he was going through computer game withdrawal earlier. That has to be as bad as caffeine withdrawal for me," Tessa said.

Kesi laughed as she squeezed the sheet into a figure eight and handed it to Tessa to hang.

"I think all three guys had this planned. Escaping while the housework is done."

"Oh, don't worry. You and me, we're not folding any of this. Not if they want dinner. I have my ways," Kesi added in a sly tone. "Notice that we haven't done the bathrooms yet?"

Tessa smiled. Kesi was one to be admired.

"Thank you for all your help today," Kesi said.

"It's the least I can do. Whatever you want

done, say the word." Tessa had tried offering her some payment for their stay, using the only currency she had changed for the trip up, but Kesi had refused, insisting that she and Nick weren't ordinary guests and that Mac always did them favors, anyway.

The jeep's engine rumbled louder as it approached.

"Thank goodness." Tessa let out a breath as she clipped the far end of the sheet and hurried toward the dirt path Mugi was coming down. He pulled to a stop and shook Nick's hand before they both climbed out.

"Hey, Nick. How'd it go?" Tessa smiled with her hands on her hips. He didn't smile back.

"Fine." He walked right past Tessa and over to where Kesi was finishing up a pair of pants. Tessa frowned at Mugi but he seemed surprised by Nick's behavior.

"Thanks again for the shirt," Nick said pleasantly enough—to Kesi.

"You're very welcome. It looks good on you."

"Got any chapati to snack on?"

"There's a covered dish inside on the counter. Help yourself."

"Leave me some," Mugi said, walking up. "I'm starving."

"Just a snack, you two. You'll ruin your lunch." Kesi stood on her toes and gave Mugi a kiss. "Did you have luck with spotting?"

"Ask Nick. He's a natural out there."

Nick? A natural in the wild? Was this reverse psychology or what? Tess tried to keep a straight face.

"We saw herds of elephants," Nick said, raking his hair back and tucking his hands into his pockets. "And a pride of lions napping under an umbrella tree in the distance, lots of different birds and elephants eating sausages." He grinned at Mugi.

"Elephants don't eat sausages, do they?" Tessa asked. She was pretty sure they didn't.

"You're so gullible, Aunt Tessa. They're not real sausages," Nick said. "They're this giant fruit elephants love but that are poisonous to us."

"I was pointing out which plants were edible and which were poisonous. It's good to know," Mugi explained.

"We have a saying here," Kesi added. "The worst place to stop and rest is under a sausage tree. If the fruit doesn't fall on your head and kill you, the stampede of elephants running to eat them will. The fruits look like long sausages but they can weigh five to ten kilograms."

"I'll remember that," Tessa said. "I'm impressed, Nick. You'll have to tell me more later. I'd like to learn stuff like that."

"Right." Nick smirked and walked off to find food.

"What did I do?" Tessa asked Kesi and Mugi.

"Nothing. He's hungry. Low blood sugar triggers bad moods. Not that they need a trigger at that age. He was fine until we got here," Mugi said.

"You know…" Kesi wrapped her arm around Tessa and led her toward the kitchen door. "He probably feels safest with you when he needs to vent whatever is frustrating him. He knows you'll love him unconditionally. With us or with others, he has to control himself."

"I suppose that makes sense. His teachers kept saying he was doing fine in class, no behavior issues, but then he'd come home and be so rude. Nothing I did was enough. It hurts."

"I was his age once," Mugi said. "My advice? Pretend he's pregnant. He'll get over it. But it'll take closer to four years than nine months."

"ARE YOU SURE you don't want to try this? I have spare supplies," Kesi said, holding her brush in the air. Tessa popped the rest of the fresh fig she'd been eating into her mouth and savored its nectar as she shook her head.

Mac had called in letting them know that he was detouring to respond to a call regarding a couple of hikers who had wandered into an unsafe area without a guide. Apparently, they'd waved frantically at a tour pilot flying overhead, but there was nowhere for a plane to land. Standard rescue was called in, but Mac was familiar with the spot and knew he'd get there faster from where he was at the time. He was doing what he was born to do. One of these days, Nick would be old enough to go up with him on potentially more dangerous calls like that. He'd have the chance to see if it was *his* calling. She could see it now. Team NickMac. Oh, to be at that young age when your life was ahead of you and you had that virgin opportunity to map it out and discover your path. Tessa wished she could be guaranteed no more wrong turns in hers.

"I like watching you paint. It's relaxing. You make it look so easy."

Tessa held her legs out straight in front of her and turned her ankles for a needed stretch as she watched Kesi brush color across a paper canvas. She gazed at the scenery beyond the river, then back at the canvas. Kesi really was capturing a certain ethereal essence with her watercolors. Kesi was all heart and soul and it showed in her work.

"It lowers my blood pressure," Kesi said. "I crumpled up plenty of attempts in the beginning, but the longer we lived here and I found time to practice, the more pleased I became with the results. There's something to be said for experience and enjoying what you do. My guess is, for you, that would be writing about fashion, so I'm sure you know what I mean."

Did she? Tessa wasn't so sure she'd describe writing her fashion column as a passion. It definitely didn't lower her blood pressure. Sometimes the incomprehensible trends raised it. Now, that last article she'd tried giving Kat…that had raised her pulse as she typed it. But that was different. Invigoration, not stress.

"I suppose," she said.

"I hear people in fashion get a lot of pattern and color inspiration from nature."

"Yes, but I don't particularly like it when they take those colors and patterns right off an animal's back."

"That, I agree with," Kesi said. "Do you like going to fashion shows to come up with what you're going to write about? Have you been to any in cities like London or New York? Watched the models on the runways? I always imagined those events would be a high-stress frenzy."

"No doubt. Actually, I haven't been. I do watch videos of some of them, but it's easy enough to gather information online. I can do my research and figure out what to write from the comfort of my own couch." She'd always thought of that as an advantage, but the minute the words left her mouth and Kesi's brush stopped, causing an unintentional bleed of azure, she could hear the ignorance in them.

"Really?" Kesi turned around and wrinkled her nose. "I had pictured you getting to travel a lot. I suppose I made assumptions when I imagined your life following the fashion industry."

"I do go shopping and try out some of the trending items," Tessa said in her defense. Shopping was a form of experience, wasn't it? Kesi sighed and went back to painting.

"You know, I took painting in school. This was before I went the architecture route. But I was told there was nothing fresh about my work. Nothing unique enough to sell. So, I applied my love of art to something more practical, like architectural sketches and designs. I'm not saying I didn't enjoy my work. I did. But after moving here…living here…feeling and breathing and tasting this place… I had the urge to paint again. I'm not my own critic, but if my experience hasn't made a difference in the artwork, it certainly has in the process. I used to try to bring things to life on canvas. Now I know that only life itself can instill that illusive quality into art…whether painting, photography…

or writing. Think about it. How does one convey an emotion or image they've never felt or seen with the same depth and layer as someone who has?"

Tessa wasn't sure whether she should be grateful or offended. She frowned and sucked the tip of her fingers to get rid of the stickiness from the fig. A sun-ripened fig straight off the tree wasn't the same as one from the grocery store. They tasted and even felt different. Was she like a store-bought fig that had never basked in the sun or absorbed its heat? She stood up.

"Have you even read any of my columns?"

"I was curious and looked them up online after we first met and Mac mentioned what you do."

Okay. Offended it was, then. She was so not in the mood to be judged. She forced a smile and resisted asking Kesi how many paintings she had sold.

"Tessa, your work is good. That's not the point I'm trying to make. I'm simply saying live a little. You're still young. Mugi and I didn't have that epiphany until we were much older."

"I understand. I do. But a person doesn't

have to experience death to write about it, do they? Or heaven forbid commit murder in order to write a bestselling mystery novel. Or what about the news? The people reporting it every night haven't experienced every story."

She wished she could retract that last one the minute she said it. She'd made Kesi's point. She wasn't the reporter in the field, the one interviewed from the front lines or with the surf crashing at their ankles right before a hurricane's landfall. She was the one sitting in a comfy seat behind a desk. Nothing she wrote or reported came from firsthand experience. She'd always come in second. Second born. Second in her class. Second to her husband. Second in work.

Tessa had only known her a matter of days, but Kesi had the ability to make someone feel like they were hanging around their mother, sister and friend all wrapped into one. And that had both positive and negative sides to it. Sometimes a person got advice and opinions from her mom or sister whether she wanted them or not. But Kesi was filling a void, too. As different as Tessa and Maria had been, they were still sisters. Maria had been the only person she'd done mundane, comfortable things with like sharing clothes or hanging out in pajamas. After she'd gotten married, most of her "friends" were merely acquaintances, usually the wives of Brice's friends or business associates. Katia was her closest friend, but Tessa often found herself holding back and respecting the fact that Katia was also her editor. Tessa never discussed things like off-days in her marriage or frustrations with the male mind and ego when she and Brice had an argument. Then again, she hadn't discussed those things with Maria, either, because her sister's opinion of Brice wasn't glowing to begin with. Anyway. All married couples had spats. Right? No one discussed them. Everyone out there had perfect, envy-worthy marriages—or at least they pretended to. It wasn't like Tessa not sharing that level of privacy with anyone mattered.

How much of a front could she put up with Kesi?

"No, I suppose you're right," Kesi said, going back to painting.

Her tone wasn't convincing.

"Where's Nick?"

Mac found Tessa resting in a wooden lounge chair in the shade at the edge of camp. Far enough from the river for safety but close enough to soak in the view. The same spot where Mugi and Kesi had been sitting his first time here. Kesi was seated nearby, working on her painting. They both turned at the sound of his voice.

"What do you mean? He was gathering firewood for tonight with Mugi," Tessa said.

"He's not in our tent. I just got back and that's the first place I went to put some things away."

"Did you check the kitchen?" Kesi asked as they all hurried toward the main house.

"He's not in the house. Mugi was at the computer. He went to look around back."

"Maybe he went into my tent," Tessa suggested. "I'll catch up." She ducked into her tent as they passed it.

Mac sped into a jog.

"Nothing," Mugi said, meeting them in front of the cottage. "I took him out in the jeep earlier, but stressed that he should never wander off on his own. I told him it's dangerous."

"I found a note," Tessa called as she ran toward them. "He ripped a page out of my journal and left this on top. And everything from my backpack was dumped on my bed, but the bag was gone. He needed something to carry supplies in. He's run away! Mac, we have to find him. This can't be happening. I shouldn't have let him out of my sight."

Mac grabbed the note from her. He knew what Nick leaving a note meant. And it wasn't good. Not out here. Especially not once it got dark. They had about an hour of light. The kid had no survival skills and was spooked by anything that moved. He scanned the bad penmanship before reading out loud.

I'm sorry. I took some food and the green thermos. I had no choice. I need to disappear and make all your wishes come true. If I end up dying out there, then good. Maybe I'll get to be with my parents again. They were the only people who wanted me around. I'm gone now so, Uncle Mac and Aunt Tessa, you can get on with your lives. I won't be a burden anymore. You don't have to argue about whose life I'll mess up. Don't worry about me, not that you would, anyway. I'll be fine. I'm not as stupid as you obviously think I am.

Damn.

Everyone was silent after Mac read Nick's last words. The mere idea of him getting lost in the wild was a lot to digest, let alone running off on purpose because of something Mac or Tessa had said or done. Mac stuffed the note into his pocket and planted his hands on his hips. He'd screwed up. This was why he'd known right when Maria and Allan had given him partial custody that they'd made a mistake. He wasn't father material.

"He must have overheard us last night," Tessa said. "We thought he was sleeping," she told Mugi and Kesi.

"We have to hurry. The sun will set soon," Mugi said.

"Do we have any idea when he left the note?" Tessa was grinding the heel of her hand against her forehead. She took a shaky breath.

"When did you last see him?" Mac asked her and Kesi.

"We went to the riverside an hour ago," Kesi said. "But he was with Mugi." She looked to her husband.

"That's about when we finished with the wood gathering. I went inside and he said he wanted to rest. We'll find him. I'll get my rifle and take the jeep. Maybe he went along the same route we took this morning."

"I'll go up in the chopper," Mac said. "I can't wait for the ground search given the daylight left. I need to start an aerial search now. Mugi, have your radio at hand. If I spot him and can't land, I'll contact you and vice versa. Kesi, stay here in case he has a change of heart—let's pray he does. Mugi, let's go. Tessa, you can stay here or go with Mugi."

"No. I'm coming with you."

"I know you're worried. I am, too. But we don't have time for you panicking up there or getting airsick," Mac insisted. "I'm gone."

He took off at a jog toward the chopper, running a mental checklist of emergency supplies he had on board.

"You're not taking off without me. We'll have a better chance of spotting him if I'm looking, too. I can do this, Mac. I can't let anything happen to him." Tessa passed him and was in the chopper before he could respond. She was right about an extra pair of eyes and Mac suspected the adrenaline rush and the obvious takeover of maternal instincts would negate any fears she had of flying. He got in without objecting and started his engine, completing a fast flight check. He glanced at Tessa, wanting to give her a last chance to get out, but the firm line of her lips and the fire in her eyes said it all. A silent understanding passed between them. They were in this together. On the same page and wanting the same thing. They both loved and cared about Nick. And for a fleeting moment, it was clear that they weren't just *acting* as guardians…they were *reacting* like parents.

TESSA'S PULSE RICOCHETED at the base of her throat and heat seemed to course through her like fuel on fire. She didn't care that she could feel every air pocket and altitude drop as Mac flew his search pattern, and the only thing that made her nauseous was the thought of Nick out there alone at night like sitting prey. She steadied herself and scoured the shrub-dotted savanna below. Mac's voice came through her headset every few minutes in response to Mugi's updates.

The older man hadn't spotted Nick anywhere in a half-mile ground radius from the camp. Mac was now over a mile out. Mugi radioed in again not long after. He'd found track marks leading off the path they'd used earlier and down a steep and rocky incline to a valley below. He couldn't take the jeep down, and it would take him too long to bypass the incline. Mac had taken the chopper there, but they still hadn't seen any sign of the boy from the air.

Ribbons of saffron and amethyst streaked the horizon as the sun hit its mark. The expanse of grass below, shimmering with amber and gold, began fading hopelessly.

"We left so quickly I didn't have a chance to refuel and don't have a spare tank on board. We'll need to either head back now, or keep the air search going as long as there's light, then take her down…make camp until Mugi can bring fuel tomorrow. I say we keep looking. I don't want him out there all night."

"Keep going," Tessa said. "Keep looking for as long as we can."

"You're smart, kid," Mac muttered as if Nick could hear him. "Find a safe spot until we get there."

TEARS POOLED IN Tessa's eyes when she heard Mac. She rubbed her nose with the back of her hand and pressed her face to the window. On one hand, she knew Mac was making the right call. The safest one for all of them. Maria and Allan had died in a plane crash. Mac and Tessa needed to stay alive for Nick. But what if Nick didn't make it? There were plenty of stealthy predators who loved the shield of dusk and dark. No doubt criminals like poachers did, too.

A group of hyenas raised their heads toward the sound of the chopper and began dancing nervously around the discarded remains of an antelope. Tessa gasped at the mental image of Nick being preyed upon. She felt Mac's hand on her shoulder and her pulse slowed a few beats.

"He'll be okay. No one could live twelve years with Maria and Allan and not pick up a few nature survival tips, and I'm betting Mugi taught him a thing or two, as well."

Tessa nodded, but kept her eyes on the ground. Nick's outing with Mugi had also made him overly confident. A little knowledge could be dangerous. She and Mac had been that age. Looking back, they thought they knew so much more than grown-ups when they were teens. But even if they had picked up a new fact or two at school, they didn't realize, then, that experience counted for something. No matter how much they learned, their parents' generation would always have a few decades of experience over them. She wondered if Nick had planned this. If, after he'd overheard them last night, he'd woken up with the intention of telling Mugi he wanted to go out and learn about the area, just so he could feel prepared to run away. She'd never forgive herself for arguing with Mac within earshot.

Something orange flicked through a small grove of acacia trees a few yards ahead of them. At first, she thought it was the sunset reflecting off an adjacent outcropping of rock and boulders, but then she spotted Nick climbing the rocks. There was no mistaking him when he looked up and began waving with both arms overhead.

"There! Oh, my God. It's him." She pointed frantically and slapped the window. She could hear Mac radioing Mugi with their status update. Mac immediately brought them down in the nearest clearing. She waited until it was safe to open her door and ducked as she ran from the chopper.

"Nick!" Tessa headed toward the rocks where she'd spotted him. Where had he gone? "Nick," she breathed as she bent over to catch her breath for a second. The ground seemed to move beneath her.

"Aunt Tessa, are you okay?" She straightened and saw Nick sliding down from the boulder above.

She leaned back against the rock, her brain finally registering that she'd been in the air and was now on solid ground.

"I am now. I was terrified when I found your note." She forced a hug on him. He stiffened at first but then hugged her back.

Mac strode right up to Nick and pulled him into his arms.

"Don't ever do that to us again. You scared the life out of me," Mac said, rubbing his knuckles on top of Nick's head. Nick let go of Tessa and hugged him back. It didn't matter that Mac wasn't Nick's dad; watching them made Tessa think of a father and his son. If anyone understood that kids needed tangible, *present* love, support and a sense of security, she did. That's what made a family. She righted herself. The fading light was blending everything into calm grays, which actually helped her head and stomach feel better. She wrapped her arms around both guys.

For as much as she loved her parents and sister, she'd missed out on a carefree, worry-free and secure childhood. But she had it now. Standing here in the middle of nowhere with Mac and Nick, she'd never felt so complete, empowered and full of love.

"I guess this means I really am stupid. I was so angry I didn't care what was out here…until I saw you guys coming. I was kind of relieved."

"Did you really think we wouldn't come after you?" Tessa asked. "Nick, I don't know what you think you heard, but you misunderstood. We love you. Life is about adjusting. Whatever it takes to figure out how we make this family work, it'll be worth it. It's not a sacrifice. Got it?"

He sniffed and wiped his face on his shoulder. "Yeah. Got it."

"I take it you were seeking shelter on a high point," Mac said, nodding toward the boulder.

"Yeah."

"Not so stupid, if you ask me. Best choice you had, considering those trees are thorn-covered and not so climber-friendly. You were thinking on your feet," Mac said.

Tessa wanted to kiss him for trying to save Nick's dignity. He probably didn't know he had it in him, but Mac made a perfect dad and uncle. He knew what a young man needed in terms of guidance and advice. She'd never heard Brice interact with Nick that way, but then again, she'd married a man who had never had any intention of having children. She didn't, either, but only because she was afraid of failing to give them the stability she'd always craved. She didn't want the burden of messing a child up. And here, she'd driven Nick to run away.

"I guess." Nick drew his shoulders back. "I would have made it. I mean, sure I was a little nervous when it started getting dark, but I think I would have survived…like you did your first time around here, Uncle Mac."

"I'm sure you would have, but why risk being a meal if you don't have to be, right?"

"I agree," Tessa said, not wanting Nick to carry his confidence too far. She couldn't stand the idea of him becoming as reckless and fear-free as Mac had been when he graduated high school.

"How badly did I scare you, Uncle Mac?"

He certainly was getting cocky like his uncle.

"Badly enough," Mac said.

"Enough to wet your pants?" Nick grinned. Tessa couldn't hold back. The kid had a sense of humor and a great memory. She laughed and Mac just shook his head.

"Let's hope you never find yourself in a situation like that. Did I mention that snakes hang around rocks for the heat?"

Nick looked behind him and stepped away from the outcropping.

"Uh…"

"That's the thing out here. What might help you if a hyena is looking for dinner could be the same thing that makes you another predator's meal. There's a lot to learn about surviving in the wilderness, but stick around and you'll learn."

Tessa put her arm around Nick's shoulders and kissed his temple. Mac had set him straight on running off. He'd done it like a parental pro.

"Come on, you two. We need to set up camp."

"Camp?" Nick asked. Poor kid was probably hoping he'd get to go home.

Tessa so didn't want to sleep out here, either, but no way was she going to become the joke of male egos. Time to suck it up.

"We got low on gas while searching for you," Mac explained. "Mugi will be out with the jeep tomorrow with enough refill to get her back to camp."

"Sorry about that," Nick said.

"I'll camp every night as long as you're safe." Tessa ruffled his hair. He didn't even pull away.

"I'll help set up," Nick said, following Mac to the chopper for supplies. "I know how to build a fire."

His latent Walker outdoorsman gene had

definitely kicked in. She wasn't so sure if that was a good thing.

MAC STOKED THE small fire he'd built. Nick had insisted on setting up the kindling and lighting it the way he'd read about in books or seen in the movies. It took a bit of finesse to hold back and let him figure out for himself that in real life stick rubbing didn't spark as fast as it did in fiction. Mac blamed it on moisture in the evening air to help the boy save face. Humidity in one of their drier months was a stretch, but Nick went with it. Then Mac showed him how to use his flint rod. Thirteen was a tough step toward manhood. Quite exhausting, too. Nick was still shifting around in the one-man tent Mac had set up. No doubt the tent would make him feel more secure than sleeping out under the open sky.

Mac and Tessa sat on the ground between the tent and the fire. They weren't too far from the helicopter. Mac wasn't about to light a fire close to it, although he did tell Tessa she could stay in it if she thought she could spend the entire night in a seated position. There wasn't much space in the model he owned. If he ever had the funds to expand Air Walker Safaris, a bigger helicopter would be on the list. Tessa had refused to be in the chopper on her own. She said she needed to be near Nick, after the scare they'd had with his disappearance, but Mac knew she wasn't comfortable with the idea of being alone out here, chopper walls or not. Night predators and poachers were enough to trigger bad dreams. As for Mac, he kind of liked the fact that she felt safer by his side. She seemed comfortable enough sitting here.

In the end, they were both adamant about being near Nick, who had initially insisted that camping needed to be "real" camping. As in, under the stars. He almost stayed outside with them, but then agreed with Mac and Tessa that real camping involved tents. Talk about growth spurts of the emotional and mental kind.

"All this adventure will either make him fall asleep instantly or make it so he can't," Tessa said.

Mac tried to ignore how beautiful she looked as she sat on the ground with her chin resting on her knees. She gazed into the fire and her big eyes had never been more soulful. He wanted to kiss her. He coughed and waved the air as if smoke from the fire had gotten to him.

"It'll hit him sooner or later. I know the rations I had weren't much for the three of us, but Mugi will get here soon after the sun's up." All he'd had were a few granola bars and instant coffee. He set his make-shift poker stick down and scooted a few feet back from the fire, next to Tessa. "You impressed me today."

"Me? Why?" She lifted her head and studied him.

"You're scared to death of flying, yet you didn't hesitate to go up for Nick's sake. And I had my doubts, but you handled the search like pro."

"Nothing like a kid to make you face your fears, huh?"

"True. But you're the one who did it and you were the one to find him." He wasn't about to let her shrug it off, even if she did shrug, turning her attention back to the fire.

"I was terrified for him."

"Me, too."

"What *are* we going to do, Mac?"

The sound of cotton sliding against polyester came from the tent behind them. Nick was still awake, which meant he was probably eavesdropping. Mac motioned toward the tent with his head and the curve of Tessa's mouth told him she understood his intention.

"I don't know what I'd do if I lost him," she added, keeping her voice natural but just loud enough for Nick to overhear. "He's a great kid. Smart, funny when he wants to be and talented. And he's family. I couldn't ask for a better kid to be a part of my life."

"I was really impressed by him today, too. He's going to grow up to be a man's man. I really enjoyed sharing bits of my life out here with him. In fact, I'd like to have more time to hang around with him. Not sure if that's what he wants, considering he ran off today."

"You think he doesn't like *us*? Maybe we were cool as aunt and uncle, but not so much as legal guardians. I have to admit, my house in South Africa is a bit…sterile. It isn't all that fun for a teen. I don't think I ever bothered to ask him what he'd like in his living space. Like a pool table or something."

"Maybe he'd rather be around dart guns and camping tents," Mac said. "I think he's pretty comfortable in mine right now, getting a good night's rest."

More rustling came from behind them before everything went quiet. Tessa put a hand over her mouth to keep from chuckling. Mac smiled back. If Nick fell asleep knowing they thought the world of him, then today was worth it. She scooted a few inches closer to Mac and leaned in.

"Are we really safe enough out here?" Her whisper caressed his jaw and it took every bit of self-control not to turn his face toward her. Their lips might touch if he did, and he knew neither of them wanted that. Not with circumstances being what they were. He kept his eyes on the fire and the trees ahead.

"I'll stay awake, and I'm armed."

"What if a lion comes? Aren't they night predators?"

"Do you want to stay in the helicopter?" Of course, she'd be there alone and he'd be here watching Nick and the fire.

"No. I'm fine."

"Generally speaking, what you do depends on the animal and situation. A defensive animal can be as dangerous as a hungry one. Take lions. They have a chase instinct like dogs. If a lion comes up, don't run. Stand still. Inch back slowly if they're not paying attention to you. Just don't trigger a chase. And Nick would be okay. They don't bother tents much. They think the walls are solid. On the other hand, rhinos are one animal you don't want to startle. They have a keen sense of smell. Vision, not so much. So if you're not downwind, you have a chance."

"I saw a movie once…an oldie…where a tribal child held a thick stick over his head to scare off a hyena. Fact or fiction?"

"Well, they can scare off if you make yourself look bigger, menacing, noisy… the whole bit. Doesn't mean they won't attack, especially if they're in a pack, but you definitely do all that to help your chances. There's nothing 'movie' out here, though. This is the real thing."

"I know. I know. I just can't stop thinking about it. Do snakes really like to curl up in sleeping bags for warmth?"

"You're not in one, Tess. Relax. I'm here."

Tessa rubbed her arms and shivered.

"That scared?"

"Cold."

"Late-August nights can get brisk, even when the days are warm," Mac said. They'd both insisted that Nick take the small blanket stored in the chopper.

"I think my body temperature is dropping from fatigue."

"Could be. Lie down. I'll keep watch and keep the fire going." It'd be warmer by the fire than in the helicopter, anyway. It didn't hold heat that well unless it was running.

She curled onto her side on the massive leaves he'd laid on the ground.

"You'll watch for snakes, too, right?" she asked. Her back was turned but her waning voice told him her eyes were closing.

"I have you covered. Go to sleep." Hopefully they wouldn't get any unwanted visitors—legless or legged—but he had a gun tucked at his lower back and a preferred tranquilizer rifle a couple of feet away just in case. He'd also shone his LED torch around the area in search of red eyes. No night stalkers turned up. That didn't mean they wouldn't.

She shivered again and put her hands between her knees in a fetal position. Mac leaned back and reached over her. He put his hand against her forehead. It felt normal.

"Sorry, just wanted to make sure you didn't have a fever. You got vaccinated before coming out here, didn't you?" He kept his voice down, not wanting to make Nick anxious if he wasn't totally knocked out.

"Yes. I don't think I'm sick. I'm just freezing. I really think it's exhaustion and the temperature drop." Her voice sounded sleepy and weak. Mac laid down behind her and pulled her against his chest for warmth.

"Does this help?"

She nodded, holding onto his hand at her waist. Within seconds, her muscles relaxed and her breathing steadied. He hoped she wasn't coming down with anything like malaria. He lay there with every intention of staying awake, but the touch of her hair against his face and the warmth of her scent lulled him to sleep for a few minutes. The call of a wild dog had his eyes jerking open. He kept his ears peeled to gauge the distance, relaxing when the sound got farther away.

He'd always been comfortable being

alone. He'd always felt *at* home out here in the Serengeti…but right now, hearing Tessa's soft breathing and a bit of snoring from Nick, for the first time Mac felt like he *was* home. This was his family.

The idea shocked him. Panic zipped through his chest. What was he doing? Warming Tessa? Yes. But still, lying here spooned against her was wrong. He slowly unwove his fingers from hers, lifted his arm up and inched his body away from hers. He sat up without waking her and considered the small supply box and tranquilizer gun within his reach. He was here to protect them. That's all any of this was. Hopefully, Tessa wouldn't get too cold…or remember being held by him when she woke up in the morning. He wouldn't be forgetting anytime soon.

He added dry wood and bark to the fire and poked until it came to life. He stared at the largest flame that swayed side to side like a woman tempting a man. Tessa hadn't done anything wrong. It was all him. Regardless of circumstances, she was a married woman. He had no business letting himself think of her as any more than a sister-in-law and co-guardian. He had no business wishing. Besides, even if she wasn't taken, this wasn't her type of life. He'd never be able to give her the predictable, secure lifestyle she wanted or needed.

He took a deep breath and glanced back at her. She was still sound asleep, but she'd curled her knees up closer to her chest, the way a person did when they were cold…or scared. He got up, took off his shirt, then covered her with it. He let himself look at her peaceful face for only a second, then walked to the other side of the fire. He was losing it. Maybe he really had been alone for too long. This was a new low for him. He raked his hair back and paced, scanning the shadows as far as the fire and moonlight would let him. He was a bush pilot. A man with sharp reflexes who knew how to handle—and was always prepared for—the unexpected. He'd never expected to see this side of Tessa, a strength he hadn't known existed. A side he liked and respected. Of all people, Tessa Henning was messing him up.

TESSA REALLY NEEDED TO GO to the bathroom. She sat up and rubbed her eyes. Mac's shirt fell to the ground next to her. *His shirt?* Her shoulder and hip ached from lying against the ground. She stretched and moved a little closer to the heat emanating from the hot coals and tender flames.

"Mac?"

He had to be nearby, or the fire would have gone out completely. She looked around but didn't see him. His guns were missing, too. Alarms went off in her head. She got up and unzipped an inch of the tent opening to make sure Nick was all right. He was still there, sound asleep. She zipped it up and went back to the fire. Maybe Mac had needed to use the bathroom, too. She wasn't going to leave Nick alone. She'd just have to hold it until Mac got back. *He better get back here right now.*

"Mac?" she tried again. The bush to her right rustled and she was answered with a strange staccato rumble followed by a sadistic laugh. Her scalp prickled. A spotted hyena slinked out of the brush with its mouth hanging open and salivating. Tessa held her arms out.

"Don't you dare. You hear me? Get out of here. Go!"

The hyena paced back and forth, laughing in a rapid succession of hee-hee-hees that made her skin crawl. Nick was in the tent. Was it lions or hyenas that didn't bother with tents? Most of the time? Something akin to a bolt of lightning flashed through her. What if Mac wasn't returning? What if he'd gone after a predator in order to protect her and Nick, but he'd lost the battle? She raised her hands over her head and started waving them like a crazy woman. This was her campsite and her kid. No one messed with Nick. "Get away! Mine! Mine! Mine! *Eeek!* Woot!" She didn't care how stupid she sounded or what she said. She was making noise until the hyena left or she got eaten. One or the other. The hyena paced one more time, then took off into the soft light of dawn. Tessa pressed a hand to her chest. She was so not going to need coffee this morning. Her hands shook but her mind felt awake. Alive.

A click sounded behind her and she spun around. Mac stood there uncocking his rifle. Boy was he a welcome sight.

"You were here?" she panted.

"I told you I wouldn't leave you. I went

to the chopper for a minute. I was literally gone less than two."

"But I called."

"You handled the situation, Tessa. You did good."

She couldn't believe it. She'd slept under the Serengeti stars and she'd chased off a hyena. What a power rush.

"Is it safe to come out?" Nick called from the tent.

"It's safe," Tessa said. *Because of me.*

MAC DIDN'T WANT to leave again, especially after he'd come home to Nick's disappearance yesterday. He'd meant it when he said that Tessa and Nick came first and he wanted to be around 24/7, ensuring they were okay, but he was really beginning to worry about the state of Air Walker Safaris. If his business went under, he'd never be able to take care of Nick.

Tessa was stronger than she thought. He'd witnessed it himself. Whatever happened with Brice, she'd get her feet back on the ground—no trouble. He wasn't sure he could say the same for himself if his business failed.

They should be hearing something from Ben soon. Kamau, Anna and Jack had their eyes and ears open and, according to their mapping of where the latest poaching victims had been found, Camp Jamba was a safe place to be. For now.

"It'll just be half a day. I have to check on things at the office before Hodari Lodge shuts me down and gives my space to someone else. The only delay would be if someone staying at the lodge wants to book a helicopter tour. I can't afford to say no."

"Don't worry about us," Tessa assured him. "Kesi promised to show me how to make her curry and Mugi told Nick about their computer. He said that if Nick helped clean up after their chickens and put in some time on a few maintenance projects, he'd let him play on it for an hour or so."

"Bribery, huh?"

"It worked. But what about you? I thought Ben said to lie low. Our connection isn't a secret, so shouldn't you be staying away from Hodari, too?"

Our connection. He knew she meant their family connection, but for some reason the words sounded even more personal.

"I'll be fine. I'll check on things with Ben and see if anything has come up with the drives and investigation while I'm there. Do you need anything I can bring back from the lodge? If you left stuff in your room, I can pick it up."

"The room. I'd forgotten. I didn't leave anything, but I think Nick did. I'm paying per night for nothing. We have no idea how long this will drag on. Will it look bad if I have you check me out?"

She was referring to the hotel room, Mac reminded himself. Man, he needed more sleep.

"It might. I think we should keep you registered until we see what Ben says. If Brice comes or sends anyone looking for you, they'll stick around the lodge longer if they think you'll be returning to your room. He knows you brought Nick to see me. He'll expect you to be there. If you disappear, he'll start searching every camp in the Serengeti and all the way back to Nairobi."

"Assuming he really is guilty."

"No matter what, the man has something to lose. Even if he ends up being clean, no smart man would let you walk away without coming after you."

As soon as the words left his mouth and her cheeks turned pink, he realized what he'd said.

"I mean, if he sees you've had a room at the lodge like you said, he won't wonder about us." This wasn't coming out right at all. "By us, I mean, if he sees the Air Walker office closed and you've also checked out of your room, he'll wonder where we all took off to. Guys get jealous. And if he's innocent, that might make fixing your marriage more difficult. The whole trust thing and..."

"He'd know Nick was with us."

"Right." Mac didn't fumble words around women. Ever. His face heated. "I just mean, bottom line, you should stay registered. Just in case. I'll give Ben a call from the office and see what he says."

"That's a lot of money per night. If Brice is guilty and gets angry when he realizes what I've done, he'll cut me off from our bank accounts. I opened one on the side about a month ago, when I was planning, but only put a little in it. He scours his books. I didn't want to raise suspicion. I need to be careful with spending."

"We'll deal with that when the time comes. It may only be an extra night or two. We'll figure it out. Safety first."

"Okay. Just be careful. Promise."

"I promise." He slapped his cap onto his head, gave her a wink just to annoy her and trudged toward his chopper. "Stay back," he yelled as a safety reminder. As if she'd come running after him like a damsel in a movie. That would only ever happen in his dreams.

SIX HOURS HAD never felt so long to Mac. He'd always lived in the moment, taking lodge patrons on tour at a second's notice, flying out to Nairobi for a private charter back to the lodge or heading off to help local friends with whatever they needed. Time had never passed so...so slowly. All he could think of today was wanting to be back around Nick and Tessa. He couldn't get either of them off his mind.

He waved goodbye to the second round of tourists he'd just returned to Hodari Lodge. The first had been a couple from London on their honeymoon and this second one was a small group of friends who appeared to be in their early twenties. Two definitely acted like a couple and the third, a sultry brunette, had gotten uncomfortably touchy-feely with him.

Thank goodness this group hadn't booked an all-day trip or an overnighter at one of the tourist campsites. The young woman had thanked him profusely after they'd paid, and had even tried stealing a hug—which he'd skillfully managed to slip away from—and then invited him to join the three of them for drinks...and whatever else he had in mind. Her words. Mac was used to dealing with customers like that and was pretty smooth at escape. Customers were customers. He had no interest in crossing that line. But for some reason, today, that client's come-on had made him want to run. As if he was a happily married man approached at a bar. He'd even blurted something about already seeing someone. What a lie. But it had worked. Sort of. He waved again at the young woman, who was lagging behind her friends and looking at him over her shoulder. It was driving him crazy that Tessa's face had come to mind when he was dealing with the customer. Tessa was another line he couldn't cross.

Since Sue was still at Busara, he passed by the concierge desk for mail. Abed, who'd been working there since Mac had started Air Walker Safaris, glanced up from behind the curved solid wood counter backed by floor-to-ceiling windows overlooking the lodge's courtyard garden.

"Mac, my man. Where have you been?"

"Oh, the usual. A few of the research groups lost track of their herds and needed some flyovers. All in a day's work." Mac leaned against the counter and casually scanned the lodge. "Any mail or messages?"

"Has Madam Sue returned to America?" he asked as he bent down to search the cubbies and drawers behind the counter.

"Just visiting her grandchildren." Everyone here knew Anna and Jack. Jack, especially, because his genetics lectures at the lodge attracted business in the form of science conference groups.

"I haven't seen your friend around, either. Are you taking messages to the pretty lady, too?"

Mac shrugged and scoffed at the notion.

"Oh, her? Not the kind of friend I keep, if you know what I mean. She's my nephew's aunt. Brought him around to visit. But you can go ahead and give me the message in case it concerns him."

Mac and Abed always shot the breeze, but given everything, all the questions sent flares up in Mac's mind. He had about a ninety per cent trust rate going with Abed. He reached into his pocket and folded a few bills into his palm. He could only hope enough shillings would cover the remaining ten per cent.

Abed handed over a small stack of mail and Mac reached out to take the envelopes while smoothly transferring the money to Abed's hand from underneath the stack. He glanced around the room casually.

"It's not necessary, Mac. How long have I known you?" Abed said.

"You're a good man, Abed. Keep it for your family." Mac hadn't meant to offend him. This whole worrying about someone else situation had his caution sensors on high alert. Abed tipped his head in thanks.

"A man called." He pulled out the yet-to-be-delivered message and handed it to Mac.

Darling, I'm back home. Thought you'd
be here by now. Miss you. Give me a
call. Love, Brice.

Mac stuffed the paper in his pocket. Here
he'd mentioned something to Tessa about
guys getting jealous. Why did *he* feel so un-
easy?

"If he calls again, tell him the boy is giving her a hard time and insisting on one
safari tour after another, so they've been getting in late. If he calls tomorrow, you can
say Mrs. Henning took a flight out to Nairobi to do some shopping and sightseeing.
It's more her style than the Masai Mara," he
said with the universal male expression for
high maintenance woman. Abed shook his
head sympathetically, then leaned forward.

"One other thing. The boss greeted two
men here yesterday. Supplied them with
drinks and lunch. He took them on a tour
of the landing strip. Stopped briefly in front
of your office, but I couldn't hear what was
said. The younger of the two seemed a bit
overzealous. Left this on his way out." Abed
gave Mac a business card. Amboseli Luxury
Tours, Inc. Mac's jaw twitched. He tapped

the card on the counter, then added it to his stack.

"Thanks, man. Grab yourself a *Keroro* after work and put it on my tab."

"Join me if you're around."

Mac waved as he headed to Air Walker Safaris. He unlocked the door—thankful it was indeed locked—and closed it behind him. He retreated into his quarters and tossed the stack of mail on his desk, then locked up the day's earnings.

Darling... I miss you.

Brice's message grated on him. The message sounded so normal. Too normal, if he listened to his gut. Too forced, given how distant Brice had been acting, according to Tessa. First the extravagant fountain pen and now a note too nice for comfort, especially if the man had been home long enough to find his office tampered with and flash drives missing. Something told Mac that a man like Brice paid attention to details. A man didn't become as successful as he was without noticing everything and staying in control.

Worse yet, Mac caught himself wondering if the guy really did miss her. If he really did love her. Because how could he not?

He needed to pass the message on to Ben. He pressed the button to boot up his system, then brushed past the cloth strips and went to his bed. He sat on the edge and considered the space. It had always been enough. He'd never needed more. Never noticed how dark and cramped it was…and lonely. Only days ago, he'd relished that feeling. It was enough. It had to be. It always had been.

Then why was he wishing he was at Camp Jamba with Tessa and Nick? Why did he feel like he was missing out on hanging around with both of them…and Mugi and Kesi. Missing out on family time. Missing home.

He scrubbed his calloused hands up and down his face, then took a deep breath. Family? Home? Was he kidding himself? Nick was his only blood relation and he didn't even know how he was going to handle having *him* in his daily life. Only now, he *wanted* to figure it out. He wanted to raise Nick. *Really* raise him. Teach him to be a man of honor. Not a man like Brice.

Mugi and Kesi had told Mac he was family and that if he ever decided that he could handle the logistics of making Jamba his home base instead of Hodari, they would welcome him. It wasn't the first time they'd mentioned it. But Mac didn't want to invade their privacy to that extent. And he liked his own, back here in his small cave. Plus, Jamba didn't have customers tracking through all day long. If he didn't have an office here in Hodari's lobby, Air Walker Safaris would definitely go under. Leaving this place would be like trying to set up a coffee shop in the middle of nowhere and wondering why there were no customers. And the lodge had a better area for him to keep his helicopter, especially during rainy season.

Besides, inviting him to stay at Jamba was different than inviting him *and* Nick. It wasn't Mugi and Kesi's responsibility to help him raise his nephew. Good a kid as he was, he was a handful. He'd proved that yesterday. Still, it'd be like growing up with grandparents around. Mugi and Kesi would be there when Mac had to work. If, after all was said and done, and Tessa decided to leave Nick with him, just as she'd planned, he couldn't think of anyone else who could watch Nick while he was out on flights. Tessa's future was up to Tessa, not him. But every time he tried thinking about how he could make things work, he came up against a rhino's butt.

Mac slapped his thighs and got up. He'd momentarily forgotten about the issue of schooling. See? A real parent wouldn't have forgotten about that. He remembered being Nick's age. How important having peers was. Even if he asked Mugi and Kesi for help, school would be an issue. Mac had told Tessa that there was no way he'd isolate the kid, and he meant it.

Everything came back to the same problems. It simply wasn't doable. Abandoning his business and moving to the city just so his nephew could attend school wasn't an option. He had to make a living and Air Walker was his life. People—wildlife—depended on his volunteer work. And even if whatever scheme Brice was caught up in got busted, there'd still be poachers out there and victims to rescue. He grabbed his bottle of Scotch, took one swig and put it back in the drawer.

He picked up the card he'd tossed on his desk. Amboseli Luxury Tours, Inc. He typed it into the search bar. *Just great.* That was one professional web presence. Clicking on a few of their links and pages made it clear just how big they were. It happened all over the world in every town. Big chain comes in and kills small, local business...or buys them out. Mac had never buddied up to the owner of Hodari Lodge. Sure, Mac was a fellow businessman. But the owner wore a suit. Mac wore khakis. And he wasn't into schmoozing. He did his own thing. Now he was wishing he'd gotten to know the owner a little better. He raked his hair back.

The luxury lodge wanted luxury tours.

Maybe the propellers were already spinning. And here he was, spending less time at work because of the Brice ivory investigation. That couldn't have happened at a worse time.

He shot Ben a quick email update, then grabbed his mail and flipped through. Bills...more bills...a letter from the lodge owner. He cranked his neck, inhaled, then opened it. *You've got to be kidding me.* Reading between the lines, they were strongly encouraging him to sell out and cut his losses. He tore the letter in half. He didn't care how impossible things seemed. If anyone thought

Mac Walker was going to crumble under pressure and sell out, they didn't know him.

He lived for the impossible.

TESSA KICKED OFF her sneakers and pulled her feet up, crisscross-style, as she sat on the chair outside her tent. She didn't know what had triggered it, but the words were flowing endlessly. It didn't matter that she'd forgotten her tablet charger back in South Africa and had no access to the documents she'd stored on it. She didn't need her fashion research or list of article ideas for the paper she was never going back to. Katia would figure out soon enough that whoever she got to cover the column this week was going to have to be a permanent hire. She didn't even need her copy of the article she'd written that Katia had refused to print. The one about her ivory trade suspicions. Nothing mattered but the glide of her ballpoint pen against her journal pages and the high she was enjoying as her thoughts bled out with the ink.

After all she'd experienced out here in Kenya's wilderness, visiting Busara and living alongside the very elephants she'd written about, that earlier article sounded hollow even to herself. As much as it would have stirred public curiosity and put pressure on people to act, it had been missing something. Something that was flowing onto the page now. Emotion. Insight.

She paused briefly to take in the chatter of primates she knew were spying on her from the branches of the fig and elephant pepper trees. She couldn't see them and it didn't matter that she couldn't identify them. All that mattered were the sounds.

It hit her that no dictionaries or universal translators were needed. If she let go and listened…really listened…she could understand every click, chatter, grunt and whistle that filled the air. They were the sounds of contentedness and belonging. They were the bustling sounds she imagined would fill a family's home during a reunion or holiday.

They were the sounds of life being lived.

Here, she wasn't standing safely behind a window looking out on the natural world. Here, she was in it. A part of it. And though she still felt like an outsider, something about being here felt right and whole and more beautiful than any part of the designer—and safely designed—life she'd been living. She finally understood why Mac loved it here. He didn't fear life…he embraced it in a way that was enviable. She now realized that all the times he'd teased her and tried to get her to take a plunge, he'd been trying to get her to love life. To feel free. He was trying to share a bit of joy with her and she'd refused. And now…oh, God…now she wished he were sharing this very moment with her. He'd understand what she was feeling and experiencing without her having to put it into words. For the first time, emotions she'd always held back flooded her.

Mac was a good man. He was everything she admired and respected and he knew *her*…her faults, weaknesses and strengths. And still, he was sticking by her side and Nick's. She could be herself around Mac. She'd never hated him. She'd hated being afraid that something would happen to him. She'd cared too much. She more than cared now.

A splash sounded and she peered across the camp toward the river. A young hippo had found relief from the sun's heat. She smiled. This place was amazing. Inspiring.

She felt like Karen Blixen writing *Out of Africa*. Out here, she didn't have to care about gaining anyone's approval to write what she wanted. She was writing for herself and because she *had* to. She needed the release. She felt the urge to put her life to paper before—like Karen, who'd left her plantation home in Kenya—she'd have to leave Kenya, too. She wanted to write down everything that had happened and all the signs she'd overlooked with the very man she'd been living with. She had to express every emotion that had choked her during Ben's interrogation. If things turned out badly…if in the end she had to go into hiding…or if something worse happened to her…she wanted her experiences to get out there. Words were eternal. If the true story she was putting to paper ever made it out into the world, then at least she would have made a difference.

"Hey, Aunt Tessa! Look at this!"

Nick came running over, his hair swept out of his face by a spare AWS cap worn in reverse, and held out, of all things, an egg. Tessa raised her brows.

"What laid it?"

Nick stared at her like she was nuts.

"A chicken. What else?"

"Okaaaay…" Not some exotic Serengeti bird or snake or something? He was ecstatic over a chicken egg?

"I was helping fix this pen made out of these really thorny branches from the acacia trees—Mugi said it's called an *enkang* and it's how the Masai people make pens to keep their livestock in because the thorns discourage predators—and while I was helping, one of the hens laid this. I actually watched it come out of her."

Ah. Now it made sense. The cool part.

"You should have seen it, Aunt T. Her vag…"

"Hey! Watch it," Tessa said, holding out her palm to stop him. "That's not what it's called on a hen."

"Whatever. Her *rear* got all pink and stretchy and…"

"Gross. Stop or you'll ruin me for eggs," Tessa said. His enthusiasm was so unexpected. Seeing him light up like this was truly wonderful, amusingly ironic as it was: Nick traveling deep into the wild Serengeti to see something as ordinary as a chicken laying an egg. She really didn't want to hear the details, though. Nick didn't care. He kept going.

"It was all wet and she just squatted there until it dried. It's still warm. Here. Touch it."

"I'll pass," Tessa said. She was appreciating "experience" but she did have her limits.

"I'm going to eat it. Kesi said she'd scramble it up for me. Talk about fresh." He winked and Tessa was floored. Mac had himself a clone.

"Mugi…"

"Mr. Lagat. It's more polite," Tessa said.

"He told me to call him Mugi. Anyway, he said that if you and Uncle Mac are okay with it, he could teach me to shoot a rifle and drive the jeep."

Now that was pushing it. Tessa set her pen and notebook down.

"You're thirteen," she said as she slipped her sneakers back on. "Isn't that illegal or something?"

"He's a lawyer, Aunt T. I think he'd know. We're in the middle of nowhere and the gun wouldn't be for hunting. I told him you guys would lose your heads over that. It'd just be for emergency protection. Even Uncle Mac keeps one. Wild animals—pythons, hyenas…"

"For the record, I scared that hyena off without a gun."

"Aunt T…remember, you want what's best for me, right?" He gave her a smug grin. "And it's not like driving a jeep would land me in jail. There aren't any police or traffic rules out here. Plus, I have great hand-eye coordination from all the console games I play and practicing driving here would be safer—no one to hit—so when we go back and I really learn to drive, I'll be better at it. More expert," he said, shaking a finger at her. Tessa sighed.

"I'm beginning to wonder what you have more of—Mac's thirst for adventure or Mugi's knack for arguing a court case."

"If I have both, does that make me twice the man?" He took off sniggering with the warm egg before she could comment.

That boy was something else. Bringing him out here was the best decision she'd ever made. The only right one, too.

She started down the path toward the cottage, but remembered her journal was sitting out. She doubled back, put it inside and headed back. The aroma floating on the air told her that Kesi had already started cooking and Tessa had promised to help out in exchange for lessons on how to make some of the dishes. She'd lost track of time while writing. Kesi appeared on their porch and waved.

"I'm sorry I forgot. I'm ready to learn," Tessa called out. Kesi shook her head.

"Mac called to make arrangements for a family that was looking for an overnight excursion. He's bringing them back with him. I could use your help."

Her help. She was needed. Valuable. No longer an outsider. It felt wonderful. She smiled and picked up her pace.

"Consider it done."

TESSA DUSTED OFF the bistro-size table and chairs in the tent that stood about five yards from hers. Kesi was spreading fresh linens on one of the beds. These tent accommodations were a little larger than hers. Large enough for two beds instead of one, so that families with younger children could stay together.

"Are you really looking for snakes?" Tessa asked as Kesi took a quick peek under the bed.

"I really am. We've never had an issue, but you never know. One can't be too careful."

Tessa had seen a copy of the release forms Mugi had guests sign. Apparently, he'd drawn up the ones that Mac used for his business, too. They were fairly comprehensive and had plenty of warnings about risk, potential injury...death. Not that different than what some of the ladies back home had talked about signing just to get their noses fixed.

"Brave parents, they are, coming out here for five days with twin nine-year-olds. I'm not sure I could do it, but I suppose it would depend on the children," Tessa said.

"It's not so bad. You visited Busara. You should have seen it years ago, when Anna first came out here. She was pregnant at the time. She got through her pregnancy and raised Pippa while living in conditions that make these look like a five-star hotel in the city. And the entire time she put her veterinary skills to good use. When we first moved here, I thought we'd made a mistake, but after a while…and after the cottage was built…it really became home. I can't imagine being anywhere else."

Tessa started on the second bed, then stopped and checked underneath. No snakes. Thank goodness.

"You've definitely made Camp Jamba a home. It's incredible. Nick is loving it. He really gets along well with Mugi and he's in heaven with your cooking."

"He's a great kid. He'll be all right," Kesi said. "What about you?"

"Me?" She thought for a minute, remembering how she and Nick had felt their first day here. Things had really changed. "You know, I'm truly enjoying my time here and there's something fulfilling and exciting about helping you get ready for visitors. Thank you for letting me help," Tessa said. She was being sincere. There was joy in being here and in anticipating getting to share the wonders of the place with others, especially the younger generation. Nick might have some fun with the visitors, as well.

Kesi fluffed the last pillow.

"I meant, will you be okay?"

Tessa stopped smoothing the bedding.

"I'll be okay. It's just that I get these moments where I feel guilty for everything going through my head. Everything I'm doing. When I got married, I vowed 'until death do us part.' I made a commitment and for most of that time, even if things between us weren't perfect, they were good. He was good. People make mistakes, right? People make wrong choices. Who decides when someone deserves a second chance and when they don't?" Tessa was so confused she wasn't even sure if she was wondering about Brice or herself. She sat down on the chair near the bed.

"My dear, only you can answer that for yourself. No one knows your life and what goes on inside you as well as you do. Don't feel judged or guilty. It's hard to share a life when you don't share the same morals and values. It makes it even harder to raise a family or to get through the bumps. There can be a false sense of security and comfort in the familiar. Change is hard and stressful and can even seem impossible. It's not until you're surrounded by people who share your beliefs, values and morals that you realize you've been in the wrong place or with the wrong person. That you're not where you're supposed to be in life."

"How do you know this for sure? You and Mugi look so happy and so perfect together. I can't imagine you ever suspecting him of criminal activity and having your life here destroyed."

"I'm thankful that's not the case. But life is unpredictable. Even we don't know what's in store for us in the future. Not with one hundred percent certainty, even if that's what we feel in our hearts." She leaned back against the dresser and looked pointedly at Tessa. "Once upon a time, I was engaged to another man. Then I met Mugi and I felt as if I'd been swept away in a flood. It took me time to get the courage to make a different choice, but with Mugi, I knew I'd met the man I would drop everything for and move to the ends of the earth with, and I knew he'd do the same for me…and here we are. Is that how you feel?"

"I'm not sure." If she had felt that way when she met Brice, wouldn't she remember? "Brice and I just happened. He was introduced to me at an animal cruelty pre-vention event—a fund-raiser—and he kept calling me and taking me out after that. He made me feel special."

"I didn't mean him."

Tessa looked up from where she was trac-ing the engraving on the chair's arm with her finger. Her pulse tripped in her chest. Was Kesi implying that something was going on between her and Mac? That she had feelings for him, the kind Kesi had had for Mugi? Tessa's face heated and she licked her lips. Did Mac make her feel like she'd drop everything and move to the ends of the world with him? The answer swirling in her head scared her.

"Why would you think…?"

"The way you look at him when he's not looking at you and vice versa. I've known Mac a long time. I've never seen him so… so grounded, for the pilot he is. I've never seen him act like a family man. Ever. Until you and Nick arrived. You've been a good influence on him. I see a lot of change in you, too, since you first arrived. You're so much more relaxed."

Her? A good influence on a man like

Mac? That notion would have been laughable back when they were kids. If anything, when she'd tried to influence him…tried to tell him to listen to his family and stay home in South Africa…he'd bolted and never returned. If she was changing him in any way, he'd end up resenting her. Was she giving off signals without realizing it?

"I don't know what you mean. Mac is Mac. Always has been and always will be. He looks out for people and is passionate about his life here in Kenya. If anyone—*anyone*—came to him with the possibility of bringing down a poaching ring, he'd have been on it just like he's been with my situation. The only thing making it more personal is Nick."

Kesi sighed and gave the tent one last perusal, then motioned for Tessa to follow her out.

"If you say so. Maybe you're right," Kesi said.

"I am. Kesi, please don't imply anything is going on. I'm still married. It's…it's just wrong. I can't go there." Guilt pounded through her veins. What was she doing?

"I'm sorry. Forgive me. I didn't mean to

make you uncomfortable. I assumed things were over with your marriage because of what happened."

Kesi was wrong. They didn't know what was on the drives yet. They hadn't heard back from Ben. She still couldn't be sure she hadn't sent everyone on a wild-goose chase.

Nothing was over.

CHAPTER NINE

"ANYTHING EXCITING HAPPEN while I was gone?" Mac asked while helping to set up a foldout table near the fire pit area. Mugi was bent down on his knees, making sure the legs on his end were locked. The Johnsons seemed to be a nice family. The Mr. and Mrs. were taking a few minutes to relax in their tent after, to everyone else's surprise, Nick had offered to keep an eye on the twins while entertaining them.

"No. Nothing you'd consider exciting, though I must say, I find your nephew quite refreshing."

Mac and Mugi turned to where Nick was showing the boys how to tie a slipknot, a skill he had only just learned himself earlier that day. Prior to that, he'd passed on his newfound knowledge of how to make a wooden toothbrush, bristles and all, from the toothbrush tree at the edge of camp.

"Look at how patient he's being. And so confident," Mugi said. "That's not the same teen you arrived with. Remember that meltdown he had right out here before we even had the chance to meet him?"

"Not easily forgotten. He's definitely not the same boy," Mac agreed. "It's good to see him like this."

"Okay, stop watching him. Let's not ruin a good thing," Kesi said as she and Tessa joined them.

They were both balancing several dishes of food. Mugi took the white tablecloth Kesi had on her shoulder and covered the table so they could set up the late lunch/early dinner.

"I'll go grab some chairs," he said.

He walked off and they all finished setting up. Mac gathered some wood so that the fire would be ready for after dinner. It was all about the ambience and experience. A lot of camps had hired help to serve the food and take care of things, but Mugi and Kesi wanted to create something different. They were all hands on. This wasn't just a camp. It was their home. But sometimes, Mac wondered how they planned to manage if things got busier...or when they got older.

Taking visitors off on jeep tours was tiring, and if Mugi was gone, that left Kesi to do all the work at base on her own. They really needed to hire at least one other person to take care of the day trips and menial chores.

The radio receiver he'd clipped to his belt sounded. It was Anna.

"I read you, Mama Tembo. Over."

"Raptor King, can you fly over? Bakhari got loose. Need help spotting. Worried. Over."

"Done. I'll be in touch. Over."

Bakhari was a baby elephant she'd rescued from a snare injury about three years ago. A favorite at Busara, and last Mac had seen, Bakhari had the beginnings of tusks, though nothing significant. He wasn't old enough to be off on his own. In wild herds, elephant babies didn't get weaned until at least four or five years of age, when their tusks, at half a foot, would start to bother their mothers. But he knew Anna was worried because, tiny tusks or not, it wasn't safe out there. Busara was Bakhari's "herd" until he got relocated to a reserve better equipped to handle the hormonal behavior of adolescent elephant bulls and their eventual transition back into the wild.

Times like this were why he liked being in control of his job. His career. He could wake up and do what he knew was right and necessary...and not have to wait on clearance from someone with authority over him. Someone likely driven by a financial bottom line.

Ultimately, he knew that organizations like KWS and their affiliates were better equipped than he was to combat poaching and illegal wildlife trafficking. And if KWS's use of drones to track poachers and stop them before they killed proved as effective as everyone hoped, then there might not be any need for his volunteer flyovers and efforts. He'd never stop volunteering as long as he was needed, but that would be a dream come true. An effective crackdown on poaching. The end of illegal killings and kidnappings of wild animals for pet sales or body parts. The authorities and the growing number of conservation organizations were not only making a difference in that respect, they were also raising global awareness and helping conservancies and research groups with their needs. Mac was only one man trying to make a difference...trying to help his friends make a difference. He hated the idea of being grounded if his company went under and he was forced to sell his chopper to make ends meet. And Anna's call reminded him why he did what he did. Failure wasn't an option.

"I need to do a flyover," he told Kesi and Tessa as he headed for his landing site.

He had a baby elephant to find.

"I KNEW MUGI could spin a story, but wow. He was really in his element as an entertainer out there." Tessa walked alongside Kesi, each of them carrying a stack of clean towels. They'd still been drying on the line behind the cottage when they were preparing for the Johnsons earlier.

"I've heard most of those stories, but I could hear them a million times over. It's in the way he tells them," Kesi agreed. "If you don't mind putting those in Mac and Nick's tent, I'll take these over to the Johnsons."

Tessa walked over to the guys' tent and slipped inside. She chuckled when she saw that neither Mac nor Nick had bothered to make their beds. She set her pile on a chair, then tied back the mosquito netting around Nick's bed and tugged his sheets straight. After setting a towel and washcloth on the end of his bed, she went over to Mac's. He'd already tied back his netting and for a moment she hesitated. She really didn't need to fix his bed. That was simply not her job, and it was…personal. Like what she did at home, with Brice. Only they shared a bed.

She ignored the rumpled mess and went to the chair to get the towels. Something black scurried out from underneath his varnished tree-stump nightstand and disappeared under his cot. She jumped before she registered that snakes didn't scurry, they slithered. But there were other lovely critters like scorpions around here. She didn't want Mac or Nick getting stung. She grabbed a decorative spear off its perch on the wall and crouched down at a safe distance. She used the tip to lift the edge of the sheet. A large black beetle hurried from its hiding place and out the door. Tessa let go of her breath.

She set the spear back in its place over the dresser near the end of Mac's bed. The bottom drawer hadn't been properly closed. He *had* been in a rush to answer Anna's call for help. She started to push it shut, but stopped. What if a snake had crawled in it? Drawers made cozy sleeping spots. She'd taken in a stray cat once, when she was Nick's age, and a few days later, woke up to the sound of mewing. The cat, who she'd named Nimbus after the cumulonimbus storm clouds that always made her worry about her parents at sea, had birthed a litter of kittens in the bottom drawer of her dresser. *Kittens. Baby snakes.* No way. She took the spear and put the end in the gap and levered the drawer open wider. Hard to see. She pulled it farther out and poked at the shirts dumped in along with a stack of papers. No snakes. Thank the universe and beyond. She had no clue what she would have done if she *had* found a snake. Or its babies.

The bottom edge of a note stuck out from under the top of the paper stack. She wasn't a snoop. Not except for when she'd broken into Brice's office. But those were extenuating circumstances. She respected privacy. But she couldn't take her eyes off the letters *Br.* She put the spear back and bent down for a closer look. She edged the paper out, just enough to see the next letter. If it wasn't an *i*, she'd look no more. Mac's papers were none of her business. It was an *i*. She pulled the entire note out.

Darling, I'm back home. Thought you'd be here by now. Miss you. Give me a call. Love, Brice.

Her blood rushed to her feet and she held onto the dresser with her free hand until she felt steady. Brice had left her a message and Mac was hiding it from her? She reread it twice. If he was home and not upset, then maybe he hadn't found anything missing yet. Her heart raced. He was missing her. He'd signed *Love, Brice.* He was calling her darling like he always did. She held the note to her chest and squeezed her eyes shut.

Trust. Traitor. If he's innocent, you're betraying him.

What Kesi had said earlier about the chemistry between Tessa and Mac came back to haunt her. She was betraying Brice in more ways than one. She couldn't deny her attraction and deepening feelings for Mac or that something about being around him felt right. She was a terrible person. But she needed to find out the truth about her husband. She needed to put this all behind her. She'd chosen to marry him and was prepared to honor her vows, but she needed to know if her loyalty was deserved. And what about Mac? Did he deserve any more from her than Brice? He didn't trust her with the note. What did that say about their relationship? About his respect for her? It didn't matter how she felt about him; he still saw her as the same naïve and sheltered teen he'd known and that ticked her off, but Mac was being himself. Overly protective. That wasn't a crime. And neither of them knew if Brice was a criminal or not.

What if Brice was playing it cool on purpose? What if the message was a way of fishing her out? She hid the scrap of paper in her pocket and closed the drawer. If he *was* trying to fish her out, then good. Let him. Because if she'd realized anything when she scared off that hyena, it was that she was willing to take the risk. She was ready to be a decoy if it meant protecting those she loved.

Forgive me, Mac.

"Brice?"

"Tessa. For crying out loud, where have you been? Why haven't you returned my messages? I've been worried sick."

Had he left more than one? Tessa bit her lip as she held the cumbersome satellite phone to her ear. She really hoped that Mugi and Kesi didn't notice it had gone missing.

"I'm sorry. I…" Did she tell him or didn't she? His message had sounded honest. Honest enough to spark her guilt. Ben had asked her to lie low. So had Mac. But he'd also kept the note from her. Why? If what Kesi had said was true, if Mac had deeper feelings for her, could he be acting on jealousy? Or was he being overly protective because he believed Brice guilty until proven innocent. Not the other way around. She wasn't sure what to think anymore. She racked her brain for something neutral to say. "Nick wanted to go on a mini safari, so I didn't have a way of checking in. I just got back to the lodge and saw your message about needing to talk to me. You knew I was bringing him up here and you know he can be demanding."

"Tessa, listen to me. I need you to stay

put. Don't talk to anyone. Don't go anywhere alone. Keep Nick with you at all times."

Alarms blared in her head and her feet felt cold. Was he worried? Or coming after her because of his missing drives? He sounded genuinely scared for her and Nick. Panic constricted around her waist like a python.

"Brice, what's going on?"

"I got home from my trip and found our house ransacked. The place was turned upside down. I had no idea if you were okay."

His last words sounded achy and distraught. Tessa's head spun. She'd misjudged him. If he came home to a break-in mess, then she'd be the last person he'd suspect of taking the thumb drives from his office. That would mean he wasn't angry or suspicious. He really was worried. Who *had* broken in and what were they trying to find? Was someone else onto her suspicions, or did Ben have something to do with this? Was someone Brice worked with or maybe someone who'd attended one of their parties involved in the ivory dealings? Katia? No way. Tessa couldn't even picture it. Someone else at the paper, maybe? Had she endangered Brice, thinking he was the danger?

"My gosh, Brice. No, we're fine. That must have happened after we left. What did the police say? Are there suspects?"

"The police think it was a simple burglary because there were a couple of valuables missing. But I don't think so. Keep what I'm about to tell you to yourself, okay? I can trust you, right?"

That was a loaded question.

She pictured herself in his office and wondered if it was now a pile of shattered glass.

"Haven't you always?"

"Tessa, I think you're in danger."

"Because of one burglary? I'm not even there."

"Listen to me. Less than a year ago, I found out that some of the companies I'd invested in were involved in illegal activities. At first, it was just suspicions, but after a while, I was sure."

"What type of activity?"

"Ivory trade. Paying poachers and suppliers under the table. Looking the other way when necessary. It's too much for you to understand. There are so many layers of contacts in what they do, so no one would ever be able to pin it on them."

The muscles in her neck tensed. That was exactly what Anna and Ben had said. *The ivory mafia.*

"We're talking men with money who know how to keep their hands clean. Dangerous men, Tessa. I had to play along to some extent because I was afraid if I didn't they'd come after my family. I didn't know the full nature of my first deal until I was entrenched in it all."

Tessa sat back on her bed, stunned. Her chest and fingers felt numb. She'd been right all along to doubt herself. Instead of staying safe and keeping her mouth shut, she'd written that damn article and pulled herself, and Nick, into a dangerous whirlpool. All along, Brice was trying to protect them and now she'd probably endangered him, too. She knew how ruthless gangs could be. If they saw Brice as a weak link, they'd kill him. And his blood would be on her hands.

"Tessa?"

"I'm here. I don't know what to say or what to believe anymore, Brice."

"I understand." His voice softened. "These past six months haven't been easy on you. I'm sorry I wasn't more present. But

I was trying to find a way to extricate myself from it all without endangering anyone. I'm afraid it didn't work."

"Are you in danger, Brice? Please go to the police. Ask for prot—"

"These people are beyond the police. Tessa… Katia's dead. Her car broke past a guardrail on her way home last night. The report says it was an accident. That she'd lost control, maybe fell asleep at the wheel. I don't think so."

"What?" Tessa's eyes stung and her head strained with pressure. "No!" She covered her mouth and started pacing. It wasn't supposed to be like this. No one was supposed to get hurt. The whole point of uncovering what was going on was to protect the innocent. What had she done? Kat hadn't just lost her job because of her…she'd lost her life.

"Maybe it was an accident," she said. *Kat dead?*

"I doubt it. Tessa, I checked her computer at the office before the authorities took it as part of their investigation."

Tessa knew what was coming next.

"You'd sent her an article that she didn't post, yet she'd emailed a copy to a private account. Someone…a mole at the company…must have found out what she was up to. If there is a mole, they know you wrote the article. And if they pass that information on…"

The truth will set you free. Or not.

"I did. I wrote it."

"Why, Tessa? Don't you realize you put everyone in danger, including yourself?"

"Brice, I wasn't sure what was going on between us. You were acting so different and withdrawn. Then Nick moved in. And I overheard some things that made me wonder if you were involved in something bad or maybe even having an affair."

"Are you kidding me? Tessa, I *love* you. I've always been faithful. And I told you the nature of my involvement. I had to put your safety, and your family's, first. *Our* family."

"My family? What are you saying? Nick's in danger?"

"I'm saying that after what happened to Katia, I did some asking around and I have reason to believe Maria and Allan's plane crash wasn't accidental. I was told they weren't just monitoring South Africa's parks. They'd uncovered information on poaching trails and border activities with Uganda. A chain they had reason to believe made its way up to Tanzania and into Kenya." He paused. "They were in the way."

She couldn't speak. She couldn't breathe.

"I wanted to tell you in person. I'm sorry to tell you this way, but you have to understand why I need you to do as I say. You're out of your league here, Tessa. I wish you'd just written your fashion report and let me deal with this. I wish you'd trusted me."

He was right. This was exactly why she didn't take risks. This was why she played it safe and stuck with her stable, secure life. Brice had given her that life and now she'd ruined everything. And Katia was dead because of her.

"I need to secure things down here," he said. "Give me a day, then I'll come up and take you and Nick somewhere safe. I can send a bodyguard if you want."

"No, that's not necessary. Mac is here." There was a brief pause on the other end.

"Promise me you won't trust *anyone*. Not even Mac. What I've told you stays between us. We don't want to endanger Nick…or his uncle. Promise."

Nick had already lost his parents. Now he stood to lose more.

"I promise."

She disconnected the call and kneeled on the floor.

What have I done?

Her breaths came in rapid-fire. She gasped, then gasped again. The room spun. *Hold your breath.* She tried twice before she managed to hold it in. She counted to ten and let it out. One more gasp and she held her breath again. *Get in control.* Her breathing finally slowed down and she laid on her back on the thin woven throw rugs that covered the hard ground, waiting for her vision to clear and her head to stop spinning.

Her mind raced. She needed to handle this. She needed to make everything right. Family. Her parents. She needed to make sure they were okay.

Tessa sat up and took a deep breath before making the call. Every second she waited for them to answer tore at her like the talons of a vulture gorging on its prey. Static crackled, alternating with a distant buzz.

"Hello?" More static. "Hello?" The sound of her mom's voice brought a tidal wave of tears. Tessa hung her head in her free hand and swallowed hard to compose herself. She hadn't seen them since the funeral, though calls were a routine. The last thing she wanted to do was to worry them.

"Mom? How are you? How's Dad?"

"Tessa! Sweetheart, it's so good to hear from you. We're fine. The weather is phenomenal today. We've had great luck with sightings."

Tessa released a pent-up breath. She couldn't hear any undercurrents of fear or worry. They were okay. Thank God.

"That's wonderful. Are you coming ashore anytime soon?"

"Not for a few weeks. Why? Do you need something? Is anything wrong?"

Tessa closed her eyes as she spoke.

"No, no. Just checking your schedule." Her voice cracked and she cursed herself for being weak.

"Tessa, I'm your mother. Something's off with your voice."

"It's the static."

"Oh, my. You and Brice are pregnant, aren't you? Oh, honey! We've been dying for more grandchildren."

"No way!" If she had tears brewing, they were gone. She didn't even want to imagine how much worse things would be right now if she were pregnant or had other children to care for. She bit back a bitter remark about grandchildren. As if her parents would ever see them more than once in a blue moon. They'd be enthralled at first, then it would be like when she was a kid: work would come first. They'd go off and she and their grandkids would be left to wonder if they'd ever see them again. Why would parents risk their lives, knowing their kids were counting on them to be around? She swallowed. She was about to risk hers for the sake of Nick. "I'm not pregnant. I'm simply away from the internet, so I couldn't check the schedule you'd emailed me. I brought Nick up to see his uncle Mac."

She always insisted that her parents send her a copy of their boating plans and travel course. Sure, they left official memos for the people they worked with, but Tessa felt better having it herself.

"Oh, well, that's nice of you to do. Maybe it'll help him cope. In fact, if he ever wants to take a trip out with us, we'd love to have him. We could keep it to a week or so. We'd actually discussed it with Maria and Allan before—"

"Yeah. Um, now isn't a great time." Like she'd ever send Nick out to sea. "So Dad's okay, too?"

"He's suiting up for a dive. I need to go check his tank."

"I'll let you go. Just…be careful. Okay? Both of you."

"We always are. Love you."

"Love you, too. Bye."

Tessa set the phone down. They were fine. She kept repeating that fact in her head, but the pit of her stomach still twisted. Telling them the truth would have only endangered them more. She had no way of knowing if anyone was listening to the call, and she didn't trust her parents not to act on the information and draw attention to themselves. Maybe they did take reasonable precautions, but there were forces of nature too powerful for people out there at sea…and there were men who were simply too powerful. Like Brice said, it would be so easy for an *accident* to happen and for the evidence to wash away.

The sound of Nick's laughter and the Johnson twins squealing penetrated her tent walls. Kesi would be needing her help. She had to get the phone back to the cottage before anyone started asking questions. She wiped her face with cool water and a washcloth, then went outside.

"There you are. I wanted to see if you were interested in stringing bead necklaces with me and Mrs. Johnson. Our female guests usually love taking home a necklace souvenir." Kesi eyed the phone in Tessa's hand.

"Oh. I'm sorry. I wanted to call my parents to check on them. Their boat's satellite phone is more reliable than their radio." Tessa gave a small smile, hoping that Kesi wouldn't pick up on her worry. "I should have asked first."

"It's fine." Kesi shook her head and took the phone Tessa held out. "They're lucky to have a daughter like you checking on them. Use it anytime."

"Thanks." Tessa bit her lip to keep it from quivering.

"Did you want to string beads?"

"Sure. I'll be there in a few minutes."

She trekked back to her tent and pulled the door flaps down. She needed a plan. *A daughter like you.* Kesi didn't realize how deep her words cut. Maria had been the daughter her parents deserved. The one who'd inherited their gene for adventure. The one who'd followed in their footsteps when it came to loving nature and research and saving the environment. She'd been a fearless risk taker, just like them. And look where it got her. She and Allan had been described as generous, giving spirits whose aerial observations had made a difference in South Africa's wildlife management. A positive spin on living dangerously. And if that made them generous, then didn't that make Tessa the selfish one? The one who, as a teen, complained that her parents weren't around more? The one who didn't care if their aquatic research would save whales because she wanted—needed—them at home? She remembered the stormy nights when she stayed up watching weather reports and listening to radio transmissions, petrified that her parents would be shipwrecked or tossed overboard. She wasn't the daughter they were lucky to have. But she was the only one they had left. And now, for all that worrying growing up, she was the one who was putting them in danger.

And for the first time, she was seeing herself without all the places, people and things that had cluttered her life. They were all crutches. Ways to avoid or circumvent her fears. But a person could only pretend for so long. She was beginning to see that now. All she'd done with her life was pro-crastinate. She had to take risks in order to really live.

There was no reason to hide anymore.

CHAPTER TEN

"I TAKE IT you're not a morning person."

Mac shoulder-bumped a heavy-lidded Nick, who was literally dragging his feet on their way to the clearing where Mac's chopper sat. He'd had no luck finding Bakhari yesterday and eventually the search was called off for the night. Kamau, over at Busara, hadn't had any more success on the ground, but the search was resuming this morning.

"In my book, it's not morning until the entire sun has cleared the horizon. It's barely light out," Nick said, slapping on the AWS cap Mac had told him to keep since the one he'd given him months ago had been left behind.

"You should rewrite your book, then, or you'll miss out on the absolute best time of day. There's nothing like waking before the sun and watching it rise from up there while everyone else is asleep." Mac pointed toward Mount Kilimanjaro in the distance, then slapped Nick on the back. "Trust me. You'll wake up in no time. You're not too young for coffee, are you?"

"Aunt Tessa says I am. The stuff tastes like cow urine, anyway."

"I see. So you've tasted cow urine?"

"You know what I mean," Nick said.

"No, really. 'Cause if you haven't, it can be arranged. There are some people who believe it has medicinal benefits," Mac said.

"Gross. Who? The Masai?"

"No. They'll drink ox or cow's blood, though. Didn't I mention that was part of their coming of age ceremony? A mix of ox blood, beer and milk? You *are* too young for beer. But if you want to try the blood..."

"You're sick, Uncle Mac. I'd rather drink three-day-old burned coffee."

"Now that's sick." Mac shuddered dramatically and got a smile out of him.

They climbed into the helicopter and Mac explained his preflight checklist and what all the buttons were for. It was nice showing Nick the ropes. Taking his nephew under his wing felt good.

The horizon transformed into blended layers of carmine red and orchid that bled into a fading lapis blue. Mac changed his course toward the savanna just east of Busara to restart his search. Nick didn't speak. He simply adjusted his headset and took in the vast expanse of woodlands and grasslands beneath them. An awe-inspiring energy surged through Mac every time he took flight at dawn. He wanted Nick to feel it, too, and from the look on his face, he did. Mac adjusted his direction again, putting the sunrise behind them. The peak of Mount Kilimanjaro to the southwest glistened with the light of dawn.

"Wow." Nick craned his neck for a better view of the mountain and the land surrounding it. Even the dark buff of barren areas and dried grasses took on the golden hues of sunrise. This was real gold. No amount of money could come close to the value of the land and life that passed beneath them. Anyone who didn't appreciate that was a lost soul as far as Mac was concerned.

"Start keeping an eye out. Let me know if you see anything, even if it's just movement or you're not sure," Mac said.

Nick nodded and leaned closer to his window. The sprawling tops of acacia trees grew bigger as Mac descended enough for them to have a better view of wildlife. A flock of white cranes startled as they passed over a bend in the Mara River and a couple of crocodiles splashed into hiding.

No Bakhari.

"There's another helicopter over there, Uncle Mac." Nick pointed at a dark green and beige chopper off to their right.

"That's KWS. The Kenyan Wildlife Service," Mac said, not sure if Nick knew the abbreviation or not. He radioed out and was told a group of poachers had been arrested overnight, a few kilometers away. Sure enough, ahead of them, just beyond a line of umbrella trees, dark smoke billowed into the air. Mac's heart sank.

"Is that a brush fire?" Nick asked.

Mac curled his lips in. That was no brush fire. Bringing Nick with him had been a mistake. He took guests on tour all the time without incident, and when they did happen to see the grim aftermath of poaching, he used it as a lesson. An opportunity to spread the fact that if they purchased ivory products, they were supporting the atrocities they were witnessing. But Nick wasn't just anyone. He was still learning to cope with death. He was just coming out of his shell. Mac had thought that the extra pair of eyes would indeed help him find Bakhari and that the baby's return to Busara might make Nick feel empowered…the way finding the boy himself had made Tessa feel when he'd run off. Now, he wasn't so sure that had been a good call. Not with the scene unfolding ahead of them. Mac wasn't sure they'd be finding Bakhari alive.

"Hey, Uncle Mac," Nick repeated, thinking he hadn't heard him the first time. "What's burning over there?"

There was no turning back now. He had to see what was going on. He needed to find out if Bakhari was down there. If he was, Mac would have to break the news to Anna. Being honest with Nick was the only choice he had.

"Tusks. They're burning tusks. After they apprehend poachers and take inventory of the stash, they burn the ivory so that it can't feed into the black market. If so much as one person gets greedy enough to sneak the ivory to the buyer—even after the poachers are arrested—then that would be as good as rewarding their actions. They can't be allowed to get away with the killings on any level. The supply and demand cycle has to be broken. Hence, the burning. Destroy it so it can't reach the market. Make sure whoever is investing their money and time to promote poaching suffers the loss, too."

Brice's name came to mind. Ben hadn't answered Mac's email yet.

A stream of curses came through his headset, but he didn't cut Nick off. He couldn't blame him this time.

"Tell me that's not what it looks like," Nick said.

Mac took a deep breath. A pile of bloody elephant carcasses...bodies without faces... lay not far from the ivory bonfire. Fury burned in Mac. Every time he witnessed a sight like this, it fueled his anger and frustration to indescribable levels. He'd learned to keep his cool because he had to. There was power in keeping one's wits about them and thinking clearly. Criminals always made mistakes. Deploying well-thought-out plans and strategies with deliberation and cooperation was the only way to fight them and put them behind bars. Mac had learned that early on.

"It's what it looks like," he confirmed.

Nick's face turned red and his eyes appeared wet and distraught.

"How could anyone do that? How can people like that exist? I don't get it. Why do evil people have to exist? Why do bad things have to happen?"

Mac reached over and squeezed his shoulder. Tessa was going to kill him when she heard about this. Mac would deserve it, too. This was a disaster, not just down there, but for Nick. More trauma for a kid who'd had enough.

"I don't know. I don't know. We just have to stick together and do what we can."

"Do you think Bakhari…? You said he was still little. They wouldn't go after a young one, would they?"

Not necessarily on purpose, but poachers didn't much care about side casualties or how little tusks were. Older elephants yielded more ivory, but that didn't mean poachers wouldn't kill for a few inches. Some would poison entire watering holes, then harvest the ivory from the dead. Indiscriminate murder. The wildlife equivalent of terrorists opening fire in a crowded mall. Bakhari had been injured once, when his mother was killed. It could happen again—or worse.

"I don't think he's there, Nick. From what I can tell based on size, the ones down there were older than Bakhari." Mac really wished he could be more certain that the young elephant wasn't buried under the heap. How would he be able to tell Anna? Or, heaven help him, Pippa. That girl loved Bakhari like other children loved their puppy or kitten. He wanted so badly for Bakhari to come walking out of the brush this very moment.

Parents dying. Their children being out there alone and in danger. Mac had a feeling that Nick was identifying with the elephants on a much deeper level. He needed to give the kid hope, but false optimism would only hurt him more.

Mac circled as he radioed the crew in the KWS helicopter that had just landed. He really didn't want to take Nick down there. The sulfurous smell of burning bone would add another traumatic memory to the mix, but Mac wanted to know if any of the crew had come across a tagged elephant of Bakhari's description. He circled one more time before the answer came through.

No. They hadn't. He exchanged looks with Nick, whose eyes widened. He sat straighter and frowned with determination.

"We need to find him, Uncle Mac. There's still a chance he's okay."

Mac nodded in agreement and flew just west of the poaching aftermath and along the river valley, leaving the bloody scene behind them.

"Keep looking."

He brought the helicopter to the far side of a tree and brush covered hill that he knew Kamau hadn't made it to, based on their communications.

"There! Over there, Uncle Mac. I saw an elephant. I don't know if it's him, but I definitely saw one by that rock. But...there's a lion right there." He pointed and, sure enough, there was a lioness stalking through the grass in the elephant's direction.

Mac circled back. That was him, all right. The sight of Bakhari's ears flapping as he stood between a granite outcropping and an acacia tree made his nose sting and the pressure between his ears released. Nick was practically hyperventilating with excitement. Mac made a pass between Bakhari and the lioness. She noticed, but it wasn't enough. She was a determined one. Probably had cubs to feed. He came in closer and this time she finally scared off. Mac grabbed his radio.

"This is Raptor King to Mama Tembo. We have your baby. I repeat. We—I mean, Nick—found him and he's okay. Over."

Mac caught a fleeting smile. Nick pulled his shoulders back with pride.

You're going to be all right, kid.

Mac landed his chopper far away enough not to spook Bakhari, while still keeping him in view until Kamau and his team arrived for transport. Nick wiped his nose against his sleeve and took off his headset.

"Just for future reference, we shouldn't interfere with the call of the wild. Every being out there has a rightful place in the food chain and babies to feed. Their mothers are meant to protect them," Mac said.

"Then why did you interfere with that lion?" Nick asked.

"Because I couldn't fly away. Bakhari's not really part of the wild yet. He was too young when he was first rescued and he hasn't been transitioned to a reserve where he can learn to cope on his own. Plus, the bigger they get, the less likely they are to have to deal with predators like lions. Their only predator becomes man. The way I see it, I was asked by his mother to find and protect him."

Anna. That's why he'd given her the nickname Mama Tembo a long time ago.

"I thought his mother was killed by poachers."

"She was. Dr. Bekker is his adoptive mother as far as I'm concerned, so see, I've been sent by his mother to protect him."

"I think you're rationalizing, Uncle Mac."

"Maybe."

Nick started to open his door, but stopped and met his uncle's eyes.

"You think you could teach me to fly one of these days?"

"Sure. Carry on the Walker tradition, huh?"

"Yeah."

"Your parents would be proud of you," Mac said. "I know I am."

MAC HADN'T STOPPED thinking about the future of Air Walker Safaris and his role as Nick's guardian. The elephant massacre they'd witnessed today and the fact that no one else had been able to find Bakhari but them only reaffirmed that there was no way he could give up his company. His work was too important. Too critical. If all he saved was one life, it still made a difference.

But he'd also gotten to know Nick, and though he was his nephew, he was beginning to feel like a son. He couldn't put words to how profoundly getting to share some of his life here with both Nick and Tessa had affected him. For all his love of independence, for some reason, seeing them embrace so much of what had come to define him meant more than any disapproval he'd ever gotten from his father. Tessa had always been the one person he'd wished would like him for who he was. The one person he wanted to share so much with. Yet that had never been possible because of her constant disapproval of him. Only lately, things seemed different between them. She was different—more trusting…more relaxed around him despite the situation with Brice. And the way she'd been looking at him when she thought he wasn't aware made him wish and want more.

The five of them sat around the dwindling flames of the small bonfire. The Johnsons had long retired to their tent. Nick was still telling jokes, challenging everyone to tell funnier ones, but Tessa was being awfully quiet. She sat there staring into the fire, smiling every so often so that Nick would know she wasn't ignoring him. Mugi appeared totally entertained by Nick's quirky sense of humor. Kesi went inside and came back out with mugs of herbal tea.

"You've all had long days. I put chamomile plus a few other relaxing herbs in this. It should help you all sleep. It may even help a certain jokester wind down," she said, chuckling at Nick. "Tessa, try it. It'll ease your tension headache."

"You always were a worrier," Mac said. "No worry, no headaches."

"I'm not the one who took Nick to a poaching site."

"Mac, here's yours." Kesi handed him a

mug. "Drink this and stop pretending you're so invincible."

Mac sniffed the mug and made a face.

"You know coffee is more my taste."

"Drink it," she said, giving him the look only maternal figures and teachers could pull off.

"Nick," Mugi said. "About poaching. Remember when you were giving the Johnson twins a lecture on it over dinner? You might want to tone down the graphic nature of your lessons to those younger than you. If we get nightmare complaints from the parents, I'm letting you handle it."

"They won't. They told me their parents let them watch all the *Jurassic Park* movies. Even the ones that came out before they were born," Nick said. "Plus, they said they told their babysitter that their parents were okay with them watching *Arachnaphobia* and she believed them. Then they kept hiding rubber spiders around the kitchen to freak her out. They've played practical jokes on their parents, too. Trust me, they're not that innocent or easily scared."

"Not innocent, huh? After the chicken I found nesting on my pillow this evening, when I was certain I'd closed up the tent, I'm not surprised you kids have been sharing practical jokes, but game on. I'll have a few of my own I wouldn't mind putting in action," Mac said.

"So long as no snakes are involved," Tessa said, pointing her finger at Mac.

"Don't look at me. Mugi and Kesi are the owners here. You should train your assistants better. No practical jokes on guests," Mac said, raising his mug to the older couple and motioning toward Nick.

"Ah, but first, you're no guest, and secondly, you have more experience with training," Mugi said. "You have a real office and an assistant. I have a wife, and a man does not even *attempt* to train a wife—or even let on that the thought crossed his mind—unless he has a death wish."

Kesi pursed her lips at him and he belted out a laugh, then grabbed her hand and kissed it. The mention of Sue reminded Mac of one more person whose life would be affected if Air Walker Safaris went under or he sold out. The humor of the evening left him.

Mac hated to ruin the fun, but everyone

was here, in one spot. If Tess thought he was a risk taker before, she had no idea. This was Mac's chance to lay it all out on the table... time for Mac to take the shirt off his back. He waited for a break in the entertainment.

"Hey, Nick. Everyone. I'd like to discuss something, and Nick, please don't run off where the lions roam or raise your voice so that our guests overhear from their tent."

Nick frowned, but Mac felt compelled to give the warning. He'd seen moods switch at the drop of a pin. Nick had that mastered. He glanced around the circle and noted he had his friends' attention.

"Air Walker Safaris is about to go bankrupt."

He'd thought he was prepared for the reactions, but he was sucker-punched by the looks on their faces. Even Tessa's eyes widened. He felt rotten. Like a failure. Losing Air Walker Safaris would mean letting everyone down: family, friends, the Serengeti wildlife he'd devoted his life to saving. But family was also important. Mugi and Kesi were the dearest of friends, but Nick and Tessa—even if she was only related by marriage—were the only true family he had left.

If he went bankrupt, there was no way the shockwaves wouldn't affect them, whether financially or time-wise, as Mac figured out how to pick up the pieces.

No matter what Tessa decided to do with her future, until Nick became legally independent, she and Mac were going to share much in their lives. They were and always would be friends and Nick's guardians. They were effectively acting as parents, and he wasn't about to let her take Nick on as a single mother. Yes, she'd been doing that, but he'd been under the impression that she had Brice around to help. Raising Nick, if they stuck to their plan of saving his inheritance for his college education, would mean Mac needed cash flow. Selling Air Walker Safaris would provide those funds. Being stubborn about hanging onto his company could have a detrimental effect on all of them.

He needed to be smart about this.

After all these years, he still wanted more—wished for more—from Tessa, even if all it could be was friendship. But he and Tessa had never shared the same outlook. She'd always be an important part of his life, but even if her marriage ended, he couldn't expect her to walk away from a life of wealth to one of bankruptcy or debt. No matter what, he was facing loss: having Tessa walk away and losing AWS and all he'd put into it. He'd lose his freedom and control. Nothing would be the same after this. Maybe his father and Allan...and Maria and Tessa...had been right to criticize his blind leap all those years ago because now he was falling.

Mac watched as Nick wrapped his arms around his waist and sat there staring into the embers that no one was bothering to keep alive. Man, the last thing he wanted was for his nephew to think his presence had caused any of this. Yes, Nick was his responsibility, but he'd never let on that the boy had influenced any decision Mac made about his business. He never wanted him to feel the burden of any sacrifice Mac might have to make. That was way more than the kid needed or deserved.

"It's not anyone's fault. Nick? Got that? Not yours. Not anyone's. I haven't been doing as well as I'd like for a while now, and someone bigger and better is sticking their claws in at Hodari Lodge. I've been getting offers to sell. Great offers. They'd involve me as a pilot, though I'd be working for someone else and would have to give up certain freedoms, like what I do with my flight time."

"You can't sell Air Walker. It's your life," Tessa said. He wasn't sure he'd heard her right, considering she'd been against him moving to Kenya in the first place. The empathy in her eyes told him she understood just how much of an emotional loss AWS would be. He'd lose a part of his identity and soul with it. He'd be following in her footsteps, career-wise. She'd found herself writing and reporting what she was told to write, not what she wanted to write about. She had someone else controlling her passion. He'd have someone else controlling his. The idea sickened him, but his dad's words kept haunting him. He needed to be responsible.

"Mac, this is sudden. Let's talk about it. Maybe there's an alternative," Mugi said.

"There is only one alternative I can think of, but I'm not sure it'll pan out." Mac hated his plan B because it meant humbling himself and admitting that even the stubborn, tough guy needed help once in a while. But it was the only way he could do what was right on all fronts.

"If there's an alternative that doesn't involve you selling out, take it," Kesi said. "I don't mean that selfishly. We appreciate all you do to help us here at Jamba, and we'll have to come up with options, as well. I mean it because it's so important to you."

"You and Mugi are an important part of my life and I appreciate that, too," Mac said. "That's what got me thinking. Why work with people I don't know or trust if I can work with someone I do?"

Mugi propped his elbows on his knees and leaned forward. Mac could tell his lawyer's mind was churning.

"Mugi, if I decide to take any of the offers seriously, I would appreciate it if you looked over the paperwork for me."

"Consider it done, but I'm waiting for your other option."

"Mugi would be insulted if you didn't ask him for legal advice. He only gives it free to special people," Kesi said.

"She's right about that. I like to be used by friends." Mugi chuckled. "Keeps all those years as a lawyer from going to waste. But I still don't like the idea of you selling your bird."

"There's a lot of money in that girl, Mugi."

"Money isn't everything."

"No, but it is necessary sometimes, and for some of us, it's harder to earn." Mac chanced a glimpse of Tessa's reaction. She was masking it if she had one. "You know how the saying goes—'If money grew in trees, most people would be married to monkeys.'"

"Some people are," Nick muttered, glancing fleetingly at his aunt. A kid after his own heart. Rude, maybe, but Mac had to agree she was married to one. However, Nick needed to learn when and how not to cross the line. He knew the boy didn't intend disrespect, but still.

"I get it, but you need to apologize to your aunt."

"Sorry."

"It's fine, but they're right. There's always a way," Tessa said.

"My therapist told me I should try not to say *always* and *never* because they're almost *always never* true," Nick said. He caught everyone by surprise with his words of wisdom. Even Tessa froze with her mug halfway to her mouth. Nick was full of surprises.

"You know, Mac, he's right. Sometimes it's difficult to see the watering hole when you're stuck in the middle of a thicket of thorn bushes," Mugi said.

Mac tasted a sip of his tea and tried not to make a face. It actually wasn't so bad after the first sip.

"Are you and Nick having a wise-sayings competition here?" Mac asked. Nick started cracking up.

"There's always a way in, a way out and a way to fix things," Mugi said.

"Is that so? Life is one big math problem? There's always a solution?"

This time Kesi laughed.

"*If* you don't have a math anxiety attack partway through the problem. The way *he* used to," she said with a smile.

"Okay, Mugi. You want to hear my option? It's to sell Air Walker Safaris to you and Kesi." There was silence. Just as he anticipated. He set his mug down on the ground. "You could consider incorporating the air service into what you're doing here at Camp Jamba."

Mugi took a deep breath and turned to Kesi. She sat down next to him.

"No pressure," Mac quickly added.

"Kesi?" Mugi looked to his wife. She nodded once and took her husband's hand in unity.

"Seems you're a better businessman than you give yourself credit for," Mugi said. "I like the idea of integrating a small flight service as part of Camp Jamba, but the answer is no."

Mac nodded. That was it. He understood and respected the decision. They were a lot older than he was. They'd come out here to semi-retire, not throw their money away.

"There's no way I'd buy you out and have you as an employee. You'd be hell to deal with. But we will consider a partnership."

Mac straightened his back. They were willing to partner? His mind buzzed as if he'd had a pot of coffee, not a few sips of herbal tea.

"I want to be clear. I realize you're a lawyer and not the financial guru and businessman I am," Mac teased. They all knew he was joking. "But I told you I'm losing money as it is and competition is moving into the area. I've been losing money while working from the Hodari Lodge with potential customers right at my feet, and that's been going on since before bigger tour companies started bidding for a spot there. So turning a profit could be a rough road from out here."

"Ah, but it's all about marketing, my friend. Having the right hook. We've been content keeping things small here, but Kesi and I were talking recently about marketing this place as a green camp. We could promote the educational experience and make sure every person, adult and child, who came through here would leave not just with an outdoor experience, but with an understanding and appreciation of the landscape and how it's at risk—from poaching to climate change. Global awareness, one person at a time."

Mugi had a point. It wasn't just the money, which was probably why Mac never made enough. The strength in the idea was in coming together to make a difference. It was in acting like a family and having each other's backs.

"Listen to me, Mac. This is how I see it. From here, you could take what's important about Air Walker and give it more impact. Your customers wouldn't be staying at a lodge owned by someone else. They'd be staying here, where we're in control. And by 'we,' I mean all of us," Mugi said.

"This would be a family business. We could change the name to Camp Jamba Walker," Kesi added.

Mac swallowed hard. He didn't miss what Kesi meant. He'd been around long enough to know that "Jamba" meant "hero." Mac was no hero. He just did what he did because it felt right and because he wanted people—families with children and any individuals with a heart for nature—to appreciate what the Serengeti was truly about. He wanted them to experience its essence. He picked up a pebble and rubbed it between his fingers. *Family business.* Where would Tessa be? Back with Brice if he turned out to be innocent? Would Nick stay? That was a whole other set of logistics.

"I know what you're thinking," Mugi said. "But she's right. The name fits. I saw that you were different from the day we first met. You love and value what you do here the way the Masai value their cattle. Cattle mean more than money to them. They believe it's their duty to watch over them. Their heart is in it. This is a chance for you to keep watch, too."

"And if it doesn't work? Then I've ruined your life here as well as your business."

"Mac, it's not like Kesi and I didn't accrue a good chunk of savings before we walked away from our careers, but even without touching those accounts, this will work. And you'll have cash flow from not paying Hodari Lodge for office space and helicopter parking. We just have to stick together and make it happen," Mugi said.

Mac was overwhelmed. This would mean staying here permanently. Camp Jamba would become home. Or maybe it always had been, in the important sense of the word.

Camp Jamba Walker.

"What do you mean a family business?" Nick interrupted.

Mac turned to Nick and ran the words through his head before he spoke. He glanced at Tessa. A faint frown lined her forehead and she didn't take her eyes off him. She'd brought Nick here. Mac was ready to give it a shot.

"Nick, how would you like to stay here with me? As in move here. Live here."

Nick's eyes widened and he jumped up.

"What? I don't get to go back home? I thought you guys changed your minds about that."

"Remember what I said about the guests overhearing," he reminded. "Now, your aunt Tessa has some things to deal with and I am trying to treat you like a mature kid who has a right to an opinion. Let's just hash this out. Okay?"

Nick's chest rose up and down rapidly and he picked up a stone and threw it into the bushes to his right.

"It would be great to have you here, Nick," Kesi said.

"You like being here, don't you?" Mugi put in.

"It's fine." Nick stared off into the darkness.

Mac knew he'd been enjoying himself a lot more than just "fine," and would continue to if he lived here.

"It wouldn't be forever, unless of course

you wanted it to be," Mac continued. "I asked Jack how they handled schooling. They've homeschooled, but now that Pippa and her friend Haki are getting older, they do some of what's called 'virtual' schooling. There's a lot of computer time involved," he added, hoping that would sound appealing. Nick shrugged. At least he was listening. Maybe even interested.

"That actually sounds like a brilliant idea," Kesi said. "Your sleep time would be more flexible, too. We'd be willing to pitch in. Between Mugi, Mac and I, you'd have solid help in any subject." Bringing up sleep time showed that Kesi definitely understood teens.

"And that would give me the chance to also teach you those other things we talked about." Mugi grinned. Everyone was agreeing and helping to convince him. Except Tessa. She just listened, lips parted as she nervously scratched the back of her hand.

"I know leaving your friends back home won't be easy," Mac said.

"I don't want to leave them. There's no one to hang out here my age," Nick blurted, then lowered his chin so his hair fell across his face. As if it wasn't dark enough outside.

"You have me there. But we could visit everyone at Busara and you could get involved with teen student initiatives in the area. A lot of older kids work together online and meet up at various lodges to organize public awareness campaigns and fund-raise to save certain species. There's even a group of teens who meet up at Hodari. If you're interested. Or perhaps you could run a sort of 'kid camp' here. You seem to have a knack for teaching this survivalist stuff. I don't have all the answers, but we could do this as a trial."

Nick shrugged again and sat a little straighter. "Sure. Maybe."

"Ben, who you met at Busara, lives with his wife and children in Nairobi. He could help us pick a regular high school out there and I'll figure out how to get you back and forth daily or ask if you can stay with them during the week and return here on weekends. We can work things out however you prefer," Mac said.

"Nick." Tessa spoke up for the first time. "I'm not abandoning you. I'd come and visit.

It's just, like Mac said, I have to take care of some things in my life right now. I think you'd be happier hanging out with Mac."

There he had it. She still wanted to drop Nick off and leave like she'd originally planned.

"Yeah, I guess being here, at least for a while, would be cool," Nick said, jerking his hair out of his face and sitting straight. "Aunt Tessa?"

"Yes?"

"I wish you could stay, too."

TESSA BARELY SLEPT that night.

It had been hard keeping up appearances with the Lagats and the Johnsons, acting like everything was normal, especially after Mac and Nick returned from their flight to spot Bakhari. She still couldn't believe he'd hidden Brice's message from her. Oh, and then there was Nick. Nick, who'd given her such a hard time. The same kid who she was so sure couldn't stand her had taken her by surprise and almost made her cry. She tossed and turned in her tent, tried to put it all out of her head. Things were settled. That was good. Nick was safe here.

Her life was a mess. He didn't need any part of it.

Despite her troubled sleep, Tessa woke full of determination. She stuffed everything she'd brought into her backpack and looked around to be sure she hadn't forgotten anything. Mac and Nick had gone up again in the chopper to help one of the park's newer research camps spot a herd of rhinos they were tracking. Mac had also promised to go to Busara and take Anna up for some overhead observations of the elephant herds. Nick was excited about going with him again. The kid seemed to have found motivation and purpose.

This was it. She hated taking advantage of the fact that they were gone, but she had to do this. Last night, the Johnsons had asked if Mugi could drive them back to Hodari Lodge so they'd get more out of their one-night stay. Taking the jeep back would give them a chance to see the Serengeti from ground level. It would take longer to get there, but Tessa couldn't pass up the chance at a ride back.

And Brice would be expecting to find her there.

She jogged to the cottage in time to find the Johnsons wrapping up their breakfast and getting their children ready for the jeep ride. She didn't care if it was a tight fit. She'd offer to have one of the twins sit in her lap if she had to. Shoot, she'd hang onto the back like ostrich bait.

"Hey, everyone. Good morning," she said.

"Good morning," Kesi greeted her, along with the others. "Hungry?"

"No, not really, thanks. I'll take a banana." She grabbed one off the table still set up outside. "So, would it be okay if I squeezed into the jeep with you?" she asked the Johnsons.

Mr. Johnson shrugged and glanced at his wife. She didn't seem bothered.

"It's fine with us. If the twins don't drive you mad," he warned.

"I don't mind them at all. They're great."

"Can I talk to you inside a minute, Tessa?" Mugi asked.

"Of course."

"We'll be right back," Kesi told the Johnsons.

Tessa followed them inside. What should

she tell them? She hated lying. They'd been so good to her.

"I wonder how Mac and Nick are doing," she said, hoping to both deflect and make sure they weren't already on their way back from their aerial search. "They left pretty early."

"You can radio and ask."

"That's okay. I'd just be bothering them and they'll probably say they're fine even if they're staring down a rhino's nostrils." Tessa almost added, "Like father, like son." "Like uncle, like nephew" didn't have the same ring, even if it fit. Team NickMac. She was glad. Worried, yes, she always would be, but she knew Nick would be safest with Mac. It was why she was confident with her plan to leave. She tried to keep her tone light. "You know how they are."

"Yes, but where do you think you're going this morning?" Mugi asked. "You're supposed to stay here and be safe until we hear more. Mac didn't say anything to us about you leaving. Does he know?"

Funny how fast a lie could brew up when someone was desperate. She had to be careful, though. Mugi *could* easily call Mac.

"Actually, I spoke to Ben Corallis. He said he needs to meet with me in person to discuss the contents of the drives and the next step. He asked me to leave Mac out of it because he'd made it clear, back at Busara, that he wouldn't let me get involved in helping. You *know* how he is. And given he's piloting that tin can with Nick in it, I'd rather he not be distracted. I'll be fine. I'm simply going to go up for a meeting. Ben asked me to keep it quiet, but I owe you two an explanation and there you have it."

"I personally agree with Mac," Kesi said. "Don't do anything dangerous. Why can't this Ben come down here?"

Think. Think.

"He said there are some other officials who need to talk to me, as well. And I think I mentioned that you had guests here at the time. If you ever meet him, you'll understand that he calls the shots. You know how important getting to the bottom of this is. In fact, we should get going soon."

"I'll wait at Hodari Lodge and bring you back when you're done, then," Mugi said.

"Oh. He said it could take a while but that he'd already made arrangements for me."

Mugi gave Kesi a skeptical look.

"Okay. Let's head out," he finally said.

Tessa gave Kesi a hug.

"Thank you for everything."

"Why does that sound like goodbye?" Kesi asked.

"It was just a thank-you, Kesi. You deserve them daily."

And yes, there was a goodbye in it because depending on how things went at Hodari, there was a good chance she wouldn't be coming back.

MAC CHECKED THE forecast on his radio and adjusted his course and speed to stay ahead of the storm that was approaching. After he and Nick had helped Anna with her data collection, they ended up staying a few hours at Busara. It was Nick who'd asked if they could. Part of that may have been because of Pippa and Haki—hanging around younger kids and acting like a role model seemed to be a real confidence-booster for him—and part of it, Mac guessed, was because he seemed genuinely interested in the elephant orphans. Like he identified with them and wanted to be sure they were well and adjusting to their new family and situation. It was a good thing, though it did tear Mac up a little inside.

It wasn't until were well on their way back to Jamba that dark clouds had eclipsed the sun. The rainy season didn't start here until at least the end of October and into November, but if a random storm came through late summer, it was a gift. This one apparently wanted to get a head start on the wet season. Mac routinely checked forecasts, but weather, as much of a blessing as it could be, also had an unpredictably cruel side. The last thing Nick needed was to be reminded of his parents' plane crash. He'd been doing surprisingly well with the helicopter flights, but he'd never hit air turbulence in one. If Tessa found out their coordinates with respect to the storm right now, she'd kill him.

His detour took them over shrubs and trees that made landing prohibitive. He'd dealt with rough weather patterns before. He could do this. But flying alone was one thing. Carrying precious cargo really did a number on a man's mind.

The chopper took a sudden drop, making Mac's insides feel like a ten-car pile-up against his throat. Nick yelped as he grabbed for the closest surface. *He's all right. Focus on flying.* He regained control but had all his senses on alert in case they hit more turbulence. *Keep her steady.*

"You okay, bud?"

"Yeah," Nick said. More like squeaked.

"Hang on. There she is."

Camp Jamba had never looked more beautiful. He landed just as the sky broke loose.

"You were brave up there. You did good," he said. "Let's get out of here."

He and Nick ran through the mud and wind to the cottage and made it through the door as lightning snapped overhead.

"We were so worried!" Kesi rushed over with a towel as Mac and Nick hung their caps on the hooks by the door. She handed it to Nick, who began drying off.

"I've never been up during a storm. My parents said it was too dangerous. That was awesome," Nick said.

Mugi tossed another towel to Mac. He didn't look good.

"Everything okay? The Johnsons?" Mac asked. Had someone had an accident? His instincts went on full alert. Had something bad happened while he wasn't available to fly anyone in for emergency care?

"The Johnsons are fine," Mugi said. "I drove them back to Hodari and they got their fill of giraffes along the way. They said to pass their thanks on to you."

"But something is wrong," Mac insisted. He looked between Kesi and Mugi. Then it hit him. Tessa wasn't there. He didn't hear any puttering around the kitchen or any other sign of her. "Tessa. Is she sick? Is she in her tent?"

Mac had seen awful malaria cases, cholera and a slew of stomach infections. He'd worried that she had gotten sick that night when they found Nick. Rain began pattering against the ground outside and lightning flashed in their window. He started for the door.

"She's not here," Kesi said.

He stopped and turned.

"What do you mean she's not here?"

"She's gone. I drove her back to the lodge with the Johnsons."

"She just left without saying goodbye to me?" Nick asked.

Kesi wrapped her arm around Nick.

"Honey, she said to tell you she'd be seeing you again soon and to enjoy your time with your uncle."

Blood rushed to Mac's head. She left? Why? What happened to staying safe?

"Why in the world would you take her there? I made it clear she was to stay here. We discussed what Ben said."

Mugi threw his hands up in the air and stalked into their living room.

What was going on? Had she decided to give Brice the benefit of the doubt? Was her devotion to her vows more important than her trust and faith in Mac and their friendship, to the unconventional yet undeniable *family* they were forming with Nick? More important than stopping Brice's criminal activity? Just as quickly as his face heated, it went cold. What if she did something stupid? Like trying to find out for herself if Brice was innocent or guilty.

"What did she say she was doing exactly?"

Kesi shook her head at Mugi.

"Tell him."

"Speak up, Mugi. Both of you."

"She said she spoke to Ben and he wanted to meet with her. Without you."

"Without me? Why? I'm the one who brought him into all this." Mac slammed his hand on a thin side table, then gripped his hair. "Was Ben there when you dropped her off?"

"I don't know what Ben looks like, but yes, there was a man waiting at the door and she told me that was him, said goodbye and got out of the jeep. I was helping unload the Johnsons' bags and she basically disappeared."

"She said, when she was here, that Ben would arrange for her transportation back to Camp Jamba and that Mugi shouldn't wait," Kesi added in her husband's defense. "We know you trust Ben."

Nick stood staring at them all. He didn't say a word. Mac went for their satellite phone, though his chances of getting through to Ben in a storm were slim. He tried, anyway. Nothing. He threw it on the couch.

"I need to talk to her. I need to go," Mac said, reaching for the door. Mugi had it blocked in two strides.

"You're not going anywhere in this

weather. You know better than that," he said, glancing pointedly at Nick.

Mac rubbed his eyes. Mugi was right. Mac had to put Nick first. Getting himself killed wouldn't be a responsible move. It wouldn't help anyone. Mugi glanced at Kesi over his shoulder, then back at Mac.

"If you want to see her, you'll have to wait for the storm to pass."

Mac understood that. What worried him was that, by then, it might be too late.

TESSA FINISHED DRYING her hair, brushed one side back and secured it with her new comb, which was fashioned with engraved, fake ivory and accented with pink, unpolished rubies. She studied her face in the framed mirror that hung in her room at the safari lodge, added a dab of lip gloss and straightened her back. She hadn't felt this fresh in days. The bath had given her time to think. The water had solidified her resolve. The makeup and hair comb...well, what beauty touches didn't boost a woman's confidence? If only they were enough to calm her nerves.

You can do this. Get your life back. Just tell him you're in this together. Convince him he can trust you from here on out. Tell him that you love him.

She held her breath, counted to ten, then let it go. One more check had her unbuttoning the top of her blouse and smoothing the back of her hair. The lingering humidity from the odd rain shower they'd gotten earlier kept making it frizz. She was tempted to throw it into a ponytail, but that would ruin the look. She was nervous. Picking on things. Brice wouldn't care about her hair.

She'd make him not care.

She was beginning to empathize with Mac's desperate need to leave the nest. Like a fledgling, he had to fly off and figure out who he was as an individual. He'd refused to be defined by his father or brother or by the fact that his mother had left him as a child. Tessa had been letting everything negative in her past define *her*. Mac had been so much braver than she was, and instead of trying to understand his choices at the time, she'd taken them personally. She'd been young and afraid.

But she wasn't a kid anymore. As insecure about the entire situation as she felt, she was strong. She had to keep reminding herself of that. She'd made the decision to leave South Africa and she'd brought Nick this far. She wouldn't let him make the same mistakes she had. She didn't want him to let the loss of his parents define him. He needed Mac as a role model. So no matter what happened today, she'd deal with the consequences. Even if it meant Mac never speaking to her or trusting her again.

She scanned the room to make sure everything was put away. Brice liked things clean and tidy. She smoothed the woven throw at the end of the bed and looked around again. She hated the creepy feeling of being watched. It made her wonder if hidden cameras had caught her stealing those flash drives at home. She shook the thought. Things were under control. None of that mattered anymore. She'd made a decision, risky as it was, and she was sticking with it. She sat on the edge of the bed to slip on the heeled sandals she'd purchased, along with the sundress, at one of the lodge's gift shops at the last minute, then smoothed the bedspread where it had wrinkled under her.

He'd show up any minute now. He said

four o'clock. It was 3:59. There was no turning back. *What's meant to be will be.*

A deep, firm knock sounded against the solid wood of the door. She pressed her hand to her chest and took one last fortifying breath,then went to open it.

Brice stood there, dashing as ever in a suit and tie. He took a step in and placed his hands on her bare shoulders, then moved them up to her cheeks.

"Thank goodness you're all right," he said.

"Brice. I'm so sorry about everything. About thinking the worst. I'm so glad you're okay and that you're here now. I missed you."

He ran his hands down her back, then drew her into a tight hug.

"I missed you, too, darling."

CHAPTER ELEVEN

MAC COULDN'T HAVE landed at Hodari fast enough. He'd left several messages for Ben before leaving Jamba, but hadn't been able to wait any longer to hear back.

He knew with every cell in his body that Tessa had lied about talking to Ben. He'd suspected that maybe Brice had somehow gotten to her, and when the storm passed he'd gone straight to his tent and found Brice's note missing. That said it all.

He ran from his landing site around the back way, through the courtyard where Nick had been cornered by monkeys, and made a beeline for his office. He opened the front door and went in…then froze. The door to his quarters was slightly ajar, which made no sense since he'd just unlocked the front and he distinctly recalled locking both when he left. Sue was still at Busara. Anna and Jack had promised to keep her there until Mac could be sure things were safe at Hodari. He shifted to the side, pushed the knob and found himself staring up the barrel of a gun.

"What the hell is—"

Ben held up a hand to silence him and pulled Mac into his quarters then shut the door. Two KWS men decked out with semi-automatics stood against the wall and another guy dressed in camo sat in front of Ben at a laptop connected to an array of surveillance equipment. Mac could only see his profile, but he looked oddly familiar. What *did* register was Tessa on screen. Tessa in her hotel room with Brice.

Ben held a finger to his earpiece, then cursed.

"Word just in from a contact in SA. No police record of any break-in at the Henning residence," Ben said.

"Break-in? What's going on here? I want Tessa out of there—*now*," Mac said, pointing at the video feed on the laptop screen. Brice was wrapping his arms around her and stroking her hair. Mac's gut burned as he started for the door, but the armed men blocked him.

"Mac, stay out of this. Interfere and you could put her in more danger. We have this."

"You don't get to give me orders, Ben. I made it clear using her as bait was out of the question."

Ben stood up and came face-to-face with him.

"She baited herself. She called Brice. If it weren't for him—" he pointed at the familiar guy "—we wouldn't have had the chance to intercept her when she got here and set this all up."

The familiar guy gave Mac a quick salute, then turned back to his work. *Mr. Johnson?* As in, the guest at Camp Jamba? Mac looked at Ben, who went back to his earpiece and the monitor without a word. Mac scrubbed a hand across his mouth. Adrenaline burned through him and anger singed his skin. She'd baited herself? Why? What exactly had Brice told her to lure her in?

"What break-in?" he repeated. "Why would you let her do this before getting your intel?" Mac hissed.

"We had no time because she'd already agreed to meet him."

"So abort. Go in now," Mac told the KWS

soldiers. He'd worked with plenty of KWS teams, but these two he didn't recognize. Neither one of them moved.

"I give that order," Ben warned. "These men are part of a team I helped train. We've worked together before. We know what we're doing."

Mac stood back. As angry, frustrated and afraid for Tessa as he was, he knew Ben was right. Any interference now could blow their plans and endanger her further. He glanced at Mr. Johnson and the others. How Ben had pulled all this off, not to mention how they all fit in Mac's quarters, defied the laws of physics, but what really threw him off balance was watching his Tessa kissing Brice on the laptop screen…and hearing her tell him how much she loved him.

TESSA FROZE AS Brice ran his hands all over her back while he kissed her, but she quickly regained control. Ben had almost clipped a microphone to her bra, but had decided against it at the last moment. Was Brice checking for one? He gently pushed her further into the room and shut the door behind him. Tessa deliberately pulled him a few steps closer to the end of the bed.

"Where's Nick?" Brice asked, kissing the side of her neck.

She stroked his chest through his Armani shirt. Brice didn't do casual.

"I left him with his uncle."

Brice stopped kissing her.

"I told you not to take your eyes off him. He needs to be with us. I need to take you both somewhere safe. Out of Africa. At least for now."

He wanted them to leave Africa? Move to another continent? Tessa swallowed as her fingers flirted with his collar.

"Brice, I think it's time he lived with Mac. I know he'll be safe with him. Whoever is after me...after us...won't bother with them. If we do get in trouble, it's better that Nick's not with us. Besides, I want this to be a fresh start for you and me. There's only so much attitude I can take and it's not fair to you, Brice. It's not fair to our marriage. I know the past six months have been hard. I'm sorry it took me so long to get over my sister's death and to realize Nick needs to be with his uncle."

Brice nodded.

"Maybe he'll be safe enough here. Perhaps not being near you is a better option. And I like the idea of it being just the two of us again, but I can't come with you. I have to head back to Cape Town to sort things out and make sure nothing else happens." He tucked her hair behind her ear and rubbed the back of her neck. Her skin prickled. He was too close to her comb. If he noticed the microphone embedded among the gemstones, disguised as one, it would all be over too soon. She stopped herself from glancing toward the micro camera hidden in the carved headboard. She drew his hand away from her hair and pressed her lips against his manicured fingertips. Mac and the touch of his strong, calloused hands filled her head. She wished Mac's arms were around her now. Brice brushed his lips against hers. "We have a little time before the private flight I arranged…"

He kissed her again and it took everything in her not to shove him away. How had she ever kissed him before? How had she ever slept with him? He rested his forehead against hers for a second.

"You're tense," he said.

"Of course I am. Katia's dead. Our home was invaded. You said these people went after Maria and Allan and now they'll come after me. I'm scared, Brice." Genuine tears formed at the thought of her loved ones being gone forever. Brice wiped them away.

"I'm here now. You don't have to worry. I've got everything under control."

That's what really worried her. She crinkled her brow and took a step back.

"But I'm afraid for you, too," she said. "Where are you sending me? I want you to stay with me. If you go back to our house, won't someone come after you?"

"I can take care of myself, Tessa."

...men with money who know how to keep their hands clean.

She needed to irritate him. Challenge his authority and his plan to get her out of the way. No one crossed Brice. Thanks to Mac and all those year of teasing, she knew all about how to push buttons. She was done with being careful. It was time to push a few of Brice's.

"What if there's a way for me to stay with you? I don't want to leave *home*, let alone Africa. I want to go back with you. I'm tougher and smarter than you give me credit for. I can make up for the trouble I've caused you. I can help you."

Brice's eyes got all stormy and he let go of her. He pulled up to his full height before walking over to the window. He glanced outside, then came back to her.

"Help *me*? You're the one who put everyone in danger. Smart? I built Henning Enterprises from scratch. You write a fashion column, Tessa. I'm one of the most influential and experienced businessmen in South Africa. On the continent for that matter. I offer to take you somewhere safe and you claim you can help me. I find that almost funny."

Tessa flinched at his words. Brice was an arrogant man by nature. She knew he had a softer side because she was his wife, but whenever they had an argument, his ego took over.

And when it did, his true feelings came out. She was nobody without him. He defined her as his wife. He'd forever be smarter than she was. In the past, that had always chipped at her confidence, but right now, after all she'd been through, what he thought of her didn't matter anymore. If he had ever really loved her, he'd never have seen her as less than he was. He'd never have spoken to her that way. Mac would never say something like that to her. She swallowed hard.

God, she wished she were back with Mac and Nick at Jamba right now. Safe…feeling at home and like part of a family…happy the way the women at Busara were with their children and…

Stay focused. Stay calm. No one knows Brice like you do. You know how his mind works. Use that to your advantage.

She stood in front of him and took the comb out of her hair.

"Brice, let me prove to you I can help. Do you see this?"

She saw his eyes flick toward the comb as she angled the gems in the light. As his wife, she always wore the latest styles. It went with her persona as the fashion columnist. She'd hoped he would pass it off as something she'd added to her jewelry collection, but now she had a better idea.

"Is that real ivory?" he asked.

"No," she said, arranging her hair over

her shoulders on both sides and slipping the comb back in. *Please don't touch it.* She straightened her dress, then smoothed her hair. "But when I saw it at a flea market in Nairobi, it made me think of that ivory-and-diamond fountain pen you gave me. I couldn't resist because it reminded me of you and what we had. I know the rubies aren't high quality, and I really doubt it's real ivory, but I don't care. I still think it's beautiful. I liked the design and figured you could have a more valuable duplicate made for me if I ever wanted.

"But that's not the point. The point is why should I run? You said yourself that people in illegal trade are dangerous. That it's such a strong web it's hard to cut loose. Wouldn't it be safer to simply regain trust? To just keep doing what you're doing instead of trying to extricate yourself from it? I may love animals, but I love you more and it's not worth getting separated or killed. We can be together, safe and comfortable. Brice, I can include photographs of fashion pieces like this in my column. That could help create a demand for the same look. Do you see where I'm going with this? It would show whose side I'm on. And it would feed the market demand for authentic pieces, even if I wrote the article about imitation ones."

He studied her face intensely and it took every ounce of courage Tessa had to not buckle under his inspection.

"It's not a terrible idea, though I'm not sure how much of a difference it'd make at this point."

"Brice, together we can make Henning Enterprises even bigger and more powerful than it is. I *can* help you. I have been, haven't I? All the parties I've thrown for you? Now that I know about your involvement in this ivory...*mafia*—from what you described it to be like when I called—I could work in a more controlling capacity at the paper. Use it to your advantage. I could keep an ear out in the social circle. Plant seeds.

"And it's good that Nick won't be with us. Do you remember being a teenager, Brice? They're naturally snoopy and too curious for their own good. And we both want him safe, right? Plus, this way, I'll have an excuse to come up here to visit him."

"And why would you need a reason to visit your nephew?"

She bit her lower lip and laced her fingers into his, then lowered her voice, as if to make sure no one in the hallway would overhear them. This was promising. At least he was asking questions instead of turning her down.

"I could be tapping into my connections, Brice. Nick's uncle Mac is a well-known volunteer with Kenyan Wildlife Service and he's worked in the area for years, helping them and other organizations track down illegal ivory. When I visit Nick, I can either plant information that keeps the Henning business trail covered or find information and bring it back to you. Information you can use to bribe these dangerous people and keep them at bay…ensure our safety. Look at this."

She let go of him, went to her purse and pulled out some papers.

"I wasn't sure I could pull it off. I wanted so much to prove to you that I could make things right. This is what I've managed to get so far."

Brice took the papers and read the first two pages, then began flipping through faster.

"Do you realize what you have here?" he asked.

Tessa nodded. "Can you use what's in there as bribery to keep people from harming us?"

Brice sat on the edge of the bed, flipping pages. Pages of falsified information given to her by Ben. Information that looked like official plans for anti-poaching crackdowns. Falsified tracking research and data on herd activity. Information that would increase poaching efficiency if his contacts got their hands on it.

"This is incredible," he said.

She kicked off her sandals and climbed onto the bed. She kneeled behind him and put an arm around his chest, leaning in as he studied the documents.

"I stole it from Mac's office files. See, Brice? As a team, we'd be unbreakable."

If he did suspect her of stealing the USB drives, then he'd believe she stole these documents, too. *It's always the quiet ones.* He reached up and covered her hand with his.

"This may work," he said.

Yes. Keep talking.

"I just want to stay alive and be with you,

but if it helps Henning Enterprises make money, then that's a bonus," she said.

"That and then some. Information like this would keep a lot of people happy and quiet. It won't just make us unbreakable, it will put us in a powerful negotiating position. The business world can be ruthless, Tessa. Money and control are the only way to keep people from taking what's yours and kicking you out the back door. And those power plays often put you in deals you never would have anticipated. But the rewards are so immense you can't walk away." He set the papers aside, then pulled her into his lap.

She gasped, not expecting the move on his part and not realizing she'd been holding her breath, praying for him to say more even though a part of her didn't want to hear it. How much did they need him to say before this could be over?

The scent of the same cologne he'd always worn made her nauseous. His touch made her skin crawl and his breath made her lungs feel like she was being held underwater. It didn't matter that she already knew the truth about him...about the man she'd given the past seven years of her life to. Hearing him confess made her feel like she was free-falling into a bottomless pit.

He kissed her, then reached up, running both hands through her hair. He pulled the comb out and tossed it onto the bed. An icy cold washed through Tessa. She wanted to scream and kick and run, but her gut told her to wait in case they needed more proof. If she blew her cover, he could get away. And he might hurt her...or worse. She listened to Mac's voice in her head, telling her to trust him and that she could trust Ben.

"You're shaking and your pulse is racing. Why is that, Tessa?"

Her eyes fluttered shut and she forced them open.

"Because I want you. You and I, we're meant to be together. I'll do whatever you want and whatever it takes to save our marriage."

He held her closer and Tessa could sense his energy had shifted. It wasn't sensual, it was threatening. Dominating.

"You did well with these," he said, referring to the papers. "But whose side are you really on? Mine? Or whoever makes you feel safe? I know you, Tessa. Isn't that all you want? Comfort. Safety. Security. I'm the only one who can give that to you."

Tessa's head began to pound. Everything was going south. She needed to think, but her thoughts scrambled in her head. She peeled herself off his lap and paced before him.

"You're right. I need you. But I'm also on your side, Brice. I realize now that I've taken everything you've given me for granted. I won't anymore. I know you can keep me safe," she said, holding his face in her hands the way she had on their wedding night, after promising him forever. She hated that her voice sounded pleading. She hated him. She'd loved him once, or thought she did. She knew now that she deserved so much more.

He placed his hands on her hips and stood.

"Someone I trust was able to get into your email accounts and erase any trails to you in terms of the article you sent to the paper," he said.

Tessa stared at him. He had her emails hacked? Married or not, she'd never shared her password. She'd had the same email account since before she met Brice. She'd wanted to retain some inkling of privacy and independence after marrying him. A sense of control, even if it was small. She didn't need him reading conversations between her and her sister or mother. Email was the one place she felt he wasn't looking over her shoulder. Was this payback for her stealing his files or had he really been trying to protect her? Or had he been searching for anything else she might know or any other actions she might have taken against him? And how possible was it to thoroughly erase trails? What about her system backups? What about computer forensics specialists?

"I did it for your safety. I didn't have a choice," he said.

"Of course. I understand. But when I spoke to Kat, I heard someone in the background. Someone overheard her talking to me. If they were the mole you mentioned before, it doesn't matter if you covered the path leading back to me. Whoever they were, they already know what I've done."

His eyes fell and he rubbed her arms.

"Exactly, Tessa. That's why you can't stay here or return home, just in case. I think

Katia was killed not only to cover tracks, but also as a warning for you to back off."

Who was playing whom here? What was he saying? That her life was a trade-off for Kat's? She was guilty of her friend's death. She closed her eyes and tried to find strength. She struggled to recall everything else he'd told her in their phone call. He'd said he was the one who had checked Kat's files and found her article. He'd gone to the newspaper's headquarters. He'd said that he'd checked Katia's computer *before* it was taken by authorities. Could Brice have really gotten to the computer before the police, if they wanted to find clues to verify her accident wasn't a suicide or homicide? Would he have had time if he'd only found out about her death after the fact? Especially given that he'd been on a trip. Unless someone had tipped him off. What if he'd checked Tessa's emails or logged into Kat's computer prior to her death? Could forensics reveal login and deletion times? Had he tampered with Katia's car? Or paid someone, so to keep his hands clean? That was more likely.

"Brice, you'd do anything to keep me safe, wouldn't you?"

"Yes."

"I'd forgive you because I know you love me, and at this point, we're in this to-gether—*till death do us part*—but did you have someone make it look like Kat was responsible for trying to red flag the companies I mentioned, just so you'd be protecting me?"

Brice's jaw popped up and down and he studied her closely.

"She was a casualty of all this, Tessa. I told you that. I can't believe you'd insinuate that I'd go that far."

"I'm not insinuating anything. It's just that this is all so stressful. I thought maybe her death was the unintentional result of trail covering." She wrapped her arms around him and rested her cheek on his chest to buy herself a minute. This time he didn't reciprocate.

Try and remember everything he said in the phone call. You need a confession... proof. Get him to trip up. He said the house had been robbed.

"I still can't believe they invaded our home," she said.

"What?"

"The burglary. It makes me nervous about you going back."

"I'm having the security system updated."

"What did they steal? You mentioned valuables. Tell me they didn't take my jewelry."

"Just items like the audio system and television."

"The necklace you got me…and the pen? Please tell me they're not gone."

He rubbed his thumb against her chin.

"No. Don't worry. They weren't taken. I took them and the rest of your jewelry to the safety deposit box at the bank before I came here."

There she had it. He couldn't have taken the ivory pen to the bank. Not when she'd had the foresight to hide it in the combination locker she used at the spa where she took yoga classes.

"Thank goodness," she said. "But they'll come back. If they want me out of the picture, they'll return. I'm a liability, aren't I?" That's how he'd always seen her, wasn't it?

She needed to go all in. Take the risk. For Nick. For Mac. For all the wild victims out there. But first, she had to think. Ben had gone over scenarios with her, but nothing fit this moment. No more pretenses. She needed Brice to fall. She walked over to the dresser and looked at herself in the mirror. He followed her.

"We'll have to leave soon," he said. He caressed her shoulders. The goose bumps she got weren't the good type. Katia had been a casualty. Who was to say he wasn't setting her up to be one, too? He'd mentioned a private plane. All it would take was a crash. Just like what had happened to her sister. Tessa had known something was off when she'd spoken to Brice from Camp Jamba. He'd mentioned believing Maria and Allan had been killed because of a pattern of poaching they'd discovered from overhead flights. A trail that ran from South Africa to Uganda and up toward Tanzania. That put the poachers at the border with Kenya.

Only days before Maria's death, she'd texted Tessa, telling her to expect an important email. She was sending it, not only for safekeeping, but because it contained newsworthy details. If Maria's copy didn't make it to the right hands, she wanted Tessa to go public with it through the newspaper, if possible. Tessa never received that email. She'd heard those details for the first time from Brice, during their phone call. At the time, she kept thinking there was a small chance he'd gotten that intel from his own sources, but now she was sure he'd been monitoring her emails for a long time. He had to have read it and deleted it. Then he had Maria and Allan killed. It was the only explanation she could think of. He made her sick.

"I'm going to end up like Maria and Allan. That's the plan, isn't it? You had them killed, didn't you?"

"You're crazy, Tessa."

"No, I'm not. Maria told me she was sending me critical information, but you intercepted it first. And the minute you read it, you knew Allan would be passing the same information on to his brother, as well as the authorities. You had to act fast. They both kept their laptops with them for work, so it was convenient that everything burned in their plane crash. But don't you think if anyone ever suspects these were all murders, they'll find the information backed up somewhere?"

His face hardened and he loosened his tie and undid the top button of his shirt.

"You took care of everything like you always do," she said, looking up at his reflection in the mirror. "For the record, the ivory pen you supposedly put in the safe? I wasn't stupid enough to leave it at home."

The color rose in his neck. He grabbed her jaw, tightened his hold and spun her around to face him.

"You should have kept your mouth shut. The kind of life I've given you comes at a price. I gave you everything you wished for and what gratitude do I get? Backstabbing."

Panic surged through her face and she clawed at his wrists and tried to pull his hands away.

Ben, where are you? Now would be a good time to step in.

"Brice, that hurts," she said, trying to loosen his hold.

"I would have protected you. I really do love you, darling. I always have. But that doesn't make me a stupid man. It makes me a cautious one."

A risktaker, but not stupid. Cautious. Mac had said almost the exact thing. But

Mac and Brice were on opposite ends of the spectrum. Their values, morals and beliefs couldn't be more different.

Mac, if I never see you again, know that I love you.

"You want to keep your parents and nephew safe? You don't want to end up like Katia? The only reason you're alive right now is because you have information I want. This isn't all of the information you managed to uncover, is it?" Brice said, waving the falsified documents at her. "You thought you could play with fire. You wanted a little taste of power. But once you saw what was on those computer drives and you realized just how many contacts I have in the ivory market, you realized you'd gotten yourself in over your head. Now here you are, trying to make nice because you know that by my side is the only safe place for you. Assuming I forgive you. I want those thumb drives back and I expect a list of every single person you shared them with or who might have had the chance to look at them when you weren't around. Nick knows his way around computers. He's on that list. Got it?"

"Then you'll just kill me."

"I won't have to. Not directly, anyhow. Your flight simply won't make its destination. It breaks my heart, Tessa. If you hadn't broken so many rules, none of this would have happened." He shoved her face away, but then grabbed her hair from behind. She felt the butt of a gun against her back. "You destroyed what we had together," he said. "I'll miss you. I mean that."

"Move!" Ben had the room cleared in seconds. He cocked his M9 and charged down the hall toward Tessa's room. Mac was on his heels, wishing he hadn't left his pistol locked in the chopper with the tranquilizer rifle. They burst in but the room was empty. She was gone. The sheer drapes that covered patio door at the far side billowed in the post-storm breeze. The racket of orders being shouted outside, clicking of triggers and Ben pulling the curtains aside all seemed to happen at once.

Brice stood, holding Tessa, in the middle of the small lawn trimmed with lush landscaping that had provided cover for an entire brigade of law enforcement and KWS soldiers, many of whom Mac knew.

Their leader, a man by the name of Farid, exchanged signals with Ben and motioned to one of his men to change positions. Ben hadn't only crammed a few guys into Mac's office, he'd used his contacts to make sure this operation was done right and nothing would happen to Tessa. Brice was surrounded. Trapped. Looking down barrels pointed at him from every tree and bush. His face turned an unnatural shade of burgundy and he pushed Tessa to the ground and dropped his handgun.

"Don't move. Put your hands slowly on your head," Farid ordered.

Brice glowered at Tessa as he obeyed.

"Tessa, move away," Ben called out from the patio, keeping his gun raised, as well.

Mac wanted to rush to her, but knew to wait until she was a safe distance from Brice. If he tried anything, Mac didn't want her getting shot.

She got onto her knees and then rose up. The expression on her tear-streaked face was enough to make Mac nervous. More than nervous.

"Tess," he said. "I'm here. Back away from him. It's over."

She took two steps back, shaking her head and glaring at Brice. One order from Farid and an officer came up behind Brice and bound his hands. Some of the men backed off while others still stood within feet, their rifles pointed at him.

"You…*you…*"

Tessa called Brice a slew of derogatory terms that were enough to make even a marine like Ben raise a brow.

Without warning, Tessa walked up to Brice and slapped him hard. Then she began sobbing in full force.

"You killed my sister! You…" She cursed and raised her hand again, but before she could deliver any more blows, Ben signaled Mac. He reached her in a few strides and pulled her away.

Mac didn't believe in violence or fighting unless it was in self-defense, but heaven help him, Brice deserved that slap. And then some. They watched as Brice was hauled away. *Scum of the earth.* Mac wished he'd gotten a few punches in for all the emotional manipulation that man had subjected Tessa to. And if somehow Brice *was* being sincere about having loved her, well, then he was one messed-up man with screwy priorities.

Tessa's shoulders sank and her arms hung limp at her sides. She stood, tears streaming down her face and her chest heaving, staring in the direction they'd taken her husband, even after he had disappeared. Mac had her braced against his chest.

"Shh. It's done. You're okay," Mac said. "Hold your breath a second. Slow your breathing. He's gone."

She buried her face into his shoulder and another sob escaped.

"I've got you, Tess," he said. "I've got you."

TESSA TRIED TO dry her cheeks with her hand and took a slow, deep breath that came out with a shudder. She couldn't find her voice, but she nodded to let Mac know she was okay and she'd heard him. He had her. Crazy Mac had her safe, supported…and he had her heart. But most of all, she had herself. She'd taken control. She'd done it. She'd brought Brice down.

Mentally, she knew his unspeakable crimes justified her actions. Emotionally she felt dirty, guilty, lost and overwhelmed by what she'd just pulled off. Where had her wedding vows gone? What happened to "in good times and bad" and "promise to love you unconditionally, to support you in your goals"? Was she at fault for breaking those vows, or did all of this qualify as "until death do us part"? Brice had caused death. And just like Mac had said with regard to wildlife and carrying a gun, no matter how much he respected animals and did what he could to preserve them, if he was faced with a life-or-death situation, he had a right to defend himself. Brice had crossed the line first. She had a right to defend herself and all the innocents affected by his actions.

Her chest constricted. She tried to inhale but her lungs filled in short spasms. She was mourning all over again. Mourning the loss of Maria and Allan and Katia. Mourning all the elephants tortured and killed because of Brice and others like him. And mourning the loss of life as she knew it. It didn't matter that she also felt relief at finally knowing the truth or that she was freed from spending the rest of her life with the wrong man, a man who controlled her and kept her from stretching or growing. Change was scary and difficult…and unstable. But at this moment, change had never felt so right.

The warmth of Mac's hands against her back and the way her cheek fit in the crook of his neck calmed her breathing. Mac was safe. Her wild and reckless Mac was more loving and caring and safe than anyone she'd ever known. He always had been. Was this why her parents and Maria and Allan had never flinched at the risks inherent in their work? Because they had each other and because they'd found a purpose beyond their own comforts? One that overshadowed fear the way protecting Nick from that hyena or preventing Mac from doing something reckless to protect her from Brice had?

She tightened her arms around Mac and let herself sink into him. She'd never felt so open…so unguarded…so consumed by an energy so pure and alive. An energy strongly reminiscent of how she'd felt when he'd held her at her sister's funeral and how he used to make her feel—as disconcerting as it was—every time he hung around just to bother her when they were teenagers. Had that been love? Was *this* love? She'd never remotely felt this depth of emotion with Brice, even if on some level she must have loved him. Tessa buried her face in Mac's chest and breathed him in. She'd always loved Mac. As much as she resented his choices and confidence because they scared her, he was the one person who knew her sister and his brother like she did, the one person who understood why her parents were the way they were and that when she vented about their choices, it came from a place of love. He was the one person she never had to pretend for because he knew the real Tessa...even if he teased her for it. He knew. He'd been there.

But risking her feelings for him back then...admitting to them...would have meant suffering more pain if something happened to him. She would have hurt more when he left to follow his dreams.

And now...now, even though her marriage was over and she'd be signing divorce papers as soon as humanly possible, if she told Mac how she really felt, he might see himself as a rebound guy. He'd think she was the old Tessa who needed someone to make her feel safe and secure. She had learned that strength and that sense of security could only come from within. She knew she had it in her. She knew now—without a doubt—that Mac Walker had always been her soul mate. She didn't need to rely on him. She needed to love him. She didn't want him to stop taking risks. She wanted him to risk loving her back.

She wrapped her arms around his neck and held tight.

"I'm sorry, Mac. I'm sorry for everything."

"There's nothing to be sorry about, except for maybe giving me a heart attack. I was really upset when I found out you'd left the camp," he said.

"I'm sorry. I had to do it, Mac. And you wouldn't have let me. I didn't want you hurt because of me. And I didn't want Nick left without either of us if the worst happened."

"You took a big risk."

"It was worth it. I understand that now. Some risks are worth it."

The entire situation was so grim, even with their success, she didn't feel like celebrating or accepting any kind of accolades. She felt nothing but deep fatigue. Utter exhaustion. She couldn't settle the slurry of thoughts and emotions whirring through her. The realization that her life would never be the same was overwhelming.

"You're right, it was. And I wouldn't have let you do it," he said, rubbing his hands up and down her arms. "But I have to admit that you were quite impressive in there. You've gotten pretty gutsy, haven't you?" Mac teased, tapping her nose. She almost smiled, but the idea that he'd seen and heard everything that had gone on between her and Brice made her uncomfortable.

"Mac, you do realize all of it was an act, right? Everything I said to him. All of it."

He tipped her chin up and looked into her eyes. Tessa wasn't sure if it was the rush of the situation or her imagination playing tricks, but something in the way his blue eyes took her in while the sun-kissed lines around them relaxed made her feel adored and—she wished—*loved*. But how could he possibly love her back? Friendship, raising Nick together...that was different. That was about caring. She didn't just care for Mac.

"I know it was. I also understand that in spite of everything, you and Brice have a history. I get that. You had a life with him. This must be so tough on you. You've been let down."

But her life with Brice had been missing something fundamental from the start. With Brice, she'd never really risked her heart because she'd never fully given it to him. Less than a year into her marriage, she'd known she hadn't married her soul mate, but he was kind to her and she'd made her choice and wasn't about to admit to her sister that she'd been right. Maybe it wasn't simply that Maria and Allan didn't like Brice. Maybe they could see there was something between Tessa and Mac that neither was willing to admit.

"We have a history, too, Mac," Tessa said.

"We do. I hope it's not just history."

"We'll work as a team. We won't let Maria and Allan down. We'll make sure Nick knows we love him." They'd always have a future together because of their nephew.

"What about making sure *you're* loved?" Mac said.

Tessa licked her lips. What was he saying? The corner of his mouth turned up and he reached into his pocket, pulling out a coin.

"How about a game of 'Get Tess to Confess'? You see, back in high school there was one 'truth' question I never had the guts to ask because I knew I wasn't the kind of guy you wanted."

Mac hadn't had the guts to do something? She never would have believed that. He used to flirt with girls all the time. But the way he was looking at her right now weakened her knees.

"What question was that?"

He tossed the coin and slapped it on his arm.

"If it's heads, you have to answer the question, 'Do you love Mac Walker? For richer or for poorer?' and if it's tails, I tell you how much I love you and always have."

He uncovered the coin. Tails. He seemed nervous. He picked up the coin and put it in her palm, then held her face in his hands.

"I confess that I love you and always have, Tessa. Be with me. I know a Serengeti camp probably isn't your idea of a nice life, but I love you and can only hope you'd give it a chance. Give *me* a chance. We can make it work for us and for Nick. I want nothing more than for us to be together forever." He kissed her and it was powerful and breath-taking and full of promise. A kiss that wiped away all the years they'd lost and the heart-ache they'd endured. A kiss that cleared away the storm.

She caught her breath, then moved the coin to her arm with the heads facing up. Mac grinned.

"I confess that I love Mac and always have, for richer or poorer, for all he stands for, for who he is…as he is…wild life and all." This time she kissed *him* to seal her truth.

"You love me? Huh?" Mac said, his cocky edge back.

"Yeah, I do. And I have another confession."

"What's that?"

"Living here with you is my idea of the perfect life."

"Does that mean after you're a free woman, you'd be willing to risk giving up that freedom again?"

"Mac, spending forever with you would *be* freedom. Freedom of the heart."

"I want nothing more than forever with you too, Tess." And with that, he kissed her.

The kind of kiss she'd only ever experienced in her dreams. The kind only soul mates could share.

And all that mattered now was that they would finally be sharing the rest of their lives together, in Kenya, with love.

EPILOGUE

Five months later...

TESSA LEANED BACK against Mac's knees as he sat on the wooden steps of Anna and Jack's house at Busara watching Nick, Pippa and Haki, along with Ben and Hope's children, Maddie, who was quite the talker, Chad and Ryan. Ryan, still a toddler, was safely perched on top of Ben's shoulders. Hope was standing in the courtyard area closer to the elephant pens, keeping an eye on all the kids. Tessa had also had the chance to meet more of their friends. Dr. David Alwanga, a colleague of Jack's who worked in research at the university in Nairobi— who also happened to be Hope's brother— had come to visit with Hope's best friend, Chuki, his new fiancée. Everyone who knew him called him Alwanga, except for Hope, who'd been calling him Simba since they

were kids. According to Hope, Chuki had
been the last person on earth that her brother
would have imagined falling for, but there
was no arguing with love.

Tessa let Mac weave his fingers between
hers and tilted her head back to smile at him.
He kissed her on the nose and rubbed his
thumbs against her skin. She loved visiting
Busara almost as much as she loved calling
Camp Jamba Walker home. It wasn't that she
didn't love South Africa or miss the post-
card views of beaches or rocky shores and
waters that stretched to the horizon. It was
a beautiful country and it would always be a
part of her, much like her new friends, Jack
and Anna, felt about America. But Kenya
was home now and she had no doubt in her
mind that it was where she wanted to be
and where she was always destined stay.
Just like she wholeheartedly believed that
she and Mac had always been destined for
each other. They'd taken a rough path getting there, but the journey made what they
had that much sweeter.

"I don't think we've ever had this many
people at Busara all at once," Anna said,
swinging past the screen door carrying a

bowl of fresh figs and mangos for anyone who still had room in their stomachs.

Jack sat cross-legged on the porch across from Sue, waiting for Noah to take his first steps. Sue slowly let go of Noah's chubby hands and they waited to see if this time he'd make his way to Daddy or teeter and fall on his butt again.

"That's true," Jack said. "We're usually outnumbered by elephants. They're probably wondering why the humans are multiplying so rapidly." He snatched a fig and held it out to Noah as bait. Noah's eyes widened and he gurgled, reaching and leaning forward at a precarious angle without moving his feet.

Kamau laughed.

"I'm not so sure. If you don't watch that Pippa of yours, she's going to have them thinking *they're* human," he said.

Pippa was trying to demonstrate that she could teach a baby elephant to use a spoon to scoop food from her hand.

Nick just stood there shaking his head.

"Kam, you'd better go rescue that poor elephant before he grows up thinking spoons grow on trees in the wild," Niara said as she sat in a chair with a pillow behind her to rest the ache in her lower back. Her hand lay on her growing belly. Kamau lifted her fingers to his mouth with an exaggerated bow, gave them a kiss and lumbered off, leaving Niara glowing even more.

"Pippa knows better." Anna sighed, watching her vivacious little girl. "She's just showing off, especially to Nick. Have you all noticed? She loves to challenge anyone older than her. Remember how she used to give Haki a hard time?" she asked Niara.

"Yes. Nick's presence here is giving Haki a break from her bossiness." Niara chuckled. "But have you noticed how Maddie keeps looking at Nick, too? I wonder if he realizes just how enamored they are of him."

"A few years from now, if he's still lucky enough to have their attention, he won't be so clueless," Mac said.

Tessa loved that blood didn't define family. Nor did species or race or history. Nothing but love did. All the children were considered cousins, not just friends, whether blood-related or not. Everyone was family here. Nick had gotten to know Ben and Hope's kids well because of a class he was taking a few times a week in Nairobi in the same school Maddie attended. He was actually adapting really well to virtual school online, with a few extracurricular activities with kids his age in the area thrown in. So far, so good. The internet really did open up possibilities. Rustic life with modern conveniences. But she and Mac were making sure he was living...experiencing things...and not just hiding behind a computer screen.

"Next time, we'll all have to gather at our place," Mugi said.

"Absolutely. We'll have a bonfire and Mugi can tell the children stories all night," Kesi added. "There's room for everyone to use a tent, so plan on an all-night gathering."

"We could time it with Pippa's birthday. Isn't it Valentine's Day? That's less than a month away," Mac said.

"Sounds good to us," Alwanga said, putting his arm around Chuki.

"Sounds great, if that doesn't make it too chaotic for you," Jack said. "When's the wedding, Chuki? Mugi and Kesi won't allow tent sharing unless we get invited to one," Jack teased.

"Well, if they're the only couple still unmarried by the time we have a bonfire, then they'll automatically have to take on baby-sitting duties. We'll divide the children up into girl and boy tents and see which of these two come out alive in the morning," Kesi said. "Kind of like being thrown in a lion's pit during Roman times."

Everyone laughed.

"Trust me, I'll be the one to win this challenge," Chuki said. "This man and a herd of children? Not a chance."

"That's probably true, but I won you," Alwanga said with a cocky grin. "I think I got the better deal."

"I think I won you, too," Chuki countered.

"Okay, you two. Enough mushiness. Set a date and get a tent," Anna said.

"Young love..." Kesi sighed.

Mac bent over and wrapped his arms around Tessa, pressing his lips against her hair. Heaven help her, she wanted to get a tent with *him* right now.

"I'm really happy you're here," he whispered.

"Me, too. I've never been so crazy happy in my life," Tessa said. Happy didn't come close to describing how she felt. She'd found the perfect ending to her story and the perfect beginning for the next one.

"I heard the word *wedding*." Hope walked up to them holding her stepson Chad's hand to keep him from escaping like Bakhari once had. Chad was like a mini marine on caffeine. "I keep telling Simba and Chuki to set a date. Ben and I are proof that when it's right, it's right, no matter how long it has been since you've met. Days or years."

"Yeah, we have a saying in America. 'In a New York minute.' That's all the time it takes to know you've found 'the one,' so I think given how long it took to find each other again, we couldn't have gotten married soon enough." Jack shared a tender look with Anna.

"Well, there's also an African saying that goes, 'Wood already touched by fire isn't hard to set alight,'" Hope said.

Jack had mentioned that she and her brother loved seeing who could slip the best proverb into any given situation. Since Jack and Alwanga worked together, he'd been sucked into their wisdom challenges. Tessa had heard so many old chestnuts in the past day, it was amusing to say the least. She related to that last one, though. Love rekindled. It fit, even if she and Mac hadn't realized the tension between them had stemmed from a deep-seated caring for each other. Love in its strongest form.

"Why else do you think Tessa and Mac here already tied the knot?" Anna grinned. "Kind of like with Jack and me. We came full circle from being best friends back in school. I suppose sometimes it takes losing what you have to see just how important it is to you."

"Only we weren't exactly best friends," Mac said. "But I'm glad we are now."

"Definitely," Tessa said, though he had been a good friend all along in an outside-the-box sort of way. But that's what she loved about Mac. He'd never fit between the lines and never tried to, but he did fit perfectly with her.

Her parents had even come up for the wedding. That had meant the world to Tessa. They kept the celebration simple, in the gardens at Hodari Lodge with everyone here today in attendance. She didn't want Brice's memory marring any part of her new life in Kenya. Avoiding the lodge just because of what happened there hadn't seemed right. She wasn't letting anyone control her life like that. And she wanted to set an example for Nick in terms of not letting the past tie you down. Thank goodness that given the situation, her divorce had been expedited.

Brice was currently in jail. He'd been given a two-year sentence and a fine. As Tessa learned, through the process, that was a pretty normal sentence. A slap on the wrist considering the pain and suffering he'd caused. But just like Ben had said, the information she had uncovered had led to arrests at the art gallery by an undercover buyer. At least it was something. Every arrest and every tusk confiscated made a difference.

"I saw your latest post," Ben said. "Great job."

She was still getting used to getting compliments from Ben. Since he and Hope worked in Nairobi, she'd only seen him a handful of times since his grand interrogation. The guy was a little rough around the edges, but had a great heart. And there was no mistaking that his wife and kids really did love him, and vice versa.

"Thanks," Tessa said. "The website has

been getting a lot of traffic lately. I love working on it. Oh, and Anna, I can't thank you enough for putting me in touch with that environmental postdoc from your alma mater. She was happy to contribute an article, and I think it was responsible for an influx of readers. Apparently, Serena Myss has quite a following."

"I'm glad it worked out. Serena got me a lot of fund-raising support back when Busara was at a critical point. I'd love to meet her in person someday," Anna said.

"Well, since my parents came here last month for Christmas," Jack suggested, "we can go visit them next time and let Serena know we'll be in town. Maybe she'll write you another post in the future."

"That would be pretty awesome," Tessa said.

Tessa had put together an online newspaper of sorts. A website that provided information and links to all the major conservation sites and campaigns against wildlife trafficking, poaching, trapping or any form of endangerment. She was using her journalism experience to report on current events as well as writing a weekly column about life in the Serengeti. In it she did just that—recounted her personal experiences and encounters with animals and even plants. Now that the site had gained momentum and a reputation for drawing in donations to wildlife and environmental organizations, she was getting some high-profile guest contributors, too. Anna included. As diverse as the site was, it placed an emphasis on raising public awareness of the blood ivory trade.

"Look, look, look! He's doing it!" Jack crouched down and held his hands out.

"He's on his own," Sue said when Noah let go of her and took four steps toward his dad before tumbling down and bawling.

"That's my boy. Come on, buddy. You can do it," Jack said. Oh, the pride on his face.

"I remember Ryan's first steps," Ben said. "Give him a few days and you'll be coming up with innovative ways to keep him corralled. You have my card."

Hope had told Tessa some hilarious stories about Ben's marine-influenced parenting tactics when she'd first met him.

Drops of rain pitter-pattered against the roof of the house and dappled the dry ground. The kids came running up the steps and into the house and everyone else followed. Tessa grabbed the fruit bowl for Anna and hurried in from the afternoon shower. She set it on the dining table and stopped to glance through the window and across the valley to the herds that passed in peace, moving on to their next grazing area, unfazed by the rain.

Sometimes it takes losing what you have to see just how important it is to you.

Mac joined her and put his arm around her. She leaned her head against his shoulder and looped her arm around his waist. Tonight, once they were alone, she'd be telling him that he'd always be a wonderful uncle, but that he was going to be a dad, too. They'd talked about it, so she knew he'd be thrilled. Their family was growing.

Busara and all its children, human and otherwise, was a special place, as was Camp Jamba Walker. Here, instead of the sands of her past, Tessa had the rich earth her future would grow on. Instead of vast stretches of waters so deep she couldn't see what lay beneath, she had an endless view of the savanna, spotted with trees whose branches reached toward the horizon and mountains that welcomed clouds as they rolled in and rivers that wove their way through the landscape with their assurance that new life would come. It was all here—from snow to sun and desert to forests and death to life—and it was all intricately and, most of all, beautifully balanced.

This was their Serengeti.

This was where they were destined to live, love and protect.

This was their home.

* * * * *

LARGER-PRINT BOOKS!

GET 2 FREE LARGER-PRINT NOVELS PLUS 2 FREE MYSTERY GIFTS

Love Inspired®

Larger-print novels are now available...

YES! Please send me 2 FREE LARGER-PRINT Love Inspired® novels and my 2 FREE mystery gifts (gifts are worth about $10). After receiving them, if I don't wish to receive any more books, I can return the shipping statement marked "cancel." If I don't cancel, I will receive 6 brand-new novels every month and be billed just $5.49 per book in the U.S. or $5.99 per book in Canada. That's a savings of at least 19% off the cover price. It's quite a bargain! Shipping and handling is just 50¢ per book in the U.S. and 75¢ per book in Canada.* I understand that accepting the 2 free books and gifts places me under no obligation to buy anything. I can always return a shipment and cancel at any time. Even if I never buy another book, the two free books and gifts are mine to keep forever.

122/322 IDN GH6D

Name	(PLEASE PRINT)
Address	Apt. #
City	State/Prov.	Zip/Postal Code

Signature (if under 18, a parent or guardian must sign)

Mail to the **Reader Service:**
IN U.S.A.: P.O. Box 1867, Buffalo, NY 14240-1867
IN CANADA: P.O. Box 609, Fort Erie, Ontario L2A 5X3

Are you a current subscriber to Love Inspired® books and want to receive the larger-print edition?
Call 1-800-873-8635 or visit www.ReaderService.com.

* Terms and prices subject to change without notice. Prices do not include applicable taxes. Sales tax applicable in N.Y. Canadian residents will be charged applicable taxes. Offer not valid in Quebec. This offer is limited to one order per household. Not valid to current subscribers to Love Inspired Larger-Print books. All orders subject to credit approval. Credit or debit balances in a customer's account(s) may be offset by any other outstanding balance owed by or to the customer. Please allow 4 to 6 weeks for delivery. Offer available while quantities last.

Your Privacy—The Reader Service is committed to protecting your privacy. Our Privacy Policy is available online at www.ReaderService.com or upon request from the Reader Service.

We make a portion of our mailing list available to reputable third parties that offer products we believe may interest you. If you prefer that we not exchange your name with third parties, or if you wish to clarify or modify your communication preferences, please visit us at www.ReaderService.com/consumerschoice or write to us at Reader Service Preference Service, P.O. Box 9062, Buffalo, NY 14240-9062. Include your complete name and address.

LILP15

LARGER-PRINT BOOKS!

GET 2 FREE
LARGER-PRINT NOVELS
PLUS 2 FREE
MYSTERY GIFTS

Love Inspired.

SUSPENSE
RIVETING INSPIRATIONAL ROMANCE

Larger-print novels are now available...

YES! Please send me 2 FREE LARGER-PRINT Love Inspired® Suspense novels and my 2 FREE mystery gifts (gifts are worth about $10). After receiving them, if I don't wish to receive any more books, I can return the shipping statement marked "cancel." If I don't cancel, I will receive 4 brand-new novels every month and be billed just $5.49 per book in the U.S. or $5.99 per book in Canada. That's a savings of at least 19% off the cover price. It's quite a bargain! Shipping and handling is just 50¢ per book in the U.S. and 75¢ per book in Canada.* I understand that accepting the 2 free books and gifts places me under no obligation to buy anything. I can always return a shipment and cancel at any time. Even if I never buy another book, the two free books and gifts are mine to keep forever.

110/310 IDN GH6P

Name	(PLEASE PRINT)	

Address		Apt. #

City	State/Prov.	Zip/Postal Code

Signature (if under 18, a parent or guardian must sign)

Mail to the **Reader Service:**
IN U.S.A.: P.O. Box 1867, Buffalo, NY 14240-1867
IN CANADA: P.O. Box 609, Fort Erie, Ontario L2A 5X3

**Are you a current subscriber to Love Inspired® Suspense books
and want to receive the larger-print edition?
Call 1-800-873-8635 or visit www.ReaderService.com.**

* Terms and prices subject to change without notice. Prices do not include applicable taxes. Sales tax applicable in N.Y. Canadian residents will be charged applicable taxes. Offer not valid in Quebec. This offer is limited to one order per household. Not valid for current subscribers to Love Inspired Suspense larger-print books. All orders subject to credit approval. Credit or debit balances in a customer's account(s) may be offset by any other outstanding balance owed by or to the customer. Please allow 4 to 6 weeks for delivery. Offer available while quantities last.

Your Privacy—The Reader Service is committed to protecting your privacy. Our Privacy Policy is available online at www.ReaderService.com or upon request from the Reader Service.
We make a portion of our mailing list available to reputable third parties that offer products we believe may interest you. If you prefer that we not exchange your name with third parties, or if you wish to clarify or modify your communication preferences, please visit us at www.ReaderService.com/consumerschoice or write to us at Reader Service Preference Service, P.O. Box 9062, Buffalo, NY 14240-9062. Include your complete name and address.

LISLP15

WESTERN WP PROMISES

YES! Please send me **The Western Promises Collection** in Larger Print. This collection begins with 3 FREE books and 2 FREE gifts (gifts valued at approx. $14.00 retail) in the first shipment, along with the other first 4 books from the collection! If I do not cancel, I will receive 8 monthly shipments until I have the entire 51-book Western Promises collection. I will receive 2 or 3 FREE books in each shipment and I will pay just $4.99 US/ $5.89 CDN for each of the other four books in each shipment, plus $2.99 for shipping and handling per shipment. *If I decide to keep the entire collection, I'll have paid for only 32 books, because 19 books are FREE! I understand that accepting the 3 free books and gifts places me under no obligation to buy anything. I can always return a shipment and cancel at any time. My free books and gifts are mine to keep no matter what I decide.

272 HCN 3070 472 HCN 3070

Name	(PLEASE PRINT)	
Address		Apt. #
City	State/Prov.	Zip/Postal Code

Signature (If under 18, a parent or guardian must sign)

Mail to the **Reader Service:**
IN U.S.A.: P.O. Box 1867, Buffalo, NY 14240-1867
IN CANADA: P.O. Box 609, Fort Erie, Ontario L2A 5X3

* Terms and prices subject to change without notice. Prices do not include applicable taxes. Sales tax applicable in N.Y. Canadian residents will be charged applicable taxes. This offer is limited to one order per household. All orders subject to approval. Credit or debit balances in a customer's account(s) may be offset by any other outstanding balance owed by or to the customer. Please allow 4 to 6 weeks for delivery. Offer available while quantities last. Offer not available to Quebec residents.

> **Your Privacy**—The Reader Service is committed to protecting your privacy. Our Privacy Policy is available online at www.ReaderService.com or upon request from the Reader Service.
>
> We make a portion of our mailing list available to reputable third parties that offer products we believe may interest you. If you prefer that we not exchange your name with third parties, or if you wish to clarify or modify your communication preferences, please visit us at www.ReaderService.com/consumerschoice or write to us at Reader Service Preference Service, P.O. Box 9062, Buffalo, NY 14240-9062. Include your complete name and address.

WPBPA16R

LARGER-PRINT BOOKS!
GET 2 FREE LARGER-PRINT NOVELS PLUS
2 FREE GIFTS!

HARLEQUIN

super romance®

More Story...More Romance

YES! Please send me 2 FREE LARGER-PRINT Harlequin® Superromance® novels and my 2 FREE gifts (gifts are worth about $10). After receiving them, if I don't wish to receive any more books, I can return the shipping statement marked "cancel." If I don't cancel, I will receive 4 brand-new novels every month and be billed just $5.94 per book in the U.S. or $6.24 per book in Canada. That's a savings of at least 12% off the cover price! It's quite a bargain! Shipping and handling is just 50¢ per book in the U.S. or 75¢ per book in Canada.* I understand that accepting the 2 free books and gifts places me under no obligation to buy anything. I can always return a shipment and cancel at any time. Even if I never buy another book, the two free books and gifts are mine to keep forever.

132/332 HDN GHVC

Name _____ (PLEASE PRINT) _____

Address _____ Apt. # _____

City _____ State/Prov. _____ Zip/Postal Code _____

Signature (if under 18, a parent or guardian must sign)

Mail to the **Reader Service:**
IN U.S.A.: P.O. Box 1867, Buffalo, NY 14240-1867
IN CANADA: P.O. Box 609, Fort Erie, Ontario L2A 5X3

Want to try two free books from another line?
Call 1-800-873-8635 today or visit www.ReaderService.com.

* Terms and prices subject to change without notice. Prices do not include applicable taxes. Sales tax applicable in N.Y. Canadian residents will be charged applicable taxes. Offer not valid in Quebec. This offer is limited to one order per household. Not valid for current subscribers to Harlequin Superromance Larger-Print books. All orders subject to credit approval. Credit or debit balances in a customer's account(s) may be offset by any other outstanding balance owed by or to the customer. Please allow 4 to 6 weeks for delivery. Offer available while quantities last.

Your Privacy—The Reader Service is committed to protecting your privacy. Our Privacy Policy is available online at www.ReaderService.com or upon request from the Reader Service.

We make a portion of our mailing list available to reputable third parties that offer products we believe may interest you. If you prefer that we not exchange your name with third parties, or if you wish to clarify or modify your communication preferences, please visit us at www.ReaderService.com/consumerschoice or write to us at Reader Service Preference Service, P.O. Box 9062, Buffalo, NY 14240-9062. Include your complete name and address.

LARGER-PRINT BOOKS!
GET 2 FREE LARGER-PRINT NOVELS PLUS
2 FREE GIFTS!

HARLEQUIN®

INTRIGUE
BREATHTAKING ROMANTIC SUSPENSE

YES! Please send me 2 FREE LARGER-PRINT Harlequin® Intrigue novels and my 2 FREE gifts (gifts are worth about $10). After receiving them, if I don't wish to receive any more books, I can return the shipping statement marked "cancel." If I don't cancel, I will receive 6 brand-new novels every month and be billed just $5.49 per book in the U.S. or $6.24 per book in Canada. That's a saving of at least 11% off the cover price! It's quite a bargain! Shipping and handling is just 50¢ per book in the U.S. and 75¢ per book in Canada.* I understand that accepting the 2 free books and gifts places me under no obligation to buy anything. I can always return a shipment and cancel at any time. Even if I never buy another book, the two free books and gifts are mine to keep forever.

199/300 IDN GHWN

Name _____ (PLEASE PRINT)

Address _____ Apt. #

City _____ State/Prov. _____ Zip/Postal Code

Signature (if under 18, a parent or guardian must sign)

Mail to the **Reader Service:**
IN U.S.A.: P.O. Box 1867, Buffalo, NY 14240-1867
IN CANADA: P.O. Box 609, Fort Erie, Ontario L2A 5X3

**Are you a subscriber to Harlequin® Intrigue books
and want to receive the larger-print edition?
Call 1-800-873-8635 today or visit www.ReaderService.com.**

* Terms and prices subject to change without notice. Prices do not include applicable taxes. Sales tax applicable in N.Y. Canadian residents will be charged applicable taxes. Offer not valid in Quebec. This offer is limited to one order per household. Not valid for current subscribers to Harlequin Intrigue Larger-Print books. All orders subject to credit approval. Credit or debit balances in a customer's account(s) may be offset by any other outstanding balance owed by or to the customer. Please allow 4 to 6 weeks for delivery. Offer available while quantities last.

Your Privacy—The Reader Service is committed to protecting your privacy. Our Privacy Policy is available online at www.ReaderService.com or upon request from the Reader Service.

We make a portion of our mailing list available to reputable third parties that offer products we believe may interest you. If you prefer that we not exchange your name with third parties, or if you wish to clarify or modify your communication preferences, please visit us at www.ReaderService.com/consumerschoice or write to us at Reader Service Preference Service, P.O. Box 9062, Buffalo, NY 14240-9062. Include your complete name and address.

HILPI5

LARGER-PRINT BOOKS!

HARLEQUIN

Presents®

GET 2 FREE LARGER-PRINT NOVELS PLUS 2 FREE GIFTS!

PASSION GUARANTEED SEDUCTION

YES! Please send me 2 FREE LARGER-PRINT Harlequin Presents® novels and my 2 FREE gifts (gifts are worth about $10). After receiving them, if I don't wish to receive any more books, I can return the shipping statement marked "cancel." If I don't cancel, I will receive 6 brand-new novels every month and be billed just $5.30 per book in the U.S. or $5.74 per book in Canada. That's a saving of at least 12% off the cover price! It's quite a bargain! Shipping and handling is just 50¢ per book in the U.S. and 75¢ per book in Canada.* I understand that accepting the 2 free books and gifts places me under no obligation to buy anything. I can always return a shipment and cancel at any time. Even if I never buy another book, the two free books and gifts are mine to keep forever.

176/376 HDN GHVY

Name _____ (PLEASE PRINT)

Address _____ Apt. #

City _____ State/Prov. _____ Zip/Postal Code

Signature (if under 18, a parent or guardian must sign)

Mail to the **Reader Service:**
IN U.S.A.: P.O. Box 1867, Buffalo, NY 14240-1867
IN CANADA: P.O. Box 609, Fort Erie, Ontario L2A 5X3

**Are you a subscriber to Harlequin Presents® books and want to receive the larger-print edition?
Call 1-800-873-8635 today or visit us at www.ReaderService.com.**

* Terms and prices subject to change without notice. Prices do not include applicable taxes. Sales tax applicable in N.Y. Canadian residents will be charged applicable taxes. Offer not valid in Quebec. This offer is limited to one order per household. Not valid for current subscribers to Harlequin Presents Larger-Print books. All orders subject to credit approval. Credit or debit balances in a customer's account(s) may be offset by any other outstanding balance owed by or to the customer. Please allow 4 to 6 weeks for delivery. Offer available while quantities last.

Your Privacy—The Reader Service is committed to protecting your privacy. Our Privacy Policy is available online at www.ReaderService.com or upon request from the Reader Service.

We make a portion of our mailing list available to reputable third parties that offer products we believe may interest you. If you prefer that we not exchange your name with third parties, or if you wish to clarify or modify your communication preferences, please visit us at www.ReaderService.com/consumerschoice or write to us at Reader Service Preference Service, P.O. Box 9062, Buffalo, NY 14240-9062. Include your complete name and address.

HPLP15